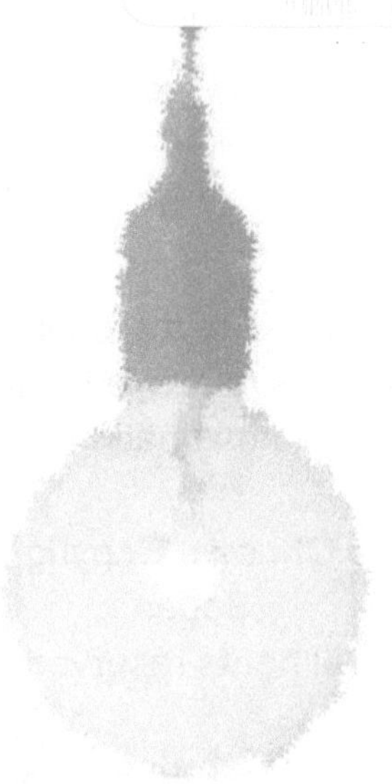

SECTOR C
THE CHOSEN

by Nina Soden

This is a work of fiction. All of the characters, organizations, businesses, and events portrayed in this novel are either products of the author's imagination or are used fictitiously.

ISBN: 978-0-9858853-3-5

http://www.ninasoden.wordpress.com
Editor: Ula Manzo, PhD.
Beta Readers: Clara Tapaninen and Gena Rawdon
Cover Design by: Nina Soden

DEDICATION

For my loving family who never lets me give up, my supportive husband who tells me every day how proud he is of me, and my beautiful children whose creativity and joy make life a journey and an adventure.

ACKNOWLEDGEMENTS

A special thank you to Ula Manzo, my patient and wonderful editor, for her attention to detail and amazing proofreading and editing skills.

Thank you to my beta-readers for being a part of this journey with me and for so freely giving your time, feedback, and encouragement to make this the best book it could be.

1

I gasped for breath as I sat straight up in bed. A warm liquid dripped from my forehead and ran down my face. I reached up with shaking hands. Blood. It had to be blood. What else could be so fluid, so sticky? I looked at my hand, expecting to find it covered in some deep burgundy gore, but it was only sweat plastering my hair to my cheek. The lights were off, except for the flickering red glow coming from the light above our door indicating that curfew was still in effect. Curfew, at least for those sector residents in the selection class and younger, is from 9:00 PM until 5:00 AM. Once curfew was over the red light would turn blue, letting us know we are approved to leave the building—letting us know it's safe.

I looked around the long narrow room, listening to the quiet breathing of the others sleeping in their bunk beds. Currently, only the moonlight lit the windows with a gentle glow, but it wouldn't be long before sunrise.

My dreams had gotten worse over the last several months. Much more vivid. Much more physical. At times, it seemed like that paper-thin space between dream and lucidity was disappearing. All I had left were the tremors. Other times, it seemed that it was only the clarity of my dreams that allowed me full awareness of my surroundings.

This wasn't the first time I had woken up unsure of where I was—*who* I was. It never took long for my memories to come back and for life as I knew it, in Sector C, to return. I wasn't sure what I was afraid of most: my dreams or reality.

I stretched out, trying to concentrate on slowing my breathing, my heartbeat.

"What the heck, A, everything OK up there?" C, my bunkmate and best friend, called softly from the bed below mine.

"Yeah. Yeah, I'm fine. Just a bad dream. Go back to sleep, C," I whispered, trying not to wake up anyone else.

C knew me better than anyone though. She jumped out of her bed and hopped up onto mine without batting an eye. "Seriously? You're going on three months straight of waking up halfway through the night with, what, panic attacks?"

"No. I'm not having panic attacks," I snapped.

"No, you're not, but you're not just having bad dreams either. You're having nightmares, but you won't admit it, even to me, and I'm your best friend."

C and I had been best friends practically since birth. We had to be. We didn't have any other choice. You see, my real name is C65A53. The "C" stands for the sector I was born into and the "65" is for the year I was born, 2365. The "A" means I was the first baby born that year, at least in my sector, and "53" means I was born on the 53rd day of the year.

C and I were born on the same day, which is rare. OK, it isn't really rare that babies are born on the same day, Sector C has lots of breeders from what I've heard. However, it is rare for more than one baby born on a given day to actually live, if any at all. There are only between twenty and thirty babies who survive, or are permitted to survive, each year. The year C and I were born, the Council only permitted fifteen births. To this day, we are the smallest selection class in the history of Sector C.

C and I always joke that we were born to be friends, but it's more like we were born to be sisters. If things had turned out differently, I might have had a brother. C65B53 was a baby boy, born only two hours after me, but he didn't survive. It's funny, the Council doesn't acknowledge the babies that don't survive and yet they still keep meticulous records in the archives of every birth. I try not to think about the babies who don't make it, and focus on my selection classmates who did survive.

For some reason that information is available to us on the link to the archives on our tablets. I don't know why – maybe to make us feel valued, having been allowed to live? A lot of other obvious information *isn't* available, though—such as where our food comes from, our clothes, and other day-to-day necessities and, for that matter, our tablets and other technology. The archives are searchable, but the results that come up are limited, to say the least.

"Hello, Earth to A. What's going on in that brain of yours?" C asked, as she pulled her long red hair up into a ponytail. Some of our classmates call her carrot-top. She's never liked that name though, so out of respect I stick to "C."

"Sorry, I was just thinking. Look, you're right, they aren't bad dreams. It's just..."

Like C, the rest of my selection class calls me A, but most people, teachers or those outside of my selection class, call me A53. That's just how things work here. Classmates and close friends call each other by letter indicator or nickname, if they have one, but others refer to us in a more formal manner, using both letter indicator and the day we were born. Considering that we don't really mingle outside our selection class, except for at events that include all selection classes and younger students. The chance of meeting someone with the same letter indicator is highly unlikely.

Someone born outside of this life would probably wonder why we don't have real names: Amy, Christy, Sarah, or any other name one might find in a book of baby names. It's simple really, moms and dads pick names like those, but we don't have parents—no one does here. Don't get me wrong, we all eventually get names. We pick them ourselves, as part of "Selection Week." But even those choices are controlled—*regulated*—based on an authorized list.

When the government was overthrown in the war of 2082, the newly-formed Governing Council established the sectors and outlawed unsanctioned procreation. Each sector would only be allowed to maintain its population. Life, death, and desertion of the sector have come to be taken very seriously. The Council has even established an advanced tracking system. All residents and selection students are equipped with an internal monitor, embedded in the inside of our wrists. These monitors not only show us basic information like time, date, and health status--they are also connected to the main sector security system. The Council says they don't use the monitors to watch over us, but merely to maintain an overview of the sector population. When someone dies or goes too far beyond the sector walls, with the exception of the external security team, their monitor deactivates. This alerts the Council and the new "population count" is registered

It doesn't happen very often that someone voluntarily defects from the sector, but it does happen. There are said to be one or two sector residents each year who leave this way. The majority of changes to the population size of Sector C are based on births, and the deaths that occur while selection students are locked up, safe and sound, during curfew.

Each year, the total number of deaths, births, and sector defectors determine how many new members will be allowed to be born the following year. When one person leaves the sector, be it through death or abandonment, another one is approved to be born into it.

If no one had defected, and no one had died, then no new births would be granted life privileges. As far as I know that has never happened. This doesn't mean no babies are born; it just means that most of them aren't allowed to complete the maturation process. In other words, they're killed. I can see where that might sound harsh—killing babies, I mean—but it's been this way for hundreds of years now. No one questions it anymore. It makes sense, really. Since our sector sizes and resources aren't infinite, neither can our populations be unlimited.

The Governing Council sets up the rules—the laws—to keep us safe. As long as we follow them, there is harmony within the community. At least, that's the idea.

"I guess I just didn't want to admit that I've been having nightmares," I confessed. "Not to myself and especially not to you. But C, you can't tell anyone. Promise me. Please."

In our society, nightmares are seen as a sign of weakness or mental instability. It's believed nightmares lead to societal indecision and disloyalty. Selection students experiencing nightmares often don't make it through the rigors of Selection Week. They end up defecting and joining the many homeless castaways outside the sector wall, in the wastelands. Sector residents who develop nightmares later in life, after they've gone through the changes of their selection, are considered cultural flight risks and are often undesired by their chosen culture anyway. I guess it makes sense why a high percentage of them end up voluntarily abandoning the sector. When nightmares are discovered by the Council, it ends in one of two ways: voluntary sector abandonment or the violent physical removal of the inflicted individual from the sector. Me, I keep them to myself.

Nodding her agreement, C asked, "What was *it* about tonight? Anything unusual?"

"They're always the same. I'm out near the wall, running, and I hear someone screaming—a boy—he isn't screaming in pain, but—*urgency*." I looked around the room, but no one else had woken up. I kept my voice low. "He starts screaming for help and I stop running."

"You stop?" she asked.

"I don't know why. I'm not afraid, I just can't move in that moment." *It's his voice, something familiar about his voice that stops me, I think.*

"Then what happens?"

"Then I hear him calling me—my name—Zelina."

"Zelina? A, you know the rules. The name you select has to begin with the letter 'A,' because you were the first birth."

"It's not a rule, it's just what everyone does."

"You're right, it's not *officially* a rule, but it *is* what the Council expects. It's what everyone expects."

"I know, but—."

"A, don't you get it?" She held up my wrist so I could see my tattoo, C65A53, there on the inside of my wrist, just above my internal monitor. "'A' is your identifier. You should be proud of it. You were the first born, and you survived! That never happens. What more could you want? Why would you jeopardize—?"

"I don't know. I can't explain it. It's not like I picked the name. It was just a dream, but I know he was talking to me."

"How do you know?"

"I don't know, I just do."

She didn't say anything for a while. I wasn't sure if she was mad, upset, or just confused. I, for one, was confused.

"Then what happened?" C asked.

"It usually stops there, but this time it went on. I forced myself forward. I walked toward his voice and his pleas got louder. I reached out and touched the wall and I swear, C, I could feel him standing there on the other side. He stopped screaming and, just as I woke up, I heard him whisper."

"What, what did he say?"

"He said, 'Find me.'" I looked up and this time C looked away.

She wouldn't meet my eyes. She stared down at her hands, picking at her fingernail. "That doesn't sound so bad, does it?" I whispered. "I mean, as far as nightmares go, that can't be all that bad, right? Maybe it wasn't even a nightmare after all." She looked up, smiling at me, but it wasn't genuine—it didn't reach her eyes.

"I don't know, maybe not. I guess," C mumbled, looking away again.

"Look, C, I'm sure it's nothing. It was just a dream, not a nightmare, just a dream."

"Right," C said a little more confidently—and, after a pause, continued, "A, I'm not gonna tell anyone, but you shouldn't either. Just in case people get the wrong idea. You know what kind of trouble you could get in if anyone really believed you were having nightmares. And I don't even want to think about what they would do to you if they found out about your name selection. The last person to select a name outside of the approved identifier list—." She leaned in close and whispered in my ear, "A, it's not a good idea."

"Yeah, I know."

"Besides, you're not the only one who's ever had a bad dream right before Selection Week. But if you want my advice, when you get on that stage, select another name." Then she smiled, her '*I've got a secret*' smile.

"Wait. You?"

"Me? Heck no! You know I've known since birth where I belong." Then she smacked me on the shoulder, almost knocking me off the bed. "Besides, so have you, you're just nervous. We were born to be friends, right?" She stared at me until I nodded.

"Sisters."

"Exactly, so that means we were born to be sisters for life, not just until Selection Week." She jumped off the bed, and as she was climbing back under her covers she whispered back up at me, "A, becoming a vampire isn't going to be as scary as you think. Especially compared to the alternative—compared to becoming a lycanthrope—you really want to trust the Council to assign you to a good breed of animal? Our luck, they'd mix up the needles and we'd wake up with rodent blood running through our veins. I don't know about you, but I would rather be a vampire a hundred percent of the time then a rat, even just for the three days a month during each moon cycle. Am I right?"

"Yeah, right."

"Besides, you're the toughest female in our selection class. Even most of the guys are apprehensive about going up against you. Just trust me. OK?"

"Yeah, OK." I said the words, but inside my stomach was churning and I just didn't think I was going to be able to make that selection. I didn't think I was going to be able to make *any* selection. When your only choices are vampirism, lycanthrope, breeder, blood donor, or becoming a castaway out in the wastelands, what choice do you really have?

Selection Week was coming, and something inside of me didn't want to—or couldn't— make up my mind. However, *my* indecision wasn't going to slow things down, let alone stop them from happening. That meant, one way or another, I needed to get ready.

2

It didn't take C long to fall back asleep. Within minutes, I could hear her breathing settle into a slow rhythmic pattern. I knew she wouldn't be up again for another couple of hours, and neither would the rest of my class.

I quietly climbed out of bed and grabbed a set of clothes out of my locker. At one end of the living space are two separate bathrooms—girls' and boys'. Each is lined on one side with shower and toilet stalls and on the other with sinks. The bathrooms were always quiet and actually kind of peaceful this early in the morning. Soon enough, when everyone waked up, the shower stalls and sinks would all be occupied with people talking, laughing, and getting ready for the day. To me, right now, the quiet was better. I needed the time to think, to figure out what I was going to do.

The steam filled the shower and fogged up the small window up above as I stood there, naked, with the water running down my face and body. Then I heard him. "Zelina, we need you. *I* need you." I turned and pushed open the shower curtain, but no one was there.

I rubbed my eyes, trying to wake myself up. *'It was just a dream,'* I told myself, but I couldn't seem to get his voice out of my head. He had sounded desperate in my dream and now, in my mind, he sounded even more so.

I turned off the water, dried myself, and got dressed for the day. It was the middle of summer so everyone would be wearing grey shorts and grey t-shirts. I was no different. The Council feels that in order to eliminate internal conflict in the sector, all members—based on rank and position—should dress the same.

Prior to Selection Week we wear grey—only grey. From birth to seventeen or eighteen, when we go through selection, it's only grey. After Selection Week uniforms are determined either by your selection or by your calling. Most people get to select between vampirism and lycanthropy. Becoming a breeder or a blood donor is what they consider a 'calling,' but most of us see it as a prison sentence. The Council selects at least one breeder from each selection class. Donors aren't selected every year, only as necessary, the Council can select up to three from a single class. The only reason donors aren't needed every year is because vampires within Sector C have free rein, once a week, to hunt outside the sector walls. They feed on the scavengers because no one will miss them if they die. Donors are afforded more security than that, with a life-guarantee for at least fifteen years after selection.

Breeders wear white, donors wear red, those who choose vampirism wear black, and the lycanthropes, no matter what kind, wear blue. The style of clothing is determined by position and personal preference, but the colors don't change.

I've never really understood the need for such strict regulations. Our society is, for the most part, non-violent; at least that's what they tell us. I haven't seen anything to indicate otherwise, at least not among the selection students. I've read stories in the archives about young children killing each other over things like shoes or jackets in the ancient, pre-sector days. Something like that would never happen here. Maybe that's why we have such strict dress codes—when everyone is so similar, there isn't anything to covet. But then again, if we really were a non-violent society the population count wouldn't drop in the middle of the night.

I brushed my teeth then stepped back to take a look at my reflection in the mirror. Light brown eyes—almost bronze—full lips, and straight brown hair. C says I'm naturally pretty, in a way that doesn't need makeup. I think it's just her way of making me feel good. Honestly, compared to the other girls in my class, I think I'm quite plain. If it wasn't for the fact that I'm, physically, one of the strongest girls in our class, there really wouldn't be anything noteworthy about me. I'd probably blend in—go unnoticed. I'm not sure that would be such a bad thing, really.

I pulled my hair back into a ponytail and slipped out the back door as soon as the curfew light turned blue a couple of minutes later. It was still a little chilly. It wouldn't start warming up for another few hours when the sun came up, but the cool air didn't bother me.

The selection class barracks are just a short jog from the obstacle course we will be required to complete during Selection Week. Although we don't practice on it during training, we aren't prohibited from spending our own time training there. I'm not sure how much time any of my classmates spend there, if any, but I've been going two or three times a week for the last two years. Recently, I started going every morning. With my nightmares keeping me up, it's either put in some extra training hours or sit in bed and wait for everyone else to wake up. It wasn't until earlier this year that I actually was able to complete the whole course without taking breaks along the way. Now, it's just a matter of getting my already acceptable time down even more.

I had already made it through the mile and a half trail run, over the ten-foot warp wall, across the pond on the one-rope bridge, and was getting ready to do the half-mile zip-line course when I heard someone calling me. "Hey, what are you doing up there?" I looked down from the platform I stood on, fifteen feet above the ground, but didn't see anyone below me. "Over here. Look to your left." I would have recognized his voice anywhere. It had filled my dreams—nightmares—for months.

Sure enough, when I looked to the left, I saw someone—a guy. He couldn't have been much older than me, but I didn't recognize his face from twenty-five yards away, staring up at me. He had long wavy brown hair and a smile that seemed to light up his face. "Stay there," I called, as I hurried down the tree and rushed in his direction, but I didn't get far. I hadn't realized how close I was to the outer wall, and within moments I came face to face with the ten-foot concrete barricade separating me from the outside world—the wastelands. Vines of ivy covered most of the wall, causing it to blend in with the brush and trees, giving the illusion of free will and an unrestrictive environment.

When the sectors were established, sturdy, high walls were built around them. We're told the wall is to keep the castaways out. Lately, I've begun to wonder if the wall is really there to keep them out, or, if *maybe* it's there to keep us in. Our leaders teach us that the surrounding area is all wasteland--mostly abandoned ruins of the world that used to thrive there. The castaways now live out there as scavengers, foraging and hunting just to survive.

"Hello?" I called out, thinking—hoping—that maybe he was still around. I scanned the trees around me, but didn't see anyone there. I hadn't seen the wall from the treetop zip-line station, but then again I hadn't been looking for it. "If you're out there, talk to me." He didn't answer—not that I actually expected him too. It was probably all in my head anyway.

Walking back to the trail, I noticed a shiny, translucent stone on the ground. It was no bigger than a coin, flat and as smooth as ice. But, picking it up, I felt a warmth in my hand. I had never seen anything like it. It looked like ice, but wasn't cold. Glass? No, somehow I knew that it was more than that. As I continued down the trail, I saw two border guards walking straight toward me. "Over there!" one of the guards yelled. I turned to look, but there was no one behind me. When I turned back, the guards were running straight for me, guns up and at the ready. I was so startled I fell backward, dropping the stone in the process. When I stood back up, the guards were gone.

To say the experience disturbed me would have been accurate. I decided not to finish my run. I could come back later to complete the course. I picked up the dropped stone and noticed what seemed like a mist right in the center of it. Then it was gone, and the stone was once again as clear as glass. Just my eyes playing tricks on me, I suppose. I'm not sure why I felt so strongly about it, but something about that shiny stone called to me somehow. Or maybe the girl in me was just attracted to sparkly things.

I ended up walking the rest of the way back to the barracks, looking back over my shoulder every few steps, wondering where the guards had gone and why they had been there in the first place.

"Where have you been?" C met me at the door just as I was coming in.

I quickly slipped the stone into my pocket. "I was on the course. Better question, why are you awake so early?"

"Very funny, ha-ha." C started dragging me out the door with her.

"C, let go. I need to shower."

"No time, they just called a sector meeting, which you would have known if you had been here or if you had been paying attention to the morning announcements. All selection class members and all official sector members who are not currently working are required to attend the meeting. Everyone else has to watch the broadcast, and it's starting in…" she looked down at her wrist, where just under the skin the time was displayed on her internal monitor. "…ten minutes. Come on. We need to go."

I glanced down at my own monitor as I followed her out. It was only twenty after seven. "The Council never holds sector meetings on such short notice."

"I know."

"What's it about?"

"I don't know."

"Why does the selection class have to go?"

"I don't know."

"We're not supposed to have to attend the sector meetings until after Selection Week."

"I know."

"Why this one?"

"I don't know."

"What did the announcement say?"

C stopped and turned to face me. "Wow. Seriously A, what is with all the questions? Why do you even care? There's a meeting. Everyone has to attend. That's all I know. Besides, we're only weeks away from being legit sector residents. How cool is it that they are actually including us? Don't question it!"

People were hurrying past us and making their way around the meeting hall to the courtyard behind it. The meeting hall had once been a chapel. We've been told they used to hold religious services there once a week. The Council doesn't approve of organized religions, so all I know about them is what I've read in books. In my opinion, religion seems a lot like a fairytale. I'd like to believe that it's all true, but no one can really know for sure, right?

"Let's go," C said as she turned and started walking without looking back to see if I was still there.

Why do I care why they're requiring us to attend? I thought. C was right. I'm still a member of the selection class so I won't have a voice in the sector until after Selection Week anyway. It didn't really matter why we had to be at the meeting or what the meeting was all about. I might as well just sit back and listen; the most that could happen was I might learn something new about our sector.

When we got to the courtyard I noticed that rows of seating that had been set up facing the gazebo. People were already filling in most of the seating and others were standing around the edges and in the back. C and I made our way to the far side and stood with the others from our selection class.

"Check it out." M126, our selection class clown, for a lack of a better description, had leaned in to whisper in my ear. "Remy came to the meeting himself. This must be important."

Remy, our sector's primary leader, in charge of the Sector C Council, was standing at the podium in front of the gazebo. His photograph, along with those of all the other Council members, hangs in the hallway outside of the selection classrooms. Even knowing he's a vampire, it never ceases to amaze me how he never ages. Year after year, he looks the same standing before us.

Remy stood there, staring out at the crowd gathered before him. "Early this morning, there was a breach in the perimeter." There were gasps throughout the courtyard. The last perimeter breach had been over twenty years ago. Sure, there had been attempts, but security is so tight that none had been successful.

Remy raised his hands, indicating that he expected silence. The crowd complied. "We've called you all here today because we want to reinforce the importance of keeping our borders secure and to remind you of the dangers of letting someone in from the wastelands. You've all heard the stories, but until you come face to face with the castaways, you can never truly understand."

Remy motioned to someone in the back of the crowd and everyone turned to look. People moved out of the way, as two of the perimeter guards pulled a wagon into the courtyard. The wagon was topped with a large metal cage, and inside it was a man—no, a boy—he couldn't have been much older than me, with long wavy brown hair and—.

"Oh no," I gasped.

"What is it?" C was up on her tippy toes trying to see who was in the cage, but I didn't want to see him. I had already seen him.

"Ahhhhhh! Let me go!" the boy was screaming as he yanked on the sides of the cage. He was squeezing so tightly that blood dripped down the bars. They had stripped him of his clothing and left him in nothing but his undergarments. Dried blood and bruises covered his arms, chest, back, and legs. The more I tried to look away the harder it was to do so.

"It has been years since a castaway was able to make it past our guards," Remy said, as he studied the crowd. "We believe this could not have happened without help from someone within our walls." Again gasps filled the air.

People began to shout back.

"It can't be."

"We must find the traitor!"

"They must pay."

Even C, standing at my side, joined in the excited bellows. "Who would do such a thing?" she shouted.

Again, Remy held up his hands and the crowd went silent. That is, everyone except the young man screaming in the cage. "We are not violent people—."

The crowd around us erupted into laughter, while I, and the others from my selection class, stood silently watching.

"Silence!" Remy's voice reverberated through the crowd. "We have visitors today..." He nodded to our class, crammed in the back corner of the courtyard like cattle in a pen. "...be *mindful*. Now, as I was saying, this creature—he means violence against us! I leave his fate in your hands. Do we send him back, banishing him once again to the wastelands..." cheers of approval filled the air, "...or do we allow him to remain within the safety of our borders as a donor to the members of our society?" 'Donor' was a polite way of saying 'food.' Vampires feed on a donor for years—until the donor is close to death—then they either *turn* them or hand them over to the lycanthropes to finish off—to devour. To think--all this amongst a non-violent people.

The crowd was torn, but it was clear which the boy preferred. "Send me back! Please, I beg you, send me back!" he cried out, as he banged his body against the bars of the cage. No matter how hard it had been for him to get inside the sector wall, or what his reasons for doing so had been, given the choice of staying as a donor or returning to the uncertainty of the wastelands, he was desperate to be banished again.

I slipped away from C's side and weaved my way through my classmates, trying to get a better look into the cage. Although I was certain it was the same boy from earlier that morning, I needed to be positive. I was almost there and could feel his cries as if they were my own. Then, he looked up from where he had finally fallen—where he had settled onto the floor of the cage. "It's you," he whispered. "You found me. Please, help me, Zelina." He reached for me through the bars, and I saw that his internal monitor was no longer glowing. It would have been deactivated when he became a castaway. But I could still see faint traces of the tattoo that had been burned off–M58M–I couldn't read the rest.

Before I could get to him, the guards were on him—shoving his arm back into the cage—and C was grabbing my hand and pulling me back through the crowd.

"What were you doing?" C snapped as we reached the back of the crowd and slipped into the street.

"Nothing. I swear. I just—I wanted a closer look." She just stared at me with her knowing eyes. She knew I was lying, but I couldn't tell her the truth. "What?! I've never seen a castaway before. I just—I wanted to see him. I'm actually surprised you didn't." I tried to turn it around on her, as if it were her actions that were out of place instead of mine.

I could hear the crowd arguing behind us. Half the population wanted him sent back to the wastelands; the other half wanted to keep him—punish him—feed off of him. I'm not sure what was decided because C quickly pulled me around the corner and out of sight. "You need to start talking."

"About what?" Playing dumb was never my strong suit, especially with C. Although she might have lacked the drive or motivation to excel in her studies like me, everyone knew she was one of the smartest girls in our class.

"A, I'm here for you, but I can't help you unless you talk to me. What is going on? Who was that?"

"How should I know? He's a castaway."

"I don't know how you know, but you do. It's written all over your face and I saw it in the way he looked at you. He knows you too."

I looked over my shoulder, you never know who's watching, but no one was there. "I think—."

"What?"

"I think he's the guy from my dream. The one I hear calling for help just outside the wall."

C just laughed and shook her head. "Seriously, the guy from your dream? That's what you're going with?"

"I swear, it's him. I don't know how and I don't know why, but it's him. He even—."

"He even what?"

"Swear to me this will stay between us?"

"I'm offended you would even ask."

"When he saw me, back there in the crowd, he called me Zelina."

"Shhh!" She clasped her hand over my mouth. "A, we talked about this. Don't use that name—it isn't safe."

The meeting broke up and people started to fill the streets. M126 turned the corner and almost ran right into me. "Oh, hey guys, where did the two of you run off to?"

"Nowhere!" C and I said in unison and probably both looking as guilty as I felt.

"OK." He looked from me to C and back again. "A, you want to grab something to eat before class?"

"Oh, I don't know. I need to shower before classes and I think C and I were going to—."

"Nope." C slapped me on the shoulder pushing me into M126's chest. "No plans. Remember, I need to go do that thing we talked about. You should totally go with him. We can catch up later, after class. Besides," she leaned in, sniffing the air around me, "you don't smell that bad. Must not have been that hard of a run this morning." She smiled and her blue eyes literally sparkled. With that red hair one would expect green eyes—the blue was always unexpected. Then she was gone, running back toward the barracks and snickering the whole way.

"I don't think you smell either," M126 said, leaning in a little to check.

"Thanks," I smiled--all the while plotting my revenge on C.

"Great, so you want to eat?" M126 was grinning from ear to ear. It was infectious, that grin.

I kept on smiling too. "Yeah, sure M, why not."

It isn't that I don't like M126—I do. He's a great guy with the looks to match, smoky grey eyes and brown hair almost as dark as mine. He has an awesome sense of humor too, but he isn't going anywhere in life. He's near the bottom of our selection class, which means he won't be selected for a higher education program or an upper level position. After Selection Week, if he's lucky, he'll be placed in some sort of service position. Otherwise, he'll end up a donor or, worst case scenario, a castaway. There's no sense in getting close to too many people here—at least not until you're past Selection Week, when life can really begin.

3

Two weeks had passed since the perimeter breach, and no one was talking about the castaway anymore. Even my nightmares had subsided. C said it was because the castaway was dead and couldn't make his way into my mind anymore. I couldn't tell her that although the nightmares had stopped, the boy was never far from my thoughts in my waking moments. M58M--I needed to know more. I needed to know why he was there—why he was looking for me, if in fact he *was* looking for me. I had searched the paper archives in the library, but I couldn't find anything about the members of any of the closed-down sectors. I would have checked the computer system files, but those are monitored and I didn't think the Council would look too kindly on my unsolicited investigation.

It is believed that many of the castaways have special abilities—such as dream-sharing and astral projection—that allow them to influence the thoughts and actions of others. This is just one of the many reasons people believe the castaways to be a threat to our way of life, and one of the reasons the Council views nightmares as a sign that someone will eventually turn to that lifestyle. If people are having nightmares they are seen as being more susceptible to the influences of the castaways. Personally, I don't really see how their supposed *abilities* are any more dangerous than a vampire's mind control or a lycanthrope's superhuman strength, but I'm not about to voice that opinion in public.

I was standing at the bathroom sink when there was a knock at the door. "Hey A, you ready to go?" It was M126. I have to admit, I hadn't been interested in going to breakfast with him after the sector meeting. So, when we actually had fun I was shocked. After that day, he started joining me for my early morning run, and much to my surprise he was actually making great improvements both during our runs and during in-class training. It was just his inability to pay attention and his sarcastic sense of humor that continued to get him into trouble during lessons.

"Yeah, I'll be right out. Meet me outside." I quickly checked myself in the mirror again and straightened my ponytail. As I was passing my bunk I grabbed C's lip gloss off the shelf and put a thin coat on my lips—something I had recently started doing.

I opened the door and almost tumbled over M, who was sitting on the steps adjusting his shoelaces while he waited for me. I couldn't help but smile as he gave me a raised-eyebrow look. "You ready to run?" he asked.

"Yeah—of course, are you?" I asked. He nodded and I took off toward the course before he could finish with his laces. "Bet you can't catch me," I called out over my shoulder.

"Oh yeah? We'll see about that." Finished with the laces, he raced after me.

I had just crossed into the tree line where the course started when he caught up and grabbed me from behind. We both went tumbling to the ground laughing. “So, you still think I can’t catch you?”

I was flat on my back and he was lying closer to me than any guy had ever been—other than on the fighting mat of course. Yet, somehow this was different. He had one leg pinning me to the ground and one arm propping himself up so he was looking down at me.

“I—um.” I swallowed, because I couldn’t speak, and he smiled down at me, only inches away. “I let you catch me.”

“No you didn’t, but you can tell yourself that if it makes you sleep better at night.”

Does he think about how I sleep at night? The thought flitted through my mind and then I was back to reality, and he was lying almost on top of me. “We—we should get started.” I pulled myself out from under him, and brushed the dirt and grass off my legs and back before turning to start running.

He stopped me before I could take my first step. “A, wait.”

“What?” My hands were shaking and my palms were getting sweaty. I had never been one to get nervous, but something about being so close to him made my insides feel like mush and my stomach feel like I was going to throw up—in a good way.

“Did you drop this?” He was standing and holding his hand out to me, handing me the shiny translucent stone I had been carrying in my pocket for weeks.

“Oh yeah, that’s—.” I reached for the stone.

“It’s so smooth.” He closed his hand around it before I could grab it. “It’s hot and cold at the same time. What is it?”

"I don't know. Just a rock I guess." I wanted it back, but didn't know how to ask for it without sounding like I cared way too much about it—about a rock.

"It's not just a rock." He shook his head, puzzled—intrigued. "Where did you get it?" he asked, finally looking up at me.

"I found it. Can I have it back? Please."

"Yeah, of course, here." He held out his hand, and as I grabbed the stone he grabbed my wrist and pulled me closer. "A—I just—I'm sorry I knocked you down."

"Don't be. I mean, it's fine—no big deal."

He reached up and pulled a twig out of my hair and tossed it to the ground before taking a step closer and brushing the back of his hand across my cheek.

"Dirt."

"Oh." I looked up into his misty grey eyes and was lost.

We stood there staring at each other for what felt like an hour but was probably only seconds. "You look really pretty today," he said, not taking his eyes off of mine.

"Thanks. I—." I could feel my cheeks getting hot and I'm pretty sure I blushed. *Note to self – wear lip gloss more often!* "We should—."

"Yeah." He stepped back and the moment was gone. We started the course, running, talking, and laughing the whole way through. He was still having some problems with a few of the obstacles, mainly the zip-line, but we were still able to finish the course in just over an hour. When I run it alone, my time is usually around 46 minutes—better than average but not as good as I want it to be by Selection Week. The course record is 39 minutes, and if I have anything to say about it I plan to break that time. Which means, I've added a solo evening run to my training in order to push myself a little harder.

We crossed the finish line after the final quarter mile trail run, and M scooped me up into his arms and spun me around. "Woo-hoo! 58 minutes 32 seconds!" He put me down, but didn't let go. For a second I thought he was going to lean in and kiss me and my mouth went dry, but he didn't. Instead he hugged me then stepped back. "Thank you, A." I guess it was a good thing, considering physical contact of an intimate nature between sector members who aren't living as a family unit is absolutely prohibited—one of the Council's rules, designed to help regulate the population, among other things.

After regaining my composure I managed only two words. "For what?"

"For helping me. I know that without your help over the past few weeks there is no way I would be able to finish this course come Selection Week. Now, I know I can, and I owe it all to you."

"Oh, yeah that—of course."

M turned and headed back toward the barracks. As I watched him go I scolded myself for ever thinking he might actually like me, for allowing myself to like him, and especially for being willing—even eager—to break the rules so openly in public. I looked around, making sure no one had seen us talking—standing so close. I didn't want anyone to get the wrong impression—like I had.

"Hey, you coming?" He had stopped at the edge of the tree line and was looking back at me with that smile. That amazing smile.

Damn it, snap out of it A!

"No, I'm gonna stretch. Just go on without me. I'll see you in class." He shrugged and headed off back to the barracks as I flopped myself back on the ground and pretended to stretch out.

What are you doing? I asked myself. *This is crazy, you can't like M! You can't like anyone!*

Yup, easier said than done. I had made it seventeen years of my life without having any emotional feelings for any of my selection classmates, and now, the week before selection and I can't seem to focus on anything but him.

When I finally made it back to the barracks, C was sitting on her bed studying for the Sector History prep-exam we had later that day. "Hey, A. Have a good run?" She smiled her knowing smile and I immediately felt myself blushing for the second time in one day.

"Um, yeah. It was fine. Why do you ask? Did you see M? Did he say something? What did he say?"

"Wow, calm down. You need to relax. Yes, I saw him, but no he didn't say anything. He just seemed—I don't know—happy." She closed her book and stood up. "Why? What did you think he might have said? Hmmm?"

"Nothing—there's nothing—nothing happened." I quickly turned away and started grabbing clothes out of my locker. I needed to make my escape, and fast, but C had other plans.

"Nothing happened?" She blocked my exit as she stood, hands on hips and a crooked smile covering her face. "If nothing happened, why was M so happy?"

"He—he was just excited about our run time, that's all."

"And you, why are you so...nervous?" She stepped closer, backing me farther into the locker.

"I—."

"Spill!" She pulled me down onto her bed and looked around. "Everyone already left. Breakfast started fifteen minutes ago. So, we're alone. Spill."

"You know M and I have been spending a lot of time training together, right?"

"Yeah, I know."

Something about the way she said it, almost curt. "What? What's wrong?" I asked.

"Nothing, sorry. I just mean yes, of course I know. That isn't news to anyone, I want the news, the juicy gossip!"

"There is no juicy gossip. Nothing happened, I swear—but..." *How can I admit to C that I think I like him? What is she going to think of me?* "I thought he was going to kiss me. He didn't," I quickly added, "but I thought he was going to."

"And?"

"What do you mean, and?"

"And, did you want him to?"

"I..." I couldn't say it. I wasn't one to break the rules, not on purpose anyway. How could I admit now that I had wanted to kiss him—that I still wanted to kiss him? "I did—I do. Oh my stars C, you can't tell anyone. Promise me you won't tell anyone."

"Wow, quite the rebel you've become. Nightmares, consorting with a castaway…"

"I never—."

"…now this—intimate contact with a fellow classmate. Tisk, tisk, A. What would the Council think?" C started laughing, but I didn't find it funny. "Oh calm down, I'm not gonna say anything. Nothing actually happened, right?"

"Right."

"Then there's nothing to be worried about." She pushed me off her bed and tossed my clothes to me. "Go clean up. Today is a big day—last day of scheduled classes, then we have four days off before Selection Week starts next week, and we have to be at the field in twenty minutes. I'm hoping you're paired up with M for today's hand-to-hand training. I can't wait to see you kick his ass." I could still hear her laughing as I shut the bathroom door behind me.

I didn't have time to shower, but I got cleaned up and we made it to the field in plenty of time to stretch before either of us had to fight.

4

I had the giggles as I knelt there on the ground. Hand-to-hand had always been my favorite part of training. I was good with the book stuff—memorization and tests—but I was great at the physical stuff. I looked around at the others, and saw M126 watching from the back row. He was smiling and even from that distance I got lost in his eyes—again.

"What the heck A? The barrel of my gun is at the back of your head and you're laughing?"

"You're right, I should be more serious. Sorry H, I'll try harder." I tried to stifle my laughing, unsuccessfully. H107 was a year younger than the rest of our selection class. The leaders had decided to move him up a year because he was excelling in his academic classes and he was able to hold his own in all the physical challenges. That didn't mean he won every fight or even most of them, but he wasn't the worst in the class either.

"You've either really gone crazy or you just don't care about losin—."

It took less than a second to throw my weight onto my hands in front of me as I threw my legs out behind me to scissor kick him. My right leg going high sent the tranquilizer gun twenty yards into the clearing and my left leg going low swept his ankles out from under him. He was on the ground, with me straddling his waist, the blade of my knife under his chin, and a stake at his chest before he finished the word 'losing.' "Who said anything about losing?"

He didn't say anything. He just laid there wide-eyed before shoving me off of him and exiting the mat. I could hear some of my classmates giving him grief, but most of them were just laughing and congratulating me.

"Wow A, great fight."

"Serious skills!"

"Thank the stars I'm not fighting her this week!"

"Damn A," C said as she spun me around. "I've never seen you take anyone down that fast, especially H. You usually go easier on him. What got into you? Still amped up from this morning's *run*?"

I looked up and M waved to me from the other side of the mat. I didn't wave back—that would have been too obvious—but I did smile. "Nothing's gotten into me. I'm just trying to focus."

"Yeah, I can see that. You're *real* focused," C said.

"No, I mean—it's just with Professor Gunner repeatedly reminding us about Selection Week I'm just feeling a little stressed. I need to be working harder both in the classroom and on the mat."

"Right, I completely understand. I mean, if anyone needs extra practice, it's you," she said. "Come on A, if anyone is *ready* for Selection Week, it's you, and you know it. But fine, I'll play along. I'll pretend it's just stress. That still doesn't explain the stake."

"What do you mean?" Although I knew exactly what she was alluding to, I tried to brush it off.

"Don't play games with me. You know precisely what I mean. Professor Gunner made you the vampire in that scenario and H the lycanthrope! Why did you take a stake onto the mat?" C didn't normally question me, especially my fighting technique, but she wasn't going to let this one go.

"I'm gonna get some water, Professor," I yelled over my shoulder as I grabbed her arm and pulled her across the field and into the locker-room. "I told you, I'm doing what Professor Gunner said. I was just trying to prepare for whatever obstacles he threw at me. It's not like I didn't take a knife too." I was looking right into her eyes—I didn't blink—I wanted her to know I was serious.

"And he took a gun!"

"So? You know how I feel about guns. They're for—."

"Cowards," she said, finishing my sentence.

"Exactly. If I can't win the fight on my own, then having a tranquilizer gun isn't going to save me. Not in the real world." I turned to leave but she stopped me.

"You're not having doubts—you're not thinking about changing your—."

"C, I don't want to talk about this, not here. Not now."

"Right," she said, glancing up at the corner of the room where a tiny dot on the camera was blinking red. The Council is always watching the new selection class. "I know. I just wanted… I mean, you're OK right?"

"Yeah, I'm fine." You could have cut the tension with a knife, but what was I supposed to say? "Come on, we better get back to class. They'll be looking for us." I turned and walked out without looking back to see if she was following me. I knew she would be.

"All right, I need everyone on the track. Give me eight good laps, and then you can get cleaned up before you grab lunch." If Professor Gunner was anything it was predictable. He loved making us run after spending two hours fighting, I think that was the wolf in him. "Focus on your breathing, it might seem trivial to you now but learning to breathe while you're running just might keep you alive someday."

"Always a flair for the dramatic, huh Professor Gunner?" M126 slapped Professor Gunner on the shoulder as he passed him, but he didn't get two steps before the Professor grabbed M's wrist and twisted his arm down and around his back, all while stepping with his inside leg and sweeping M126 down to the ground. M might be improving, but there were still areas he needed to work on. Besides, Professor Gunner has been at this a lot longer than any of us and he didn't mess around.

"Damn." T240 squeezed in between C and me, whispering, "If he weren't ten years older than me or if I weren't just a selection student—."

"Don't say it, T," I stopped her.

"Come on A, you can't look at him and not want to touch those biceps. I mean he's just so yummy." T240 giggled and her golden highlights seemed to sparkle around her face giving her an almost angelic glow.

Still holding M down, Professor Gunner seized the teachable moment. "Now, if you had been more aware of your surroundings, M126, you might not be lying flat on your back right now." Then, casually, he looked around at the rest of us. "What do I teach you? A.R.C. What does it stand for?" He looked around as everyone just watched. "Anyone?"

"Aware. React. Control," I answered.

"Very good, A53. Now, M126, did you have anything else you wanted to add?"

"No sir."

"All right then, get up and start your laps." He looked around at the rest of us as we stood there staring at M lying on the ground. "All of you, go! Lunch is getting cold while you just stand there."

"Mmm, I'm ready to eat—."

"T, stop. Please, just stop," I snapped.

"Whatever," she rolled her eyes then took off jogging behind the rest of the class.

I could see the embarrassment in M's face as he turned away from me. "Hey, come on, run with me," I offered, reaching down to help him up. "Sorry about that."

"No worries. If you hadn't answered, we would probably all still be standing around waiting for someone to figure out the answer."

"Well, not all of us. You'd still be on the ground."

"Ha ha, very funny," M said as he took off running. "So, think you can catch me?" He was still laughing when I caught up, about halfway through the first lap.

Two miles flew by and M126 and I were two of the first to finish. C never was much of a runner, so by the time she made it back into the locker room I was already showered, dressed, and heading out to the chow hall. "Hey, you gonna wait for me?"

"Yeah, I can't. Not today, I need to eat quick and then read up for the Sector History prep-exam." I ran out and straight over to the chow hall to grab lunch, but I didn't stay and eat with the others. I knew C was getting worried about me, or maybe she was just pissed, but what was I supposed to do? We were closing in on the biggest week of our lives and everyone seemed to know exactly what they wanted—everyone but me. I had no idea what I was going to do.

I needed to figure things out, and fast, but I also needed to find out more about the castaway who kept haunting my thoughts, even though he wasn't actually 'talking' to me anymore. There was only one person I could think to talk to about it—Teagan—but I had tried several times over the last couple of weeks and never could figure out what it was that I wanted to say—or ask. Considering this was the last opportunity I would have to talk to her before Selection Week, I didn't really have another option.

Teagan was the only non-Council sector transfer in the last ten years. She had been born and raised in Sector M, but after the Council declared that sector no longer relevant and decided to close it, she got out. No one ever talks about how it happened—who approved the transfer, or why she was permitted to transfer before the sector was burned down—it just happened. That was supposed to be enough of an explanation, at least for those of us in the selection class. We don't rank high enough in the community to warrant anything more, but I was hoping she would share.

I knocked on her office door. Teagan was one of the selection counselors. Each year, she works with students in the selection class who are approaching Selection Week, to help determine their best fit in our society. I had already met with her two or three more times than anyone else in my class, but I never seemed to leave feeling like I had gotten any closer to a decision.

"A53, what are you doing here? Did we have another appointment scheduled?" she asked, as she pulled the door wide open, guiding me in.

"No. I'm sorry to bother you. I just—."

"What is it? Are you still worrying over your selection?"

No. Yes, but that's not why I'm here, I thought.

I nodded, because I couldn't find the right words to explain how I was actually feeling.

"You don't need to worry. I've seen your scores. You have amazing scores in all of your physical training, your test scores are at the top of the class in your core courses, and I've even been told you have one of the top five run times on the selection course—."

"How do you—who told you that?"

Teagan just smiled. "You're very impressive, both physically and intellectually and, believe me, it isn't going unnoticed." She meant it to be comforting, but it was anything but. "Vampire or lycanthrope, it doesn't matter what you decide. With your scores, the Council is sure to assign you a great position after Selection Week. I wouldn't be surprised if you're selected for one of the higher education programs. Doctor, engineer—your scores could get you any position you want. You just need to trust yourself."

"Right, trust myself." Teagan had no idea how hard that was. How do you trust yourself when your instincts are telling you to run and everyone else is telling you to choose?

"Is there something else?"

I shook my head and stood to leave, but my mouth deceived me. "Can I ask you something?"

"Of course."

"The castaway they found a few weeks back—."

Teagan quickly glanced past me, to an upper corner of the room. Looking back over my shoulder, I saw the familiar blinking red light. I had never noticed the camera there before, but it didn't surprise me. I'm not sure why I had thought her office would have been a safe place to talk. Wishful thinking, I guess.

"A53, we must not speak of such things," she said sternly as she picked up a pen to make a quick note. "The Council has handled the incident, and they have taken precautions to ensure the safety of our community. There is no need for you to be worried or afraid." She took a deep breath, smiled, stood up, and took my hand as she led me to the door. Out in the hallway she closed her office door and leaned in close and hugged me goodbye. "You are one of the top students in your class. The Council has high expectations for you—but I'm not the only one who has noticed your…" she pulled back slightly, "…indecision lately."

"I just—."

"We can talk, but not here." Then she pulled away, grabbed my hand and slipped a small folded paper into my palm as she shook my hand. "Thank you for stopping by. I'll see you again at your next appointment."

"But next week is—."

"Goodbye now." She didn't wait for me to respond before going back into her office and shutting the door between us.

I made my way to the training facility, gripping the folded note tightly in my hand as I walked. I passed two of the younger classes on their group runs through the streets, and several of the sector members as they walked to work, or back to their homes. Even a few of the Council members were gathered in a group just outside the training facility that morning.

"Good morning A53," one of the Council members called out to me as I passed.

"Um, good morning Blake—I mean, Councilman Blake. I'm sorry." I glanced down at my wrist and my internal monitor was glowing 12:40. "I'm sorry, I—."

"There is no need to apologize." He looked down at his own wrist and then quizzically back at me. "Where are you off to in such a hurry? Is this not still your lunch period?"

"Yes, it is, but I have a prep-exam—Sector History. I just didn't want to be late. I was hoping to do a little more reading before class started."

"Well then, I suppose you should get going."

"Right. Thank you." I turned to leave, but Councilman Blake stopped me.

"A53."

"Yes?" I turned back, slowly, afraid he might ask me about the note I was holding.

"I'd like you to stop by my office after your class is finished."

"Me?"

"Yes. I'd like to discuss your future here in Sector C."

"But, I'm just a selection student. I haven't even—."

"No matter. Let's say three o'clock, shall we?"

"Um, sure. I mean, of course. I'll be there." I stood there watching as he turned back to the other Council members who were quietly whispering, watching me. Then, they all turned and walked off toward the center of the sector where the Council offices are located. It's easy to spot a Council member by the sector insignias they wear: usually a gold pin worn over the heart, in the shape of an archer's arrow. However, sometimes it's embroidered onto their clothing and for the female council members worn as jewelry, such as hanging from a necklace, wrapped around the wrist as a cuff. I've even seen Councilman Iris wear a small gold arrow wrapped like a ring around her finger. The arrow signifies the force with which the Governing Council had won the war. Although they didn't actually fight with bows and arrows, they were cunning, fast, and precise, as they see the arrow to be, and as they teach us to be when training.

What could Councilman Blake want with me? I was in my own world when M grabbed my elbow, startling me back to reality.

"Hey A, ready for the exam?"

"No." I looked up at him. "I mean yes. Yeah, I'm ready. I just—I need to stop at the restroom first." *Why did I say that? WHY DID I SAY THAT?!*

"OK." He let go of my arm and I could feel my skin tingling where he had touched me. "Well, I'm gonna grab a drink at the shop. You want anything?"

"No thanks."

"OK, well, I'll just see you in class then."

"Yeah, OK, see you in there." He was gone, and I was once again left feeling utterly stupid, watching him walk away.

M was far from being the best looking guy in our class. Take D and F, for example. They were both *almost* pretty, in a manly way of course. And always at each other's throats, half-seriously, as if there were some kind of deep and basic difference between them that they couldn't set aside. Then there was N—tall and blonde, and always taking everything way too seriously, with that level blue-eyed gaze. Even H, who I had taken down so easily this morning—that sweet baby face of his made him look even younger than he already was, but in a really adorable way. But I had never felt drawn to any of them, or any of the others, the way I had been, recently, to M.

In the bathroom, I quickly checked under each stall door before locking myself in the corner stall. The bathrooms were the only place the Council didn't permit cameras, so it was a safe place to read the note Teagan had given me. I tried not to make too much noise as I unfolded the small, tightly-folded paper.

Behind your barracks tonight at 23:00

I read those six little words over and over in my head. "23:00—but that doesn't make any sense. That's after curfew." *Why would Teagan call me out after curfew?*

"A, is that you?"

I didn't move—I didn't breathe. How had C found me? Was she following me? I hadn't even heard the door open.

"A, I know you're in here. I heard you talking. Is someone in here with you?" I waited for what felt like an hour, but was probably less than a minute. “Fine, whatever. I just wanted to let you know class is getting ready to start. If you don’t want to be late, you should probably come now.”

I heard the door shut as she left the bathroom, and all I could think was, *what am I doing?* C had been my best friend since birth. If there was anyone in the world that I could trust, it was C—at least it should have been. So, why was I so worried about talking to her? Maybe it was because they had ingrained in us how important Selection Week is, how vital we are to our community, and how dangerous and uncertain our futures would be if we chose to defect. No, I knew that wasn’t it. I was just scared. “Crap!”

I ran out of the bathroom, slamming the door behind me and calling out, “C! Wait up, I’m sorry.” As I turned the corner I ran right into her and we both ended up on the ground. “Hey,” I began, not sure what to say next.

“Hey.”

“Listen, I’m really sorry. I’ve just been crazy these last few weeks. Lack of sleep and all.” She just looked at me. C has a way of making you feel two feet tall when she’s mad at you. “I shouldn’t have taken it out on you. I just—I didn’t want my problems to become your problems.”

“See, that’s where you’re wrong. Your problems *are* my problems, A. We’re best friends. Nothing is ever going to change that. So when you’re stressed I’m stressed. You used to lean on me. We used to lean on each other, but lately I feel like you don’t even want me around. It’s like you’ve replaced me with M or something and, honestly, I just don't see the appeal." She pushed herself off the floor and adjusted her shirt.

I jumped up after her, not even looking down to see what my disheveled clothing looked like. "No, I do need you. M doesn't mean anything to—."

"Wow. Tell me how you *really* feel, A." M126 said as he turned the corner.

Crap!

"No, M—I didn't mean—."

"It's cool. Whatever. We were just training buddies anyway, right? Sorry if I was cramping your style." I'd never heard him sound quite so hurt before, and his eyes seemed—sad.

What have I done? What have I done?

"You weren't. I didn't mean it like that. I was just—M, please. Just give me two seconds to explain." I turned back to C who was standing there shaking her head at me—at the whole situation. "C, please, you know you're my best friend. You're my sister, and you know I want—no, *need* you around. I'm so sorry, but you're also the only person I know who will always be there for me, so I know you'll forgive me." I turned my back to her, grabbed M126's hand and pulled him around the corner and quickly into the girls' bathroom, leaving C standing there alone in the hallway.

Inside the bathroom I locked the door as M126 just stared at me. "Um, you know I can't be in here right?"

"Yeah, I know."

"So, what am I doing here? I mean, clearly I don't mean anything to you, so—."

I kissed him!

5

The warning bell rang, out in the hall, and I quickly pulled away. "We should go."

M126 still had his arms wrapped around my back and wasn't letting go. "Yeah, but shouldn't we talk about—?"

"No."

"No?"

"I mean yes, but not now. After the exam, OK?"

"Sure, you want to meet out at the course around three?"

"Yes. No. I mean, I can't. I have to go to Councilman Blake's office at three." He gave me a funny look that mirrored exactly what I was feeling. "I don't know. He didn't say why." I answered his unspoken question. "Can we meet after that? How about after dinner tonight? Say, six-thirty?"

"Yeah, OK. I'll be there." He glanced back into the bathroom. "So, this is what the girls' room looks like. Smells better than the men's room." He laughed, and then pulled me closer. "You should go first. I'll give you time to get around the corner, then I'll follow you out."

"What if you get caught?"

"Maybe you should have thought about that before you dragged me in here."

"Oh, I—."

"I'm kidding. I'll be fine. I'll just say I had to go really bad and I couldn't make it to the men's room."

He was smiling. *Oh that smile.*

"Um, OK."

He kissed me again, then with his hand on my lower back he guided me toward the door. I looked back for only a second before leaving and hurrying down the hall toward class.

Both M and I were in our seats before the final bell rang. C was eyeing me from her seat on the other side of the room. I just smiled at her, pulling my textbook and my computer tablet out of my desk as if nothing had happened.

Professor Kade, one of the first Sector C residents, and a vampire long before the war of 2082, stood in front of the class. To say he was old would be an understatement, but with his shiny black hair and perfect skin he didn't look a day over 21.

Kade taught both Sector History and, for those students who were interested, U.S. History. I can't remember what the "U.S." stands for, but it had something to do with the territory before the war, when it was still divided into states. "Please clear your tables. We will be taking the Sector History prep-exam this afternoon. The results of this exam will be taken into consideration as the selection committee puts together your individual exams for next week. Remember, each of you will experience Selection Week differently. That means that your tests, like your fight selections, will be based on the Council's perception of your potential. I suggest you focus today. This test is more important than you might think."

On his desk was an old fashioned timer, which he picked up and tossed from hand to hand. *I am not going to miss that thing,* I thought as I watched.

"When you receive your results, I suggest you pay close attention to any areas in which you have not scored within the accepted range." Professor Kade is soft-spoken—so soft-spoken it's eerie. C thinks he is sexy, but he just creeps me out.

The older vampires have a way about them: it feels like they can see right through you—into you. Who knows, maybe they can.

"Go ahead and log into the test center now. You'll have one hour to complete the exam. Make sure you read each question carefully and review all of your answers before submitting your tests." As he spoke we logged in and, like clockwork, as soon as the last student was ready, he placed the timer on his desk and the faint ticking began.

I hate that thing, I thought to myself. Professor Kade was the only instructor that still used the old fashioned timers. All the other instructors would set the timers on our tablets, when time ran out the tablets turned off. It was so much better than the constant ticking while taking a test.

I stared down at my tablet. In the top right corner of the test center app was my name C65A53, like always. Below that, there were seventy-five multiple choice questions. Intimidating? Yes, but I had studied and prepared just as hard as anyone else, if not more. However, there was no way I could have been ready for what happened next.

I was about ten questions in when my mind started to wander. I glanced up and saw C shaking her head. *Focus A, focus*, I told myself, and looked back down at my own test, but it wasn't my test anymore. My right hand or what should have been my hand now had a scar along the inside of my thumb. It was the scar C had gotten when we were only six years old. I looked at the top of the tablet and sure enough where my name should have been, was C65C53.

"What the—?" I dropped my stylus and it rolled off my desk and fell on the floor beneath my seat.

"A53, are you all right?" Professor Kade stood up and started down the aisle toward me.

"Yes, I'm fine. I was only startled." Everyone was staring at me as Professor Kade bent down and handed back my fallen stylus. "I thought I saw a spider on my shoulder, but it was just my hair. Sorry."

"Right. Everyone get back to work," is what he said to the class, but what I heard was, *"Focus, Your future depends on it."*

When I looked back down at my test, it was once again mine.

Taking deep breaths I focused on each question individually. I used my stylus to select each answer one by one before moving on. I got stumped on question forty-five: 'What is the primary function of the archives keeper, other than to maintain the history of the sector?' Of course E popped into my thoughts right away. Everyone knew he was destined to one day run the archives. He thrives on all things old—old movies, old books. History had always been his favorite subject. He always said, *if you don't study history you'll be doomed to repeat it,* whatever that means. So, if anyone knew the answer, it would be E. As soon as I thought about him I *saw* his hands in front of me. He was holding a black stylus, just like mine, and I could see on his tablet he had selected: '(b) to share the histories, good and bad, so that we don't repeat them.'

I took a deep breath and looked down at my tablet. Sure enough my vision was correct: '(b) to share the histories good and bad, so that we don't repeat them.'

Interesting, I thought. *This could really come in handy.*

I finished the exam in just under fifty minutes. I looked around but most of my classmates were still focused on their tablets. I thought about reviewing my answers again, but I couldn't seem to think of anything other than the visions I had had. *Visions*—I'm not even sure that is the right word, but I couldn't think of anything else that fit. I had never heard of a selection student having visions. In fact, I had never heard of anyone having visions, at least not in Sector C. I sat back in my chair, trying not to think too hard, while I waited for the rest of the class to finish. I needed to focus on something other than the exam, and I did.

My mind kept drifting back to the bathroom and M's hands on my waist, his arms wrapped around my back, and his lips—.

"OK, time's up. You need to submit your tests and put your styluses down." Professor Kade interrupted my thoughts—not that he cared I'm sure. "You know the drill. We'll go question by question. Make sure you're taking notes on any questions you answered incorrectly. You won't be able to take your tablets with you tonight, so you'll want your notes to study over the weekend."

"Yeah right," J102 laughed. "I can think of better things to do this weekend." J was always up for adventure. No doubt there were antics planned for the coming unscheduled days.

"I'm sure you can, J102. However, with Selection Week only days away I think you might want to consider spending some time preparing."

Isn't that what we've been doing our whole lives—preparing? I thought. It just seemed like maybe J was right—maybe we deserved a little break before the biggest week of our lives.

"How many states were there before the Governing Council divided the territory into sectors?" Kade asked.

"48," F97 yelled from the back of the class where he and J102 sat whispering back and forth.

"Wrong. Anyone else?" E82, Mr. Historian, quickly threw his hand into the air. "Anyone else? Anyone other than E82?" He waited but no one responded. "Fine, E82, what is the correct answer?"

"50 sir. There were 50 states: Alabama, Alaska, Arizona, Arkansas, California, Colorado—."

"Very good, thank you. You don't need to list them all. Next question: how many sectors were developed when the Governing Council was first organized? C53, what answer did you have?"

I looked over at C, who stood and read from her tablet. "The Council established fifty sectors, sir. One in each state. However, there are only twenty-five still remaining today."

"That's correct. Can anyone tell me how the Council originally selected the locations for the sectors?"

I knew the answer and probably should have raised my hand, but sitting behind R201, the biggest guy in our class, I had the perfect opportunity to hide in plain sight without being noticed. Besides, Q190 quickly raised his hand and started answering before he was even called on. "They were military bases, sir. Before the military became obsolete, that is."

"Correct, it seems you have been listening this year. And, Q190, do you know the name of the base that once existed where Sector C is now located?"

"Of course, sir. Sector C used to be called Fort Hood. When the territory was still divided into the fifty states, Fort Hood was located in Texas." Q answered confidently. He has never been the brains of our selection class, but he does love Sector C and has been very vocal, since we were all young, about the fact that what he wants most in life is to become part of the sector security team. That means he has to know everything there is to know about our sector.

Texas, I thought—I had always thought Texas was a strange name, but then again we go by numbers and letters, so I can't really judge. We were required to learn the names of the fifty states along with so many other useless facts about the old world—facts that don't even matter now.

"...A53, can you list them for the class?"

"What?" I had been daydreaming. It wasn't the first time I had dozed off in class, but it was the first time Professor Kade had caught me. "I'm sorry, can you repeat the question?"

"Not getting enough sleep? Did you need to go to the infirmary for a sleep sedative?"

"No. No, I'm fine—I swear—sir." I looked around and everyone's eyes were on me for a second time. When I glanced back at M126, he was smirking.

'Are you all right?' C was mouthing. I just nodded and rubbed my eyes.

"I'm sorry. What was the question?"

"Of the twenty-five remaining sectors, which sectors have the highest population counts, and who are their primary Council leaders? Please list them."

I stood, because that is what he expected. "Sector A – Xavier, Sector B – Caiden, Sector C – Remy, Sector D – Bram, Sector E – Uriah, Sector N – Miles, and Sector Q - Amara." I could see out of the corner of my eye that C was quickly shaking her head. "I'm sorry, I didn't mean Sector N. They were deactivated two months ago."

"Three." Professor Kade corrected me.

Hmm, if we keep this up, I thought to myself, *in about a hundred years there might not be any sectors left.*

"Yes, I'm sorry, three months ago." I quickly sat down. I didn't want to be the center of attention any longer than I had to be.

Professor Kade watched me for a little longer, then turned to address the rest of the class again. "Now then, this was your last scheduled class before Selection Week. I'll need you all to turn in your tablets before you leave the classroom. If you want to take your textbooks with you, to study up for next week, please do. Anything else that is left in the desks after today's class will be thrown out, so make sure you take all your personal belongings with you."

"Excited to get rid of us professor?" Class clown M asked from across the room.

"If I say no, will it make you leave any quicker?"

"Um, I—."

"No, M126, I am not excited to get rid of you. Having only fifteen students this year has almost been like a vacation. When the next class moves up in two weeks, I will have thirty-two. But, I wish you all well, and I am looking forward to seeing how you perform next week."

Yeah, me too.

Everyone started pulling their things out from the shelves under the tables and piling them up in front of them. I just sat there listening—thinking.

"You will have the next four days off. Do not look at them as free time. Although you will not be required to attend classes, it does not mean you shouldn't be continuing your studies and your training on your own time."

The bell rang again in the hallway, pulling me out of my daze. When I looked around the room everyone was already up and out of their seats heading for the door. I followed suit, quickly gathering everything from under my table and placing my tablet on the table as I headed out the door.

"A53, could you stay for a minute, please?"

First Councilman Blake and now Professor Kade? What is going on?

"Of course." I turned back to Professor Kade's desk and set my things on the desk closest to the door. "Should I sit?"

"No, you may stand." He looked up at me from where he sat behind his desk and waved me forward. "You're a very bright young lady—."

"Thank you."

"Don't thank me yet—let me finish." He glanced at the door, which had just clicked shut behind the last student. "You're a bright girl, but you push yourself too hard, physically and mentally. If those were my only worries, I wouldn't be worried about you at all. However, it seems you continue to align yourself with others..." He paused, looking for the words, tasting them in his mouth, "...with *another*, who is less than desirable."

"I don't know what you—."

"I've spoken with Professor Gunner, and he agrees that you are exceeding even the very high expectations we had for you. We also agree that even though you could easily test at the top of your selection class next week there is little hope of you being given a desirable placement within the community. That is, unless you show the Council that you can make better choices when it comes to those you associate yourself with."

"But, I—."

"Now then." He stood and smiled across his desk at me. "You must understand, or at least learn to accept, that you cannot possibly anticipate every obstacle that you will face next week. And, if you try, you will fail. Selection Week is rigorous, both mentally and physically, and without the proper rest you will never survive it." He circled his desk, stopping to put his hands on my shoulders. "You can't do everything on your own, but those you choose to align yourself with must be carefully selected. Do you understand?"

"Yes. No. I don't know. I thought the whole point of Selection Week was for us to be tested and make our selections alone. Our futures within the sector are supposed to be based on who we are as individuals, right?"

He didn't answer me, only walked to the door and held it open for me. "I believe you have a meeting with the Councilman. You mustn't be late."

"How did you—?"

"Run along now." He shut the door behind me as if I didn't even matter.

6

As if the next five days weren't going to be stressful enough, Professor Kade's advice, or warnings, played over and over in my head as I walked to the Councilman's office.

"It seems you continue to align yourself with another, who is less than desirable." I couldn't figure it out. Did he mean C, M126, or one of my other selection classmates? Why would any of them be less than desirable? Sure, M126 hadn't been doing so great in the physical challenges, but that had changed over the last couple weeks. He was working harder and even putting in extra time. Besides, I haven't *aligned* myself with anyone, at least not publicly. We're all classmates—it's a little hard to avoid any one of them.

"You cannot possibly anticipate every obstacle that you will face…"

"Duh, tell me something I don't already know!" That was exactly the reason I had taken a knife *and* a stake onto the mat with me that morning—to be ready for what I couldn't anticipate.

"You talking to yourself?"

"What?" I spun around and H107 was standing right behind me. "No!"

"I kind of think you were."

I turned to walk away. "I don't have time for this, H. I need to get to the Council offices."

He quickly followed me up the road. "That was a great fight this morning."

I couldn't help but laugh. "You mean when I kicked your ass?"

"Yeah, then." I could tell he was still upset about losing—his neck and cheeks were turning red the way they do when he's embarrassed—but he was trying to keep it together. "Listen, I know you think I'm not worth your time, and maybe I'm not, but I've seen how you helped M. I just thought that maybe—."

"Wait." I turned to look at him, eyeing him up and down like you would an opponent—sizing him up to see if he was serious or just messing around. "Are you asking me for help?"

"Those you choose to align yourself with must be carefully selected." Professor Kade's words rang in my head again.

"Moving up a selection year was never my choice. The Council didn't give me a choice."

"And?"

"If I hadn't been moved, I would probably test at the top of the class during next year's selection. But, as it stands, I'm not ready for next week." He wasn't lying, and even if he had been trying to sound strong his body language would have given him away: slumped shoulders, shuffling feet, eyes on the ground.

"H, Selection Week is roughly five days away. If you're—."

"I know." Unfortunately, H had never really fit in with our class. He was smaller than the other guys and because he hadn't lost all of the baby fat in his face he appeared softer too. So, when he looked at me now in that innocent almost naïve way, I didn't know what else to do.

"What do you expect me to be able to do in five days?" I was about to tell him I couldn't help him, but then I saw it—the fear. There was no way he would make it outside the wall as a castaway, and although he could hold his own in our class he wasn't big enough or strong enough to get placed in a security position. His classroom grades were decent, but not good enough to earn him a placement in an advanced education program. So, that meant he was either going to be placed as a donor, or, if he was lucky, he might be given some low-level grunt job, as a service worker somewhere. He was in the same place M had been just weeks before, only M had made the decision to change early enough that it had worked.

"OK."

"OK? OK, as in you'll help me or OK, as in—?"

"OK as in I'll help you, but it isn't going to be easy, and if you fight me I'll quit. Do you understand?"

"Yes. Yes, thank you!" He grabbed me and hugged me, quickly releasing me and stepping back. "Sorry. I didn't mean—."

"It's fine." I said. I looked around, but didn't think anyone had noticed. "Don't worry about it." Looking down at my monitor, I saw that it was 02:55. "Listen, I really do have to go now." I started jogging off in the direction of the Council facility, but before I turned the corner I called out after him, "05:30, tomorrow morning—be out at the selection course!" Then I was gone.

I made it to Councilman Blake's office with two minutes to spare, and sat down on one of the over-stuffed couches in the lobby as his assistant went in to let him know I had arrived. There were plastic plants in the corners that looked like they hadn't been dusted in years and photographs on the walls that were so old they had started yellowing.

"Councilman Blake will see you now," she announced as she came back into the room. She held the door open as I walked through, then she quickly walked away, allowing the door to click shut behind me.

"Good afternoon, Councilman Blake." I looked around the room, nervous, not knowing if I should sit down or remain standing.

He was half standing-half leaning on his desk watching me as I struggled with the decision. "Please, have a seat."

"Thank you." I took a seat and couldn't help noticing that his office was decorated much more nicely than the lobby. The cherry wood table, desk, and bookshelves looked like they had just been polished, and the plush tan carpet and heavy burgundy window drapes were spotless.

My stars, why did he call me here? I thought.

"You're probably wondering why I called you here," he said, as if he had just read my mind.

"No sir. I mean, yes, I guess I am. Is there something I can do for you?" *Of course there's nothing I can do for him. He's a Councilman. He has people who have* people who do things for him.

"Actually, there is."

"Oh."

He walked around to his chair and took a seat. There was a full four feet of solid hardwood between us—the top of a beautifully renovated old desk—with nothing but a single manila file folder on top of it.

"I've been reading your file," he said, with his hand resting lightly on the folder.

"My file?"

"Yes. You are a very..." he paused, and I wasn't sure if it was for dramatic effect or just to scare me. "...impressive...young girl. Bright, and somewhat fierce on the combat mat."

"So I've been told," I mumbled under my breath. It seems more and more people are taking notice. I wasn't sure if that was a good thing or not.

"Excuse me?"

Crap, did I say that out loud?

"Nothing. I'm sorry sir." He just stared at me across the desk. He went completely still, like a statue. It's a skill all vampires develop over time, and it is one of the things that make them exceptionally eerie and yet intriguing in my opinion.

"No need to apologize." He watched as I squirmed in my seat. "You do that often don't you?"

"What, sir?"

"Apologize, when it isn't warranted, when you're uncomfortable."

"No, I don't think so. Maybe, I don't know. I'm sorr—." I stopped myself. He was right, I did apologize too often. Apologies when appropriate are fine, but when unwarranted they are seen as a sign of weakness, especially among the vampires. Since I am one of the strongest students in my selection class the last thing I need is to be seen as weak to the members of the Council. "No, sir." I corrected myself. "I apologize when I feel it is necessary, and only then as a sign of respect."

"Fine." He nodded his head slightly and turned his attention to the file on the desk in front of him and I felt a weight lift off of my shoulders. "As I was saying, you are a very impressive young girl. Your scores in class are all above average, and your scores on the field are exceptional."

"Thank you, sir."

"You should be very proud." He waited for me to respond, but I didn't. Pride is not allowed among the selection students. It isn't until you have passed Selection Week and are accepted into the community as an official member that you're permitted to openly show pride in your accomplishments. Prior to Selection Week your accomplishments are seen as the result of proper training and guidance and therefore any honor they deserve is awarded to your instructors. "Have you thought much about what you would like to do, after Selection Week is over?"

"I'm still considering my options, sir."

"Well, your scores are certainly high enough that you could select from any number of advanced education programs." He looked at me, through squinted eyes. "However…" he paused as he thumbed through the pages of my file a bit more.

"Yes, sir?"

"Well, I probably shouldn't say this but, unofficially of course, the Vampire Council would be more than welcoming should you choose the vampirism injection rather than the lycanthropy injection." He closed my file as he said it.

"The Vampire Council, sir?"

His eyes met mine and he smiled. "Of course I mean the Council as a whole. I only meant to say that if you were interested in working with the Council, there might be a place for you working directly with the Vampire Council *representatives*." Then, when he smiled again, he exposed his fangs, something completely against Council policy unless used in battle.

"I—." I stood, too quickly, obviously alarmed. "I must go, but thank you for giving me something to think about." I backed toward the door, not wanting to take my eyes off of him, but he beat me there. Inhuman speed—another of the perks of vampirism. One second he was standing behind his desk and the next he was gone. When I turned around he was blocking the exit.

"No need to be frightened," he said, as he pushed open the door.

Yeah, easier said than done.

"Think about what I said. We're all eager to watch your performance next week."

"My performance?"

"Of course. The battles fought during Selection Week help you make your mark—your reputation—among the sector residents. Although we won't be in the room with you, I assure you we will all be watching."

I walked out without saying another word. I didn't even acknowledge his assistant as she waved goodbye. I needed to get back to the barracks and find C. If anyone could set my mind at ease it would be C.

7

It took a while, but I finally convinced C that I was truly sorry for hurting her, and begged her to forgive me, and she finally gave in. I explained everything, from my first encounter with Councilman Blake, earlier that day, to exactly what had happened in his office. "He really showed fang?" C asked in disbelief, or maybe excitement. "That is so cool!" OK, mystery solved, it was excitement.

"It was not cool, C. It was creepy, very creepy." I looked around and saw a couple of the other students—Q190, R201, and T240—hanging out on bunks at the other end of the room. Leaning in I whispered, "Besides, it's inappropriate, unless he was warning me or challenging me or something. What do you think it meant? Was it a warning? Should I be worried?"

"I don't think it meant anything. It isn't a secret that we've been more than just leaning toward vampirism. Maybe he knows. Maybe that was his way of giving his approval." I didn't agree, but I didn't tell C that. "Besides, his fangs aren't what you should be focusing on. He basically told you that after next week, if you choose vampirism, they will place you in a position working for the Council. That means no more schooling, no patrolling the sector with the security teams, no crappy service job – not that you ever had to worry about that, but still. A guaranteed job working directly with the Council? That's amazing, A!"

"Yeah, about that."

"What?"

"I don't know. It's just the way he said it, he referred to the Vampire Council as if it was a separate entity from the Council. Like the lycanthropes and the vampires work separately or something. It was just weird, that's all."

"I'm sure it was nothing. You have no idea how lucky you are, do you? I would give anything to be in your shoes right now."

"Yeah, lucky." If I was so lucky, why didn't I feel it?

"Seriously A, I'd give anything to have a job working anywhere near the Council. Hell, I'd make their coffee for them if they gave me a desk and a phone to staff."

"You would not."

"Would too."

"Give me a break, C. You would hate working a desk job. You're meant for more—you'd love security work, but even that I think is beneath you."

"OK, yeah, whatever. I enjoy fighting, but seriously, how much fighting could security around here really do? The castaway they found a few weeks back was the first one to be capture in what, five years? Even back then it wasn't a full sector breach, External security was able to stop the castaway attack before they even made an attempt. It had been what, twenty years since someone had gotten over the wall before now?"

"At least."

She stood up and started shuffling through her locker. "I would need more action than that to keep me interested."

"Well, you're not going to get it answering phones all day. Besides, you've got the brains to be accepted into an advanced studies program, you just need to prove it to the Council next week." She turned and looked at me as if she didn't believe me or wasn't sure I believed what I was saying. "I'm serious," I assured her. "Admit it, you would be so excited to get chosen for one of the engineering programs. I see the way you look at the cameras around the sector and I know you've taken your tablet apart more than once. If you had let Professor Kade see that side of you, you might be looking at something more for yourself than just—."

There was a commotion at the front door—arguing, yelling. Both C and I ran to see what was going on, as did everyone else in the room.

R201, the most rugged, masculine member of our selection class, got to the door first. The rest of us piled out after him.

There, in the middle of the yard, were D77 and F97—fighting, for the third time that week.

"Get off of me!" F97 yelled, as D77 sat on top of him, holding him down by the shoulders.

"Do you know how easy it would be to sink my fangs into you right now?" D77 laughed.

"Um, hello… you're human! No fangs to sink in."

"Yeah, well, not for long."

F97 jerked his body around, under the weight of D77, and quickly bucked him off. F97 was bigger and stronger, when he had the advantage, and right then he did. He swung and caught D77 clear in the jaw, knocking him out cold. "Well, how easy do you think it would be to sink your fangs in now, pretty boy?" 'Pretty boy' was a nickname D had earned years ago because of how mad he would get if anyone messed up his face during a fight. Well, that and the fact that it *would* have been a shame to mess up that face, and he did keep his nails immaculately manicured.

F97 stepped over D77's body and headed straight toward us. F was every bit as attractive as D, but in a more animalistic way. Somewhat taller, broader across the shoulders and slim at the hip, he didn't just walk—he stalked across the yard.

We all moved out of the way, except for R201 who stood right in his path. "I knew you could take him," he smirked. "It's about time you taught that fanger a lesson."

"Wow, fanger? Really?" C spat at him. "You might want to take some time off from your daily workout. It seems, the bigger your muscles get the smaller your brain gets."

"Look carrot-top, I can't help it if you have some love connection with the vampires, but I'm not going to pretend that I like them. But hey—if you want to come over to our side—go shifter—I'd be more than happy to play *family unit* with you after Selection Week." R201 laughed, and it was deep, like a grunt or a growl.

C turned and headed back into the barracks, pulling me behind her. "It's C—not carrot-top! And no, not interested!"

"What about you A? I know you haven't decided yet. Want to come over to the dark side?" R201 laughed and as the door was shutting behind us I could hear them all laughing.

"What does he mean you haven't decided?" C snapped, as she turned to face me head on.

"What? Nothing. He doesn't know what he's talking about, C."

"You sure?"

Do I lie to my best friend again, or is it time to tell her the truth, the whole truth?

"A, snap out of it." C snapped her fingers in front of my face. "Are you sure?"

Truth!

"Look, C. I know we've talked about doing the whole vampire thing since—forever, but—."

"Oh my stars, he was right."

"No! No, he isn't right. Just listen to me." *Great. If I had to be stuck in this conversation or between a rock and a hard place–literally–I think I would choose the latter.* "C, like you said before, we were born to be friends, for life. It doesn't matter if I choose vampirism or lycanthropy. That won't change the fact that you are my sister. Besides we live in a sector where everyone gets along. Why should—?"

"Right. Everyone gets along." C scoffed and turned away, walking toward the bathroom expecting me to follow--which I did. "What imaginary world are you living in A? Why do you think we have a curfew in place? So the vamps and lycanthropes can get together at night and party? NO!" She looked back, making sure she wasn't talking to herself. "You've heard the screams that fill the night air. Sure, they try to keep it away from our quarters, but we still hear it. They play nice during the day but when the sun goes down, and all of us mere humans are tucked safely in bed, their real nature—their beasts—come out."

"I'm not stupid. I get that things aren't perfect here, but—."

"Not perfect? In the last three months our population count has dropped by seventeen residents. Vampires don't die of old age or disease and there isn't a single virus that a lycanthrope can't fight. So, you tell me how fourteen vampires and three lycanthropes just suddenly vanished. I'm not stupid enough to think they all just up and jumped ship into the wastelands. Are you?"

She grabbed her lip gloss off of her shelf and tossed it at me. "Here, why don't you go ahead and keep this. Not sure I need to be sharing it with a... What? Where do your loyalties lie, A?" She didn't wait for me to answer before walking away and slamming the door behind her.

8

I wanted to fix what I had apparently broken with C—again. It seems like all I had been doing lately was fighting with my best friend and then trying to make things right again. But I didn't have time to think—or worry—about her right then.

Dinner was already starting, and I had plans to meet M126 at the course afterwards. My insides were tied in knots, and I wasn't sure I'd be able to eat, but I headed for the dining hall anyway.

During breakfast the selection students have the dining hall all to ourselves. During lunch and dinner we share it with the lycanthropes. Vampires are different. They only eat once a day, and sometimes less often, and so during the dinner hours the upstairs is reserved exclusively for them. I've never been up there, but from the stories I've been told, they lay out the donors on tables and gather around for group feasts, with multiple vampires feeding off each donor at the same time.

Lycanthropes eat regular food, except during the three days of the full moon cycle: the night before the full moon, the night of, and the night after. On those days, they feed on the donors that are no longer useful to the vampires. I've also heard many of them get permission to hunt off-grounds, outside the sector wall. Other than that, they share the dining hall with everyone else. They eat meat, meat, and more meat at every meal, because their metabolism is so high they burn calories just sitting still. So, in order to maintain their energy and strength for shifting, they typically eat three to five meals a day. When the sectors were originally established, the Governing Council made sure each sector had farmlands and cattle ranches within its walls. We grow our own produce and breed cows, pigs, and chickens. I can't help but think with as much as the lycanthropes eat, we will one day run out of cattle.

Those that have never seen a lycanthrope eat should count themselves lucky. Dogs are more civilized than hungry lycanthropes.

I stood in line, filled my tray, and found a seat with the rest of my class. "Hey O, mind if I join you?" O154 is, by far, the prettiest girl in our class. She has fair skin, long golden-blonde hair, and the clearest blue eyes I've ever seen.

"Sure, but where's C?" She was looking around me to the cafeteria line I had just left. "You two haven't been glued at the hip as much lately. Everything OK?"

"Yeah, everything's good. I think she's just getting dinner a little later."

"Oh."

At that moment, as if it had been planned, the door to the dining hall slammed open and in walked C with three of our classmates hooting and hollering behind her. She looked like the queen in a parade. *Perfect timing*, I thought, but I just smiled across the table at O as if I hadn't noticed. Maybe O154 wouldn't say anything.

"Hmmm, that's interesting." Nope, she wasn't going to let it go.

"So, how did you guys do on today's Sector History prep-exam?" I asked the others at the table, trying to change the subject. I couldn't stop myself from staring at C, though, as she passed by with D77, T240, and W351—all students I knew were either leaning toward or openly committed to vampirism. Even though we weren't technically supposed to declare our allegiance before Selection Week, in order to prevent others from swaying our decision, there were more than a few students who had.

E82, the brains of our class and the one everyone agrees will probably end up running the sector archives one day, jumped right in. "That test was a joke. I didn't miss a single one. You think Professor Kade was going easy on us because he knows we're all stressed about next week?"

F97 threw his dinner roll, hitting E, right in the face knocking his glasses off and into his mashed potatoes. "You're such an idiot, E."

Although E didn't throw anything back, it didn't stop the rest of us from joining in. In seconds, everyone at our table was covered in food, and laughing. I had all but forgotten about C and her new minions. I was wiping the mashed potatoes off my face when I looked up and saw M walking toward us.

"Food fight, huh?" he asked smiling down at me.

There's that smile again.

"Umm, yeah. E started it!" Everyone except E laughed.

"Did not!"

"You kind of did," F said. "I wouldn't have hit you in the head with a dinner roll if you hadn't been such a brain!"

"You know that's not really an insult, right?" E said as he slid his glasses back on. He wasn't the best on the fighting mat, but trying to take him in a battle of wit or knowledge wasn't a smart move.

"Whatever. I'm out of here." F stood up. "Anyone else want to hit the lake to clean off?"

"I'll come," J102 said, hopping up from her seat. J wasn't exactly the quiet type. With her dark brown hair and chocolate brown eyes she could have been very pretty, but she was more 'one of the guys' than anything else. She was always ready for fun and she didn't really care what other people thought of her. She never wore makeup, always had dirt and grass stains on her clothes, and I'm not even sure she knows what a hairbrush is for.

"I could use a swim," O said, as she started cleaning the table around her.

"Yeah?" N152, said—seriously, as usual. "Then count me in." Everyone turned to look at him, and his cheeks immediately turned pink. "I just mean that—." He wasn't one to easily joke himself out of a tight spot.

"You are aware of the sector policy governing physical contact, are you not?" Councilor Serenity asked from only inches behind him.

Councilor Serenity's name should not be taken literally. She might look like a goddess, standing taller than most of the guys in my class with golden blond hair and a perfectly chiseled body, but I think she selected her name just to mess with people. She oversees the sector security unit, and to say that she is anything but serene would be putting it nicely. I once heard that she was one of the main instigators of the war of 2082. Supposedly, that is what earned her a position on the

Council, but other than hearsay there isn't any real proof.

"Yes, Councilor Serenity," N152 answered crisply.

"Good. Then you won't mind sitting this little field trip out, will you." Clearly, it wasn't a question.

His eyes darted to O, and a look of disappointment washed over them both. "No, of course not Councilor."

"Then I have an assignment for you." She took a couple of steps back and N152 turned, obviously intrigued. "Once you have sufficiently cleaned yourself up, meet me back here at the dining hall. We'll discuss the…" she glanced around the table, briefly meeting me eye to eye "…project. But don't delay. You need to be back in your barracks before curfew and this assignment is time sensitive."

As she walked away, without turning back, she called over her shoulder, "The rest of you should be mindful of the time. You wouldn't want to find yourselves down by the lake after curfew." Then she was gone—up the stairs to the vampires' private dining area.

"What was all that about?" O asked quietly.

"Who knows and who cares," F interrupted. "Let's go before it's too late." They all piled out, N heading toward the barracks to get cleaned up and the rest of them heading toward the lake. Only M and I were left standing at the table.

"So…you thinking about getting cleaned up too, or are you ready to—?"

"Yeah, no, I need to shower." I was covered in mashed potatoes and gravy. There was no way I was going to try to have a serious talk with M when I smelled like the dining hall had thrown up on me. "Have you eaten yet?"

"No, I had something to take care—." He was shuffling his feet—a nervous habit he's had for as long as I can remember. "It doesn't matter. But, I'll still be there at six-thirty. So, you get cleaned up and then we'll—."

"Talk."

"Yeah, talk."

9

It didn't take me long to shower, dress, and get to the course. In fact, I was early and glad because it gave me time to think. Physical contact, outside of established family units, is forbidden. What M and I had done, and especially me pulling him into the girl's bathroom, could have been grounds for exile from the sector. I knew that I couldn't let it happen again. I just didn't know how I was going to avoid it.

I sat with my back up against a large oak tree, just inside the tree line, close to the start of the course. M would be there soon. I closed my eyes and my mind started to wander back to the bathroom, my back pressed against the door and M's lips pressed against mine. Then, it was as if I could feel his hands on my hips but when I looked down it wasn't my hips I was looking at—it was a table, covered with food—the dining hall. I could see my tray—steak, mashed potatoes, and corn—only it wasn't my tray. The hands were masculine—the right hand holding a fork and the left one fiddling with a piece of foil—no, wire, about the length of a pencil.

"Hey, you sleeping?"

I was jerked out of my dream—vision—by the sound of M's voice. When I looked up he was smiling down at me and holding out his hand to help me up. I took his hand, and he pulled me up and into him. His other arm went around my waist like it was the most natural, innocent thing in the world, but I knew better. I quickly pulled away. “We can’t. We—if the Council finds out—.”

“A, no one is out here. No one is going to find out.”

“I’m just—.”

“I’m scared too.” He finished my thought with his own, and he was right, I was scared.

I was scared and excited and a million other emotions I had never known existed. All I wanted in that moment was to feel his lips on mine one more time.

“I brought you something.” He took a small step forward.

“You did?” I closed what little space was left between us.

He looked around as if he had heard something, but I hadn’t heard a thing. Then, he put his hand in his pocket and pulled out what looked like a wire spiral. “It was you,” I said, remembering the vision I had just had.

“What?”

“Nothing, sorry.”

He held it out to me, and I wasn’t really sure what to do or say. “Take it, it won’t bite,” he laughed.

“Um… I, OK.” I took the wire from him and rolled it around in my hand. It was lighter than I had expected. When I looked closer I could see that it was hollow inside and there was a small loop at the top. “What is it?”

“It’s copper wire.”

“No, I mean—.”

“It’s a charm.”

"You mean, like a good luck charm?"

"No, not a good luck charm. At least, I don't think so." He knelt down and started untying his shoe, and then pulled the lace all the way out. Standing back up he explained, "I didn't have time to find a chain, but I will."

"A chain, for what?"

"Do you have that little stone you always carry around? The one that looks like glass."

"How did you know I still—?"

"I've seen you playing with it. You had it earlier today during the test. I just figured you'd still have it on you."

Thinking back, I couldn't remember having it out during the test, but then again I hadn't realized I was holding it when he startled me out of my daydream—my vision. I had stuck it in my pocket as he pulled me up off the ground. Had he noticed it then too?

I put my hand in my pocket and pulled out the small, shiny stone. He plucked it out of my hand, and instantly I wanted it back. "Watch this," he moved even closer as he slid the stone through the slit at the top of the wire spiral. "It's a perfect fit," he said. "I knew it would be." As he strung his shoelace through the loop on top he told me to turn around.

I turned and he slipped the shoelace necklace around my neck. "Can you lift up your hair?"

I swallowed. I could feel a tightness starting in my chest. "Yeah," I managed to say as I pulled my hair up off my now-exposed neck. After tying a knot in the end of the lace his hands rested on my shoulders. I let go of my hair and leaned back into him, holding the charm in my hands. "It's for me?" I asked.

"Yeah," his voice was soft, and although I couldn't see him I could feel him smiling as he answered.

"Thank you," was all I could think to say. No one had ever given me anything like that before—anything personal—anything special. Closing my eyes I could almost see us standing there in the woods—close—too close—not close enough. I turned and his arms went behind my neck and pulled me closer to him. He leaned in and just as his lips were about to touch mine I heard the cracking of a twig. I pulled back. "Did you hear that?"

"Hear what?"

I scanned the tree line, but didn't see anyone. "I swear I heard someone walking along the path."

"A, there's no one there." He turned me back toward him. "We're all alone."

"Do you think—I mean, we're so close to Selection Week. Maybe we should wait."

"Wait?"

"I just think—."

M pulled back. I couldn't tell if he was mad or just hurt. "A, you know that even after Selection Week… this… it still won't be allowed." Then he took my hand. I don't think I had ever really held hands with a boy, not like that. "I really like you, A. I've liked you for a while now, even before we started training together. I don't want to make you—."

"You're not. It's just if anyone were to find out—."

"It doesn't have to be wrong," he pleaded. "If we both want the same things."

It doesn't have to be wrong. Does he mean that? I stepped back trying to fight the urge to hold on tighter. I needed air—space. *What do I really know about M?* I thought. *Not much.* I didn't even know if he was leaning toward vampirism or lycanthropy. Hell, I didn't know which *I* was leaning toward anymore.

"What do you want, A?" He asked as he moved farther into the woods.

"I don't know." At least I was honest. I watched as he paced the edge of the trail, until he stepped off the path and moved behind a large tree, where I couldn't see him anymore. "M?"

"I'm here."

I followed his voice, and as I passed the tree I felt his arms go around my waist and pull me into his arms. My back was against the tree, and his body was pressed up against me, holding me in place. His mouth was inches from mine, and I wanted to close the space. "What do you want?"

I whispered, "I want—."

"What do you want?"

"I want—." I was breathless, and my heart was pounding in my chest.

"Just say it," he demanded.

"You! I want you!" Then, he kissed me. It was hard and long and I could feel his body reacting to my touch just as mine was reacting to his. His hands were around my waist and then they were at the sides of my face, before long they were exploring the sides of my thighs.

Just as I was ready to give in to him I saw us again. It was as if I was standing off to the side, staring through the trees. I could see us, up against the tree, closer than two selection students should be. I stepped back and as I did a twig snapped under my feet. I looked down at my hands, but they weren't my hands, they were too masculine. I knew it was another vision, but I couldn't tell whose eyes I was seeing through. I focused on the hands. Masculine, strong, but with long slender fingers. There were cuts along the knuckles of the left hand. *He must be left-handed.* It was a passing thought but it made sense. When I'm on the mat my strongest punches are with my right hand. I'm right-handed, which means that my right hand takes the brunt of a fight. Why would he be any different?

I felt M pull away from me and the vision stopped. "Wait. Stop!" I wasn't sure if, in that moment, I was talking to M or to the mystery spectator.

M stopped. "What is it?"

"I…" I quickly looked around, but didn't see anyone. "Someone's watching."

"How do you—?"

"Don't ask me how I know, I just do. We need to get out of here, fast, before anyone else comes." We both started jogging toward the main path, but we didn't get far before M had to stop and pull his shoes off.

"I guess I should have grabbed a new lace instead of giving you mine," he smiled.

"Sorry."

"Don't be."

As we made it out onto the road. I looked down at my monitor.

"It's 20:53, M. Curfew is in seven minutes. Did you know it was so late?"

"It can't be," he said, checking his own monitor. He looked back at me, and I could see how confused he was, too. "I had no idea."

"Let's go." We ran the rest of the way back to the barracks. Once inside, we went our separate ways—he to his bunk and I to mine. Sitting up in my bed I had a clear view of him leaning up against the wall in his bunk across the room. *What am I doing?* I thought, but the answer didn't come.

I rolled over, and held my new wire charm in my hand, close to my heart. He had made it for me. What that meant I wasn't sure, but I was excited to find out.

10

I lay there in bed staring at my monitor, watching as time passed minute by minute. 22:35, only twenty-five minutes until I was supposed to meet Teagan behind the barracks, and I still had no idea how I was going to get out without the alarms going off.

I don't know how things are done in other sectors, but here in Sector C the general population—those still going to school and waiting for "Selection Week"—sleep in the barracks. Those who have already gone through "Selection Week" and have chosen to stay and work within the sector live in either the studio apartments that used to be called hotel rooms or the multi-family housing developments. Where people are placed depends on a number of factors: their selection, their job, and whether or not they have chosen to live in a family unit or alone. Then there are the sector Council members. They are considered our sector leaders and protectors and report directly to the Governing Council. Most of them have plush housing in the old officers' housing developments located near the center of the sector.

Slowly, I sat up in bed and looked around the room. As far as I could tell everyone was sound asleep. *Do I get dressed or just go out there in my pajamas?* I didn't want to get caught wandering around after curfew wearing nothing but a t-shirt—not that I wanted to get caught in my regular clothes either. Getting dressed seemed like the lesser of the two evils.

Normally, I wouldn't change so out in the open, but I didn't want to risk waking anyone else by walking back and forth to the bathroom more than once. So, I stripped down to just my underwear and then, grabbing a clean outfit out of my locker, I tiptoed to the girls' bathroom to get ready. I didn't turn the bathroom light on—I didn't want to chance anyone noticing it.

22:53—only seven minutes left. I was dressed and ready, but the red light above the back door was warning me not to try anything. Normally I wouldn't, but what choice did I have? I reached out, and just as I grabbed the door handle I was thrown into another vision. It felt so real. I was outside, behind the barracks, and I was kneeling down by a vent grate. I could feel the pebbles digging into my knees through the blue cloth of my pants. *Blue pants? I'm a lycanthrope,* I thought. I felt myself picking up a screwdriver and starting to work on the screws around the vent grate. Then I was back, standing there at the door about to set off the alarm.

I quickly let go of the door handle and stepped back. I searched the walls to the left and right of the door and there it was, behind a trash bin, a square vent grate just above the baseboard, maybe eighteen inches square. Kneeling down, I grabbed it by the edges, not wanting to make too much noise, and slowly pulled it toward me. Sure enough, the screws were loose, and the grate came off easily. I waited for the alarm to go off, but it didn't. *Hmm, it doesn't seem like it should be this easy,* I thought.

22:59. Counselor Teagan should be there any second. I stuck my head through the vent. It seemed to be large enough, barely, so I crawled the rest of the way through. When I made it all the way out, I saw a dumpster I could easily hide behind just ten feet away. There was no way to put the vent grate back in place, so I just had to hope no one would notice that it was missing. I sprinted to the dumpster, and waited for Teagan to show up.

Fifteen minutes passed before she got there. "I'm sorry I'm late, but I had to make sure it was safe."

"*You* had to make sure it was safe?" I exhaled. "*You're* allowed to be out here, I'm *not*."

"I know, and I'm sorry I couldn't meet you under different circumstances, but this was the only way. You know that don't you?"

What was I supposed to say? *No! Hell no! Why didn't you meet me in the dining hall for dinner? We could have sipped tea and chatted over dessert.*

"I do," I lied.

She looked back over her shoulder toward the vent I had used for my escape. "How did you know that I had loosened the screws?"

"That was you?" I asked.

She nodded.

"When?"

"Earlier this evening, when everyone else was in the dining hall eating dinner."

"But you—."

"I've answered a question for you. Now you answer one for me. That's how this is going to work. How did you know I loosened the screws?"

"I didn't know it was you. I just knew they were loosened."

"How?"

I thought about making something up—telling her that I noticed bits of dust and dirt on the floor by the vent—but what good would lying do? "I saw it—no, I felt it. No, that isn't right either—."

"You had a vision." It wasn't a question, but I answered her anyway.

"Yes, I think so."

"How long have you been having them?" She was intrigued. I could see it all over her face, and I started to wonder if I should be here—if I should be talking to her—trusting her.

Those you choose to align yourself with must be carefully selected. Professor Kade's words rang in my head again. *Carefully selected.* He had me second guessing everyone around me and my own instincts.

"A53, you're safe with me. Your secret is safe with me." She stressed the last part, and something inside of me told me to believe her.

"I will answer you," I started, "but first—."

"You want to know about the castaway."

"I do. When I saw him there, in the cage, he reached out to me." I didn't tell her he had called to me. I couldn't tell her that he had called me Zelina. I wasn't ready to share everything. "I saw his wrist and I saw that his internal monitor was turned off. I've never seen that before."

Teagan grabbed her own wrist as if remembering something, but I didn't know what it could have been.

"Then I saw his identifier tattoo, "M58M—." I couldn't see the rest. It looked as if the skin had been burned away, and parts of the tattoo along with it."

Counselor Teagan stared at me clenching her jaw; then, she took a deep breath. "What is your question?" Her hazel-green eyes glistened under the night sky and in that moment she looked as if she had taken on the weight of the world.

"You came from Sector M. Do you know him? Is it possible that he was looking for you?"

"Micah was one of my students, but no, I don't believe he was looking for me."

"Micah? So, you knew him well?"

"Yes, I did."

"You were an instructor?" Thinking of Counselor Teagan as a teacher didn't feel right. She had been in Sector C for almost five years, but she had stepped right into the role of selection counselor. I never would have guessed that she had been an instructor.

"I was. I taught Sector History. When I came here…" she looked down, "…it just didn't make sense to leave the teaching field altogether. Counseling made the most sense."

"What happened to him? Did he defect during Selection Week?"

"No, not at all. He was a brilliant student, and strong. He sailed through Selection Week. He was one of the most promising young lycanthropes in Sector M. That was ten years ago." I could see her remembering it like it was yesterday. "A couple of years later, while completing his higher education courses he was attacked—injured. After that, he was reassigned. He started working as my aide." There was sadness in her voice, an emotion I wasn't used to.

"Why don't you think he was here to find you?"

"Nope, your turn. How long have you been having visions?"

I looked at my monitor: 23:32. I knew I needed to get back into the barracks soon. I was starting to feel exposed. "It started the day they found him, the castaway—Micah. Maybe earlier, I'm not sure." *Should I tell her about the nightmares?* It's true, he had been in my nightmares, but I wasn't sure if he had been controlling them or if I had been. *Were they my visions or his?* I decided to tell her. "I had been having nightmares for months before that, always the same. It wasn't until I saw him there, in the cage, that I realized he was the one I had been dreaming about." When I looked up I could see in her eyes that she understood.

"That means he had been here for a while. Maybe not within the sector wall, but close enough."

"Close enough for what?"

"Close enough to connect with you," she answered--as if it was the most obvious thing in the world and I was stupid for not having realized.

"How is that even possible? I mean, I've heard the castaways have the powers of dream-sharing and astral projection, but why would they target me?"

"It isn't that the castaways have powers. In fact, most castaways do not. Micah was special. His abilities started when he was very young. His father once told me—."

"His father?"

"Yes. You see, not all of the sectors are run the same way. In Sector M, we were raised in family units.

Births were still regulated by the Council in order to maintain population, but once a healthy child was born it was released from the hospital and assigned to a family unit. It wasn't like here, where children grow up together with caregivers assigned to them as jobs."

"That's…" I couldn't think of the words. I've read about families in the books in the archives and I've seen old movies where 'traditional families' are depicted. I've always wondered why the Council abandoned them. "It sounds…wonderful."

"It was, but it was also destructive. The family unit structure was one of the main reasons that Sector M was eventually destroyed. Families were torn apart when children went through Selection Week only to defect, or choose a side that went against everything their parents believed in." Again she rubbed her own identifying tattoo. "You see, people need free will, and too often children were basing their selections on what their parents wanted and not what they felt in their hearts. Sector C does it right—at least to some extent—by not allowing children to get attached to parents. The Council allows the younger generations to decide for *themselves* what the right life path is for them—the one that makes the most sense for each individual."

"Our selection is still influenced. Maybe not by parents, but by our friends—our selection classmates—*our* families."

"It isn't the same. When selection students go their separate ways there are some hurt feelings, but in time everyone moves on. When families are torn apart by the decisions riots break out and chaos ensues."

"Yes, but don't you think we are also missing out on so much as young children?"

"In what way?"

In what way? I asked myself, but I didn't know the answer. I just knew that there was something missing, something warm and comforting—something I couldn't give a name to. "I don't know."

"A53, every once in a while, a baby like Micah… like you… is born. Your powers develop on their own and at their own speed. Some can communicate through dreams or through astral projection. Others have visions of the past or even future events. There really is no way to know all the possibilities. But you need to learn to use those powers. They can be very helpful to your future. Especially if you are thinking of—."

"I don't know what I'm thinking, not yet." I cut her off because I knew what she was thinking. I don't know how, but I knew she was wondering if I was planning to defect. "Besides, it's dangerous. I know what would happen if anyone were to find out I'd been having nightmares or visions as you call them. I can't take that risk."

"Right. Well, I can say that there is a reason why it is believed that so many of the castaways have those special powers." She didn't have to explain any more than that. I knew what she was trying to tell me—that one day I would probably be out there too, fending for my life, scavenging in the wastelands.

"Why did Micah end up—?"

"I left Sector M shortly before the Council deactivated the sector and burned it down. I'm not sure what happened to him when that transpired. I imagine he tried to get out. Maybe he burned his arm in the fires. I really don't know." She looked away. "His monitor would have been turned off when the Council deactivated the sector—everyone's would have. I can't imagine what they—."

Counselor Teagan glanced down at her own monitor: 23:54.

"You should get back inside. We'll talk again, I promise." Then she turned to leave, but before she slipped out from the shelter of the dumpster she turned back. "Thank you for trusting me. I promise you won't regret it."

After she was out of sight, and I was sure no one else was around, I sprinted back across to the vent, and slipped back inside. I pushed the vent cover back into place, and tiptoed back to my bunk. I drifted off to sleep thinking about Micah. Micah. Putting a name to his face made everything seem that much more real.

11

The next day, our first real day *off* in twelve years, seemed exciting at first. I wasn't really sure what I was going to do with myself. Normally, I'd have classes to attend or at a minimum morning physical education and fight training. There hadn't been a single day in the last twelve years when I didn't have something scheduled or someone to listen to other than myself. Even during the three days of the moon cycle each month, when so many of Sector C's lycanthrope population seemed to disappear, we had been required to attend morning classes. I lay there in bed thinking of all the wonderful possibilities.

"Hey A, you getting up anytime soon?"

I rolled over to find H standing at the side of my bed all dressed and ready, but *ready for what,* I wondered.

"What?"

"It's a quarter after five, you said to be out on the course at 05:30. I was just getting ready to leave and saw you still in bed."

Crap. So much for a day to myself.

"Oh yeah, sorry. I'm getting up right now. Why don't you head down to the course and start stretching."

Why did I agree to this? I asked myself as H turned and headed for the door, shoving a donut in his mouth.

"Spit it out and I won't ask where you got it from. I don't even want to know how old that thing is," I said. "Besides, it won't help you."

"What?" He looked back, mumbling around the donut. "Oh, right. Sorry." He tossed the small piece he was still holding into the trash basket next to the door as he left.

It didn't take me long to get ready. It never does. So when I got to the course I was only half surprised to find H just messing around instead of doing what I had told him to do. "You do remember I said that if you don't take this seriously I'd quit, right?" H quickly snapped into motion and started stretching. "Not like that. Follow me." He was going to need more work than I had anticipated if he wasn't even able to stretch correctly.

I started by stretching out my upper body and walking him through each step. Once it seemed like he was following along, I stopped talking and just did my normal routine. This session was as much for me as it was for him. Halfway through the stretching routine I heard twigs cracking under someone's feet. I turned to see who or what it was, but no one was there.

"We know you're there, you might as well come out," I called.

"We know who's what?" H asked, looking around. "Are you talking to yourself again?"

"No, I'm not talking to myself again—and I wasn't talking to myself yesterday either."

"OK, whatever you say."

A few seconds later M stepped out of the trees and onto the path. "So, you're training with him now?" M was looking down at H, who seemed fairly clueless, and M didn't look happy.

"He asked me for help," I explained. "I thought he could join us—."

"You still want me here?"

"Of course. You're my…" *What is he to me? We aren't a family unit, but we've been acting like one. He's my…*

"Hell yeah, we want you here. At least I do. You're the whole reason I'm here," H chimed in just in time.

M looked confused as he stared at H. "I'm the reason you're here?"

"Yeah man, I mean, you used to be one of the worst fighters in the class. You couldn't even make it two miles around the track without throwing up at least once."

"Um, yeah, thanks for the reminder."

"No, my point is once you started training with A, you skyrocketed to the top of the list. There's probably only two or three guys who can beat you in a fight now—and maybe A of course." He laughed and looked back at me. "I'm not sure there's anyone who can win on the mat against her." They shared some sort of *guy moment* I didn't quite understand—nor did I care to understand.

"Right," M said. "Anyway, it's about time we get started. Today is our first day off in years. I don't want to spend the whole day on the course."

We walked to the starting line and it dawned on me that H might not be as familiar with the course as M and I. "So, H, when was the last time you ran the course? Do you remember what your time was?" I asked. "We'll try to aim for having you beat that time today."

"Um, yeah, right. I was on the course about four—no five—years ago. When we all walked it as a class." I stopped dead in my tracks. "I don't remember how long it took us," he confessed.

He is seriously expecting me to work miracles here, I thought.

"So, you've never actually run the course?" M asked, taking the words right out of my mouth.

"No, but I'm a pretty fast learner."

I laughed. I flat out laughed, I couldn't help it. "Oh my stars, H. I'm not a miracle worker you know."

"Yeah, I know. I just—."

"A, come on." M was shaking his head. "He just needs a little help is all. He knows you can't make him the best in the class in five days. He just wants a little help so he isn't as nervous about next week."

I looked from M to H and back again. Whatever guy moment they had had back there must have been a good one. "Yeah, OK, you're right. I'm sorry." H was smiling now. Maybe having M on his side was all he needed. "If you're going to make it through the course, you need to pace yourself. It's not going to be easy. It starts with a one and a half mile trail run and finishes with a quarter mile trail run."

"No problem, I can run. I'm not the fastest in the class, but I'm not the slowest either."

"Good," I said. *Maybe there is hope.* "Between the two runs are a number of obstacles. We'll go through each of them today until you are able to do them without help. The first is a ten-foot warp wall. It's the hardest obstacle on the course, so you're lucky it comes first. You won't be as tired when you get there. Next is the one-rope bridge that goes over the pond. It's about fifteen feet long. It's not hard, but if you don't do it right, or if you don't have enough upper body strength, you could get stuck in the middle and end up having to drop down into the water and swim back to try again."

"Why not just swim across?"

It was a good question, and maybe in the real world that's exactly what you would do, but it's an obstacle course and that isn't the point. I took a deep breath before answering.

"Because the challenge is to get across the bridge, not to see if you can swim. After the rope bridge there is a half mile zip-line course, a twenty-foot vertical rope ladder, a twenty-foot horizontal rope ladder, a low crawl obstacle, the tire run, and then finally a forty-foot balance beam to cross. Once you make it through all of that you still have the final trail run and then you're done."

"Once I make it through? You mean *if* I make it through don't you?"

"No, you'll make it through. It might not be any time soon, but you'll make it through." M said.

"Yeah, OK. So, how fast do I have to do it to—?"

"Don't worry about time, just follow me. If you can't keep up just stay on the track. Either M or I will circle back to check on you. Just make it through the trail run. When you get to the ten-foot warp wall, I will be waiting for you on top. Got it?"

"Uh, yeah, got it."

I took off with H and M still standing there at the start line. I looked back. "M, get him moving, please!"

I heard M behind me yelling at H to start running. Then I heard their footsteps running in unison. I zoned out, listening to the rhythm of my own footsteps and focusing only on the dirt of the path in front of me. I love that moment during a run where the rest of the world seems to slip away and all that's left is me and the ten feet of path up ahead.

When I made it to the top of the warp wall I couldn't see either of them on the path behind me. *How can M be that slow? We run almost every day!*

It took them about seven more minutes to make it to the wall. I really should say it took H seven more minutes. Belatedly, I realized M wasn't there yet because he was busy encouraging H to keep running. I guess I should be thankful M was there to help. I'm not sure I could have handled H on my own.

"I know I said not to worry about your time just yet, but you're going to be timed on this course in only four days," I called down from the top of the warp wall. "It might be hard, but you're going to have to push *yourself* through the obstacles. No one is going to be there to convince you to take that next step or to tell you to keep going when all you want to do is sit down."

"Look man, the warp wall isn't really all that hard," M told H as he scuffed his shoes on the dirt a few feet from the base. "Watch what I do, and then try it yourself." He ran at the wall, took three steps up, and pushed off—flinging himself toward the top ledge. The fingertips of one hand grabbed the top edge, and he swung himself so he could grab on with the other hand too. Then, it was just a full-body pull-up to get himself on top of the wall. M wasn't even winded as he climbed up and stood next to me.

"Hey."

"Hey." I couldn't help but smile as his shoulder brushed mine. There wasn't a lot of room at the top of the wall, so standing close was a necessity—a wonderful, tempting necessity.

"See, that's not so hard is it?" M called down to H who was just staring up at the wall as if he was getting ready to vomit.

"Right. Not hard at all," H mumbled to himself.

"Now you try," I said. "Don't worry, we're gonna stay right here until you make it." I looked over at M. He didn't seem to mind the idea of staying either, no matter how long it took.

"You know this could be a while, right?" M whispered.

"I'm counting on it." I tried to hide a smile as I turned back to H who was scuffing his shoes on the dirt just like M had. "Maybe he'll become a bull or a horse. He's already got that whole pawing the ground thing down. Now, if he can only charge the wall and reach the top." We watched as he made his first attempt, unsuccessfully, and then his second, third, and fourth. "Just keep trying. You'll get it, you're closer every time."

"Yeah, right," H mumbled from below. "Hey, can I take a break?"

"Yeah, two minutes. You should stretch though, don't just sit there."

M laughed. "I remember when you were that hard on me."

"I was never that hard on you." I sat down, dangling my legs off the front of the wall and leaned back. M followed and as he sat back his hand brushed along the side of mine. My whole body reacted to his touch. “Hey, I was wondering—.” I stopped, unsure of how to ask it—whether to ask it.

“What?”

“Have you given any thought to what you want to do after next week? I mean...” *Vampire or Lycanthrope – if you had to choose right now, what would it be?* “...do you know what you’re—?”

“You want to know what injection I’m going to pick. Is that what you’re asking, A?”

“I mean, I know it’s none of my business really, and we’re not even supposed to be talking about it. I’m not trying to sway you or whatever. I was just wondering if you—.”

“I had always thought lycanthrope, but recently I’ve been thinking—I mean, you’re going with the vampirism injection right? Both you and C seem to have known what you wanted for years.”

“I don’t know what I want.”

I looked down and H was about ten feet away, just sitting there, leaning against a tree. “Time to go again!” I called out to H, and he reluctantly stood up.

“I just figured—.”

“A lot has changed recently, M. I mean, just yesterday, Councilman Blake basically told me that if I select vampirism I could work directly with the vampire Council members after Selection Week, but I’m not sure that’s what I want to do.”

“Wow. I mean, wow.” He seemed surprised, or maybe jealous. “That’s amazing, A. I’m hoping for a position with the guard. Maybe now, after everything you’ve done for me, I might actually get it. But, in terms of which injection… I really don't know. You're right, a lot has changed recently." He leaned in and I could feel his breath on my neck. "Maybe you and I… maybe we could decide together what—."

"I got it! I got it!" H yelled as he grabbed onto the ledge of the wall, interrupting the moment—before he slipped and tumbled back to the ground. "I don't got it."

I looked at my monitor. We had already spent twenty-five minutes on the wall. "Why don't you go down and show him one more time?" I said to M.

"Yeah, OK. But, we're not done here."

"I know." I smiled as he leapt off the wall and landed lightly and safely on the ground below. Knowing that M wanted to decide our futures together—it was more than I could have hoped for. More than I should have hoped for. However I didn't know if I really wanted to be responsible for deciding his future? What if we didn't work out, what if he resented me?

By the time we made it all the way through the course—with plenty of rest stops along the way—it was lunchtime. I never had the course take that long before, even my first time. However, admittedly, we had done most of the obstacles, other than the trail runs, a few times.

"Well, we don't really have an accurate time for you, but at least you know you can complete each of the obstacles," I said as I sat down to stretch near the end of the path.

H followed suit, but instead of stretching he lay flat on his back and stared up at the trees. "Thanks for doing this."

"No problem," M and I answered together, then laughed. We had had more fun in the hidden moments than H could ever have known. Not that anything had happened, but those shared glances, brushing up against each other, and the way M's little finger had settled on mine as we sat at the top of the warp wall for almost forty-five minutes—it was all very risky and exciting.

"What?" H pulled me back into the present—only half-questioning M's and my amusement.

"Nothing, it's nothing." I stood up and brushed the leaves and dirt off my legs. "I'm gonna go get cleaned up for lunch. Why don't you two finish stretching and we can all meet at the dining hall."

"What, guys aren't allowed to shower?" M said, laughing.

"Do you *ever* shower after we run? I mean, seriously?"

"I shower—OK, no but—."

"I rest my case. I'll see you at lunch in…" Glancing down at my monitor I saw that it was already 12:32. "…fifteen minutes."

As I took off jogging toward the barracks I heard H saying, "I can't believe she still has the energy to run. It's going to take me fifteen minutes just to walk to the dining hall."

"It's less than a block away," M answered.

"I know," H groaned.

I made it back to the barracks, grabbed fresh clothes, and was in the shower in no time. The warm water always felt great on my sore muscles after running the course. Today was no different. I closed my eyes and just let the water run down my back. The events of the previous day played over and over in my mind: my visit to Teagan's office, the Sector History prep-exam and my talk with Professor Kade, my discussion with Councilman Blake and his unofficial offer, and of course my time in the woods with M.

As the warm water washed over me, it was suddenly almost as if I were back there, in the woods. One second I could feel the rough bark of the tree cutting into my back as M's body pressed into mine, and the next I was seeing it all happen from outside of my body. I looked down, but they weren't my hands. It wasn't my body. *Scraped knuckles… left-handed… grey sleeves.*

I gasped for breath as I literally fell out of the vision. I opened my eyes and I was sitting on the floor of the shower with the water running down my face. "Who the heck was that?" I asked out loud to no one at all.

"It's just me—O." O154. Perfect timing, yet she had no idea what was going on behind the thin shower curtain.

I scrambled up. "No, O. I'm sorry, I wasn't talking to you. I was just talking to—." *Great, now I'm gonna sound crazy,* I thought. "I was just talking to myself." I turned off the water and reached out for the towel hanging on the hook outside my shower.

When I stepped out, O was washing her hands at one of the sinks. "I do that too." She was smiling as if we had just shared a little secret, a moment.

"You—?"

"Talk to myself," she said. "Sometimes, not all the time. I mean, I'm not crazy or anything." She was smiling. Somehow, pretty little blonde-haired O was always smiling.

"Hey, I'm about to grab lunch with M and H—you want to join us?"

"Sure."

"Well, give me five minutes and I'll be ready to go."

"No problem, I'll be on my bunk. I wanted to finish a drawing anyway." O was, for lack of a better word, an artist. Not like the ones I've read about in the archives, the painters and sculptors, but she liked to draw. She was actually pretty good at it too. It's too bad there aren't any positions within the sector requiring that skill. We don't learn art in classes. It's not a valuable skill, at least not in our world.

12

We sat in the dining hall, with M and H talking nonstop about the course. They were going over what obstacles we needed to work on the most, and telling O she should join us the next morning, but I wasn't really listening. I was watching—waiting. "Hey, who in our class is left-handed?" I asked to no one and everyone.

M and H exchanged looks, but it was M who answered. "I don't know. Is anyone left-handed?"

"There has to be at least one," I said, sounding confident but beginning to doubt my own vision. The guy in the woods the night before had been a selection student. He had been wearing a grey shirt—I had seen the sleeves. But—*What if he wasn't from my class? What if he was younger? Maybe he didn't even know what he was seeing.* I could only hope the last part was true.

"Well, well, well. Look who finally decided to make an appearance today. What have you guys been up to all day?" T240 said, as she strolled into the dining hall, flanked by U277 and W351. Leaning in toward me, she whispered in my ear, "We all knew you were buddy-buddy with M now, but come on, don't you think you're digging pretty deep if you've gone and scooped up H too?" She stood back up. "I mean really A, you're supposed to be our selection class leader. You've got the test scores to prove it and even the fighting skills, but why, oh why, would you pick these losers to hang with?"

W laughed along with T, but U just shook her head. "What?" T asked, staring her down.

"Nothing, I just—."

"You just what?"

U looked back and forth between M and H. "I just… I don't think they're losers. I mean M is almost at the top of the class now and H, he's pretty smart. Why else would the Council put him in our class?"

"Whatever. You think they're so cool, why don't you just hang here with them?" T and W walked off, not bothering to look back. If there actually was an official class leader it could easily have been T—she was a real 'take charge' kind of girl. W, on the other hand, could have done a lot more with what he had—both brain-wise and body-wise. W pretty much coasted through life, and he didn't do too badly, but he didn't do too well either.

M, H, O, and I just sat there looking up at U, who suddenly seemed awkward and alone. "You can you know," I said. "Hang here with us, if you want."

U did stay with us. We finished eating and headed back to the barracks to change. H thought it might be fun to hit the pool for a while and since we still had three more free days before Selection Week, I thought, *why not?*

It's hard to understand that while being a selection student there isn't much free time. Days are filled with class time, field time, meal time, and sleep time. Socialization takes place mainly around the fighting mats, in the barracks, and in the dining hall. Our instructors have told us that after Selection Week a whole new world opens up, but I'm not buying that until I see it for myself. If the distant cries I hear late at night after curfew are any indication, I'm not so sure the new world is really for me.

We were all taught to swim when we were little, and in the free time we did have the spacious, high-ceilinged pool room was a popular hangout. I sat on the edge of the pool watching the others splash about. Something just didn't feel right in that moment. I couldn't explain exactly what it was, but if I had to try I'd say the room had gotten darker and the air thicker. For a moment I wasn't sure I could take a breath, but the feeling passed.

I sensed someone behind me, and turned to see C standing a few steps away, staring down at me. "So. You go running this morning?" she asked.

"Yup. Like every other morning. You know…" I stood up. "…you could always join us."

"Us, as in you and M? Yeah, I don't think so. I wouldn't want to be—."

"It's not just me and M anymore." Her eyebrows lifted in that *do tell* sort of way, but she quickly stopped herself. C never did like backing down from an argument first. "H came along today. I'm trying to help him get ready for next week."

"Wow, good luck with that."

"I know, right?" We both laughed. It felt good—like nothing was different. "No, actually, he isn't that bad. He's just younger. He made it through the course, and we did each obstacle a few times. I pushed him pretty hard, but he hung in there."

"Wow, I'm actually impressed. You, I can see doing it, and maybe even M, but certainly not H."

"Well, it's not just me that's going to have to do it in a few days. So if you want to see them in action, you can join us tomorrow morning. I even think O might be joining us tomorrow."

"I don't—."

"When was the last time you ran the course?"

"I don't know. A year ago maybe."

"Well, part of how the Council determines the position they assign you after Selection Week is going to be based on your time on the course. I get that you already know what your selection is, but don't you want to be assigned a great job too? I know you don't want to admit that you want to get into one of the advanced education programs, but even if all you want is to be part of security, you're going to need to do well on the course. Unless you prove yourself—."

"A..." I could tell she wanted to say yes, that she wanted this petty fight between us to be over, but she just wasn't ready to give in. "...I can't. Not tomorrow, I already have plans, but maybe the next day."

"Yeah, sure. Well, you know where I live if you change your mind."

"Right." She turned and headed off toward the dressing rooms. She didn't come back out, and I wasn't surprised.

"Hey, you OK?"

"What?" I turned back to the pool to find M bobbing up and down at the edge. "Oh. Yeah, I'm fine. I thought C was going to join us, but I guess not."

"Oh, well H and O just left. I think they're heading back to the barracks for a while. Did you want to—?

"No. I mean, I don't want to leave if you don't." The pool had almost cleared out. Only a few others were left at the far end.

"Then you want to get in? I mean, we can do laps or something, if you want."

"Laps? What, you didn't get a good enough workout this morning?" I couldn't help but laugh.

"No, I mean, yeah, I did. I just thought maybe you would want—."

"We could play some pool-ball. Maybe a game of wolf?" Pool-ball is just like basketball, but in a pool. When you play wolf, each player picks a spot and tries to make a basket. If they get the ball in the hoop the next player has to match their throw or gets a letter added to their score. The first player to reach WOLF loses.

"You seriously want to play wolf with me? You know I'm amazing at pool-ball right?"

"Amazing huh? That's a pretty bold statement."

"Trust me, it's true."

"We'll see." I jumped in, splashing him in the process and quickly swam toward the net to grab the ball before he could get it.

He beat me there.

Holding the ball over his head where I couldn't reach it, he just laughed. "Not how you pictured this going, is it?"

"Or maybe it's *exactly* how I pictured it going." I jumped up, startling him, and grabbed the ball out of his hand. I tried to turn and swim away but he grabbed my waist under the water and pulled me back so that my back was resting on his chest.

"I... We should—."

"Right." He quickly let go and we put some space between us. No one seemed to have noticed, but there were always the cameras in the corner of the room, and whoever was sitting at the other end staring at the monitors. "So, wolf."

"Yeah."

We played, he won, and then we played five more games. He won them all. We were the only two people in the room now, and we sat on the edge of the pool with our legs dangling in the water. "You know, you'd think you'd let me win at least once," I said as I nudged his shoulder with mine.

"Let you win? Why would I do that? You don't go easy on me on the fighting mat."

"Yeah, but... this is different."

"No. Not really."

"I guess you're right."

He didn't say anything for a while, and I was starting to wonder why we were still there. Just as I was about to ask if we should leave he stopped me. "Have *you* given it any thought?"

This is it. This is the moment. I turned to look at him, and he was staring right at me—through me. His grey eyes seemed to glisten, reflecting the movement of the pool water.

He looked up at the camera in the corner and then back down to the pool water. "You think they can hear us?"

"No. Well, not if we're quiet. I don't think so anyway."

"Like you, I don't want to sway your decision. I just, well, I like you and I figured if you like me too, then—."

"I do."

"Good. I'm glad."

"I just... I don't want you to base your selection on me. Not if you know what you want. It's just that, I'm not a hundred percent sure what my selection is going to be. I've always thought I'd select the vampire injection, but lately... I don't know."

"Yeah, but if you can get a position working with the Council's vampire representatives... I mean, you can't really turn *that* down, right?"

"Right. I mean, I guess not." *He's right, isn't he?* I asked myself. I couldn't really turn down a position with the Council, could I?

"Just think about it, OK? I want to be with you. If that means we both end up selecting vampirism then I'm OK with that. You just let me know. That is, if you want to be with me too."

"I—."

"What are you two doing?" The door from the dressing room opened behind us, and the building security guard interrupted our conversation not a moment too soon.

"Um, we... We're just talking."

"The pool's closed. Closed a half hour ago. You'll need to get dressed and head out."

"Oh! Sorry!" M and I replied in unison, then jumped up and headed to our separate dressing rooms to change. The moment was over, and if I were to be honest with myself I wasn't upset about the interruption. I didn't know what I would have said next, let alone what

I should do. I needed some time to think, and I planned to take these next few days before Selection Week to do just that.

The next three days turned out to be pretty much the same. We spent our mornings on the course, ate lunch, and then spent the rest of the day running around the sector having fun. It's one thing to study the sector map, but to actually have free reign of it—I had no idea how big the sector really was and there was no way we were going to be able to see all of it in just three days.

In the late hours of the evening before Selection Week was to begin, I sat on my bunk, books spread around me, getting ready to study. It's never too late to cram, right? But as soon as I picked up my Sector History book I felt it happening again. My hands were hurriedly flipping through the pages to stick something inside. I gasped for breath as I pulled myself out of the vision.

"Hey, you OK up there?" C called from the bed below mine.

"Yeah, yeah I'm fine." I hung over the bed to see her. "You reading too?"

"Everyone is. It's weird right? I mean, exams start tomorrow, and until earlier today everything seemed normal. Now… I don't know, everything seems so uncertain."

"Hey, C. You're going to do amazing this week. You're so smart, tough, and honestly, you've known what you wanted all your life. There is no way you're going to fail." Hanging upside down from my upper bunk, I felt my cheeks getting warm as all my blood flowed to my face.

"Thanks," she said. "Now sit back up before your head explodes." We laughed and a few people around the room hushed us, as if laughing wasn't allowed.

"Oh, get a grip," C called out. "If you don't know the answers yet, you're not going to know them by tomorrow."

And one by one everyone in the room started to laugh. Maybe that's all we needed—all anyone needed—just a break in the tension.

I sat back up on my bed and cautiously picked up my book again. No vision. I flipped through the pages, and there it was—a small folded paper stuck in the middle of chapter three. When I unfolded it, I recognized Teagan's handwriting right away.

Tonight, same time, same place.

Yeah, sure, I don't need rest the night before Selection Week starts. What was she thinking? I wondered.

13

I sat out behind the dumpster, waiting for Counselor Teagan to arrive. She was only five minutes late this time, which is practically on time for most of the people I know. "I'm glad you got my message. I couldn't figure out any other way to get to you—not without the Council noticing."

"You're lucky I saw it. I hadn't planned on studying tonight, at least not Sector History, but everyone else was reading so—."

"It's a good thing you did." She glanced over her shoulder where I saw two sector residents passing. She drew me farther back into the dark corner where we couldn't be seen, and said, "You're being watched."

"I know, but how did you know?"

"I'm the Selection Counselor, which means I'm also on the board that will be testing you next week. We had a meeting earlier today, and your name came up. A number of the board members, mostly Council members, are extremely nervous about your testing. One of them, Councilman Serenity, announced that she suspected you of violating the rules governing physical contact with another sector member. She requested to have you followed. Her request was granted."

"Wait, when was that meeting?"

"This morning, why?"

"Someone has been following me for the past five days. It didn't just start this morning." I tried to remember when I felt it last—it was out on the course earlier that morning, while training with M and H.

"Are you sure?"

"Yes."

She gave me a steady, level gaze, and moved in closer. "Have you done anything, even something small, within the past five days that could confirm her suspicions?"

Images flooded my mind. The feel of M's lips on mine was still so fresh. The warmth of his touch. What was I supposed to say? Do I lie and risk losing her trust when she does find out the truth, or do I admit what I've done and hope that she isn't going to turn me in?

"A53, have you done—?"

"Yes." My voice quivered, but not in fear. It was the excited memories of what I had done. I wouldn't have given up a single second of my time with M over the past few weeks, even if it meant punishment by the Council.

Teagan nodded thoughtfully. Finally, she said she wouldn't turn me in, but I could see she wasn't exactly happy with me either. She listened to my side of the story and waited until I finished before she laid it out for me, in no uncertain terms, what it would mean for me if, in fact, Councilman Serenity had proof to show the rest of the Selection Board.

"It could mean being banished from the sector, in which case the Council would most likely have you removed prior to testing tomorrow morning—both of you. Or, it could mean involuntary placement." I waited, but she didn't elaborate on that possibility, and I was guessing involuntary placement, at least in her opinion, was worse than being banished.

"What do you mean by involuntary placement?" I wasn't sure I really wanted to know, but I did want to be prepared for every possibility.

"They could decide, no matter your scores, to place you as a breeder, or a donor, or—."

"Or?"

"Or, they could choose your injection classification—vampirism or lycanthropy—no matter your selection of choice. That probably doesn't seem all that bad, but trust me, living as someone you're not, or something you never wanted to be, isn't as easy as some might think. It is, I mean would be, in my opinion, the worst punishment they could give you."

"Are you saying that you—?"

She didn't answer, and that was answer enough.

"They can't really do that, can they? I mean, how could they? It goes against everything our sector stands for. You've said it yourself so many times this year—Sector C is based on free will, allowing its members to decide for themselves what their future holds. How can they justify a punishment that goes against that?"

"As you said, it would be a punishment. Punishments are not meant to please the wrongdoer. They are meant to teach you a lesson." She looked down, searching for something to offer in the way of encouragement—guidance—hope—but she came up empty. "I'm sorry, A53. I wish that I knew more. I will hope for the best, and in the morning we will both find out what the Council has in store for you."

"When? Will you be able to warn me? Will they do it in front of everyone else?"

"A53, you need to try and relax. I don't know if the Council will let the rest of the selection committee know or if they will handle it on their own. You might find out at the same time I do. We will just have to wait and see what tomorrow brings."

"Yeah, easy for you to say."

"Not really. I've been where you are, or at least in a similar situation. I know it isn't easy, but I'm here for you. I told you that you can trust me, and you can. Do you understand?"

"Yes."

"Then go back in and try to get some rest. You'll need it, whether they let you test or not."

A single tear escaped my eye. It was probably the first time I had cried in over twelve years, and I wasn't about to let her see. "Fine, I'll be ready." I turned and squirmed back into the barracks through the vent grate without looking back.

14

"A, wake up." M was nudging my shoulder. "Hey, you OK?"

Apparently, if someone else was waking me up, my internal alarm clock had failed me for the second time in less than a week, but what did I expect? I had gotten maybe two hours of uninterrupted sleep all night. My brain kept replaying the conversation with Teagan, and when I finally fell asleep I kept being startled awake by nightmares about what was going to happen to me this morning.

"Yeah, I'm fine. What time is it?"

"It's 07:40. We have to be out at the course in twenty minutes. Big day, remember?"

Twenty minutes? I sat straight up in bed misjudging how close I was to the edge and fell out straight into M's arms. He caught me. "Oh. Sorry."

"No need to apologize," he smiled, as he stood me up. "You sure you're OK?"

"No, but it doesn't really matter now, does it?" I could read all over his face that he was confused, but I didn't have time to explain, nor did I know how. "It's only going to take me five minutes to get dressed."

"I'll wait. We can walk to the course together." He smiled. "Maybe you can tell me why the top student in our class seems so nervous."

I wasn't so sure that was a good idea, but then again, if Serenity already had the proof she needed, it was going to incriminate both M and me. We might as well face the firing squad together. "Yeah, OK. Just give me a few minutes and I'll be ready to go." I grabbed a change of clothes and dashed into the bathroom. I didn't shower, but I figured I could do that after I finished the course. That is, if the Council even let me go through Selection Week. If they didn't, and they sent me out into the wasteland, then maybe not showering would help me blend in. A shiver ran down my spine, I didn't want to think about that right then.

When I got back to my bunk, M was sitting on C's bed flipping through my Sector History book. "You know, cramming this morning isn't going to do you any good," I said, jokingly—trying to ease some of my pent-up nerves. It didn't work.

"Yeah, you're probably right," he mused, without looking up. "Hey—what's this?"

It was the note from Teagan: *Tonight, same time, same place.* "Oh, that's... It's from C. A note to meet her."

"From C?"

There's no way he's going to buy this, I thought. "Yeah."

"I thought you two weren't speaking right now."

"No, we aren't. I mean, we are, but yeah, things are rocky. But, that's old." I grabbed the note, folded it back up and shoved it back into my book and tossed the book onto the shelf. "I just use it as a bookmark now." I glanced down at my monitor: 07:50. "Ten minutes. We should go." I turned to leave, not waiting for him to respond.

As we walked to the course I gave M the abbreviated version of what had happened, and might be happening.

"You mean they did see us?"

"I think so."

"Then why haven't they said anything until now? Why would they let us finish out the last week? Why make us wait until the first day of Selection Week?" M asked, without giving me time to answer.

"I don't know. I think we just need to go and see what happens. Maybe everything will be fine. Maybe I'm worried about nothing."

He stopped just before we came to the tree line, and turned to me. "A?"

"Yeah?"

"Whatever happens, I'm here for you."

"I know,"

"Do you?"

"I think so, yeah."

"And? I mean, we're in this together, right? It isn't just you out there on your own. I want to be with you, here in Sector C, or out there, wherever we end up."

"Let's not worry about that, not yet. We still have time, OK?" I smiled but I don't think it reached my eyes. Something just didn't feel right. "Come on, we need to go."

We stood there—the whole selection class—all fifteen of us, and no one said a word. We had been told to be at the course at exactly 08:00 and we were. Not a single person was late.

Time slowly passed and it was 08:15 with no sign of any of our instructors, the Selection Board members, or the Council.

This has to be a test. They're probably watching us, I thought to myself, but I didn't look around to find out. Instead, I began to stretch. If they were going to expect us to run the course I wanted to be ready. M and H both followed my lead. Pretty soon more than half of the class had joined in. By the time we finished stretching, and I felt completely warmed up and ready, I saw Professor Gunner, Counselor Teagan, and Councilman Ash walking up the path.

Councilman Ash was in charge of all selection student events and recreation activities, including Selection Week. From what I've heard, he designed the obstacle course as well as most of the physical and mental testing we would be going through. Although I have never personally spoken with Councilman Ash, I have seen and heard him speak numerous times over the last twelve years in the selection program. He doesn't give off any warm and fuzzy vibes, so I'm not expecting him to go easy on any of us this week.

"A53, can you please join us for a moment?" Professor Gunner called and all the hairs on my body immediately stood up.

Oh shit, this is it, I thought. I glanced over at M, but then quickly looked away. Being in trouble for my actions was one thing, but I wouldn't take M down with me, not if they didn't already know about him. And if they did know about him—I'd find a way to protect him anyway.

"Yes, professor?" I smiled up at Professor Gunner while also acknowledging Teagan and

Councilman Ash. Showing respect to your elders is extremely important in Sector C and even if my suspicions were correct, and they did decide to punish me for my actions, I wasn't going to give them any more ammo to use against me.

"Thank you for taking charge and leading the class in stretches this morning," he said, while staring over my head at my classmates behind me. It wasn't the response I had expected, but I was thankful for that.

"But I…" I looked back and everyone was wide-eyed, stunned, looking right at me. I cleared my throat and spoke up. "…I can't really accept credit for that, sir. I was merely trying to prepare myself. If they joined in, then the credit should be given to each of them."

"Hmmm. The girl shows modesty," Councilman Ash noted, as he jotted something down on a pad of paper. "I hear you run this course quite often. Is that true?"

"Yes sir. I try to do it at least once a day, usually early in the morning before classes begin."

"And the rest of your classmates, are they as dedicated as you?"

"I—I don't think that is for me to judge sir. There are a couple of others who have been running the course with me in the mornings, but other than that you'd have to ask each of them."

"Right," he smirked, jotting something else on his mysterious notepad.

"I'm sure they are committed to their own success, sir." Why I was defending my classmates, the majority of whom had probably never even tried running the course, I had no idea.

"Did you know that I designed the course?"

"In 2085," I answered. "From what I read you took down the original obstacle course that had been here when Sector C was still Fort Hood, before the sectors were developed. Then you designed and built this course in order to test both the mental and physical stamina of potential sector residents. It wasn't until 2089 that the first selection class completed Selection Week and was tested on the new course." I was confident in my response and knew, from the look on his face, that I had been correct.

"Who holds the current record for completing the course?"

I looked back at my classmates again. I wanted nothing more than to end this interrogation and take my place back with them, but I had a feeling this was only the first of many interrogations I would be dealing with this week. "You do, sir. Your time was exactly 39 minutes. No one has ever been able to beat your time."

"That is correct." He exchanged looks with Professor Gunner and Counselor Teagan. "I hear that you have come close—that you have hopes of beating the record this morning."

I could hear gasps and whispering behind me. "No sir. My fastest time is 46 minutes. It would be very difficult, if not impossible, to shave off another seven minutes this morning. Especially," I added after a pause, "while sharing the course with so many other students."

"Then you will not share the course," he said, and turned to Professor Gunner. "This one will be tested separately, first. I want to see her capabilities. If she really is all that you and Counselor Teagan have claimed, then maybe Councilman Serenity's allegations—her evidence—can be...overlooked."

I could feel my heart racing. *Councilman Serenity's allegations? Her evidence? They know. They all know.*

"You will begin in five minutes," Professor Gunner stated, and he, Teagan, and Councilman Ash headed toward the starting line.

"What was all that about?" C asked, rushing to my side with M and H right behind.

"I..." *What am I going to do?* "...I don't know, a test, I guess."

C grabbed me in her arms and hugged me tight. "You can do this A. Just don't think about it. You could run this course in your sleep."

I pulled away. Was this the same girl who had been ignoring me for the past week? No. *This* was my best friend who had stood by my side all my life.

"Thanks."

"You got this," she reiterated. "Now go make the rest of us look bad." She smiled and something inside of me let go—relaxed. She was right. I was ready.

I stepped up to the starting line and nodded when Counselor Teagan asked if I was ready. "When you hear the air horn you can begin. Your monitor has been re-set to indicate your runtime so that you can monitor your speed. It will be activated as soon as the air horn goes off. We will be waiting for you at the end of the course."

15

The air horn went off and I didn't even hesitate. C was right, I could run this course in my sleep, but I wasn't sleeping and I intended to give it everything I had.

Just as I was completing the first mile and a half trail run I glanced down at my monitor: ten minutes seventeen seconds and counting. I was making great time, and I made it up and over the 10-foot warp wall with little effort on my first try. I snapped into my harness and climbed up onto the rope bridge. It took me all of a minute forty-two seconds to get across the bridge to the first zip-line obstacle.

The zip-line course is a half mile long, but the hardest part is climbing the ladder to the first obstacle and then climbing down at the end. It took me seven minutes to complete the course and I was on to the vertical and then the horizontal twenty-foot rope ladders. These had always been my least favorite obstacles—the way they sway back and forth as you climb. I'm not afraid of falling but it isn't something I look forward to either. By the time I jumped down from the horizontal rope ladder my monitor read twenty-six minutes twenty-nine seconds.

I only had four more obstacles to go, and I knew that even on my worst days they didn't take me more than fourteen minutes. I had made great time on the course so far, and if I could just push myself to complete the next four obstacles in twelve and a half minutes I would break Ash's record.

I hit the dirt and dragged myself across the field for the twenty-foot low crawl obstacle, and then jumped up and dashed through the tire run. I could already see the break in the tree line where the final quarter-mile trail run started, but I had to cross the forty-foot balance beam first. I was climbing the ladder to the top of the balance beam when I looked up and saw Councilman Ash standing at the top. "What are you—?"

He started crossing the beam and I quickly completed the climb to the top, and stepped onto the beam behind him. He didn't look back. It was as if he didn't know I was there. Then I noticed it, he wasn't wearing the insignia of the Council. He hadn't yet been assigned to the Council.

Seriously? A vision right now? I shook my head, snapping out of the moment, and continued across the beam.

I made in to the trail and started running. My monitor said thirty-six minutes and fifty-one seconds. I had two minutes and eight seconds to cross the finish line in order to beat the record by one second. I found that zone, the one where nothing in the world exists except for me and the ten feet of ground in front of me, but I made the mistake of glancing at my hands, causing me to trip, falling forward onto the dirt path beneath my feet. I was holding a piece of paper—the words were blurry but I tried to focus. The more I focused the clearer the writing became. It was Teagan's handwriting. *Now? You've got to be kidding me.* She was sending me a message.

Control your urge, do NOT beat Councilman Ash's time!

"What? Why?" I asked aloud as I came out of the vision and back to the trail and the trees all around me, but I already knew the answer. No one had ever beaten his time. If I did it now he might not look favorably on me throughout Selection Week exams. I looked down at my monitor, thirty-eight minutes and ten seconds. I knew I was almost at the end of the trail, and soon they'd be able to see me coming. I could easily finish in under thirty-nine minutes, but I resisted the urge—I fought the impulses telling me to go-go-go. My body was shaking and my muscles were beginning to hurt. I had never pushed myself that hard for that long before, and I knew if I didn't cross the finish line soon I was going to end up crawling across it.

Just as my monitor switched to thirty-eight minutes fifty seconds I took off full-speed ahead, and crossed the finish line exactly seven seconds past Councilman Ash's record.

I dropped to my knees as C and M ran up to me with the rest of the class following close behind. "Oh my stars A, I can't believe you're done already."

I couldn't breathe—I couldn't speak. I just lay back and closed my eyes as my head touched the ground.

"A? A, are you OK?"

"Is she OK?" Gunner asked.

"I'm… I'm fine," I answered, not sure if I really believed it myself. M helped me sit up and I started stretching out my legs before the muscles had a chance to tighten up too much.

"Well, I know I told you to go out there and make the rest of us look bad, but damn, A, I didn't mean *that* bad." C knelt down at my feet and lifted my legs up one at a time to help me stretch.

"Yeah, about that. Sorry."

"Are you kiddi—?"

"No need to apologize," Councilman Ash interrupted. "That was quite an impressive run. I wish I could have seen you on each obstacle."

Thank the stars you couldn't, I thought. *The last thing I need right now is you seeing me stop at the end.*

"No matter, I'm sure the security footage captured most of it. I will enjoy watching it later," he said with a slight smile.

"Security footage?" My eyes darted to Teagan, she was the one who had warned me to slow down. She couldn't also have warned me that I was being recorded?

"Only to ensure that each student completes every obstacle. How else did you think we knew you were running the course so frequently? I've been fascinated by your—skills—for quite some time now. Well, you deserve some rest, don't you think?"

I wasn't sure if I was supposed to answer him or not, so I stayed quiet. "Why don't you head back to the barracks, while the rest of your class completes the course? You should have plenty of time to clean up, get some breakfast, and meet us back here to watch your classmates finish."

"I—thank you—." He didn't let me finish before he turned and walked away.

"Professor Gunner, please send me the final times after everyone has finished. I will want to review them before they are taken to the Selection Hall."

"Yes sir," Professor Gunner called out as he made his way through my classmates—my friends—to my side. "That was quite a run indeed." He reached out to me. "Let me help you up."

"Thank you, Professor."

"Do as Councilman Ash said. Go get cleaned up and get some food in you. If this morning is any indication of the week to come, I have a feeling he has more in store for you."

More in store, WHY ME?! I wanted to scream it, but I couldn't. I didn't need to ask, though. I already knew the answer. Because I had broken the rules. Maybe, instead of questioning, I should just be thankful he was letting me test instead of throwing me out into the wasteland.

16

I hurried through my shower and breakfast but made sure I grabbed an extra energy drink. I had a feeling the adrenaline rush I was experiencing from my morning run was going to fade and the lack of sleep was going to hit hard. I got to the course just in time to watch M cross the finish line. He was the third student to finish, with a very impressive time of just over fifty minutes. He had pushed himself hard and I could tell he was just as surprised by his time as Professor Gunner was.

"Well, well, well, M126, it looks like you've been practicing."

"Yes sir," M said, slightly out of breath but still standing.

"I'm glad to see it. I look forward to seeing what else you can do this week." Professor Gunner turned back to the finish line as a few more kids appeared at the tree line to run the last stint.

"Oh my stars, M. You did amaz—."

He grabbed me around the waist and swung me around before I could finish.

"Ahem." Counselor Teagan interrupted M's little celebration and he quickly put me down.

"He was just excited, that's all." I quickly explained.

"Well, he can express his excitement while keeping his hands to himself." She looked straight at M. "Can you not?"

"Yes ma'am, I can. I'm sorry."

"No apology necessary, just be mindful of…" she looked over her shoulder at Professor Gunner and the rest of the class, "… who else might be around."

Wait, was she giving us permission with a side of warning? While I puzzled over her odd choice of wording, she turned and walked away, back to Professor Gunner. M and I just stood there—silent—confused.

"Here, I think you need this more than I do." I handed M my extra energy drink and he smiled as he twisted off the top. He downed it in about three seconds.

"Thanks, I owe you one."

"You managed a time just over fifty minutes. I think you owe me more than just one energy drink," I said.

"Yeah, you're probably right."

R201 was the last student to cross the finish line. He's big, really big, and unfortunately that probably hurt him more than it might have helped him with a lot of the obstacles. It was written all over his face as he ran in the last ten yards; he was hurting and he hated for anyone to see it. Even though I despised him for his incessant 'fanger' comments and relentless abuse of the vampire culture, I didn't altogether hate him. The truth is, he wasn't completely wrong in his feelings. I'm just not sure I believe the lycanthrope community is really any better.

"Seventy-two minutes eighteen seconds," Professor Gunner announced as R201 crossed the finish line. "Not exceptional, but not entirely unfavorable for someone of your size either. Good run!"

R201 looked relieved. "Thank you, sir." Since we were kids, he had wanted to join the external security team under Councilman Donovan, and doing well during Selection Week could ensure his position. Councilman Donovan is a lycanthrope, and has been R's personal hero ever since Donovan captured a band of castaways who had planned an attack on the sector. The castaways hadn't penetrated the sector wall or anything, but there were enough of them that they probably could have done some damage if Donovan hadn't found them first. Ever since then, R has strived to be the biggest, toughest, and strongest selection student in the class, in hopes of piquing Donovan's interest.

Counselor Teagan was double checking everyone's times on her chart as Professor Gunner gathered the class. "You've all done really well this morning, as I knew you would." His eyes met mine and he paused for a few seconds longer than what would normally feel acceptable. "I'm proud of each of you and you should be proud too."

We don't show pride, it isn't in our nature. OK, maybe it is in our nature but we aren't permitted, or hadn't been permitted until this week, to display those types of feelings. It was going to take some time getting used to the new rules moving forward.

"You will have the next two hours to get cleaned up, eat, and pack up your personal effects."

"Pack? Already?" U277 asked from the back of the group. U was one of the few students who hadn't already shared her preference—vampirism or lycanthropy—with the rest of the class. She was friends with everyone and was a naturally caring person. She had always seemed genuine in her friendships with everyone. I honestly had no idea which way she was leaning.

"Yes, pack. You will no longer be staying in the barracks. You will spend the rest of Selection Week in the Selection Hall. This should not be news to you."

"No, of course not," she answered. "I just thought we'd have more time."

"Time is a gift and unfortunately you have little right now." After a long pause Professor Gunner took a deep breath and continued. "You will each have a private room and can leave your belongings there." There was stirring and murmuring as we looked around at each other, trying to process this shocking news. "After Selection Week is over you will be transferred to housing within the appropriate areas throughout the sector, based on your selection and job placement."

We all knew we would be leaving the barracks during Selection Week, and yet I still wasn't prepared—it seemed that no one was. I should have tried harder to work things out with C. We had been bunkmates for years, and now… We would be separated during Selection Week, and after that we might not even be living or working in the same community.

"Only pack your personal effects. There is no need to pack more than a few changes of clothing. You will not be wearing selection student grey after this week. Don't bring any textbooks or study tools. You won't have an opportunity for any more last minute cramming."

He finished talking, but no one moved. "Go now! Time has not stopped for you." He looked down at his monitor and continued, "One hour and forty-eight minutes remaining. Be outside of the Selection Hall at precisely 13:00 to begin the next phase of testing."

Selection Week really does bring with it a new life, I thought.

The mood in the barracks as everyone packed was somber. No one talked, but you could feel the thoughts floating through the air like a thick fog. I didn't have much to pack—my toiletries, a couple of books I enjoyed reading just for fun, and a few photos of me, C and the rest of our class that we had taken over the years. I was sifting through the photos and remembering all the great times we had shared, and wondering how I could even be thinking of doing anything that could separate us.

"Hey, you want this?" C held out her lip gloss to me as she shoved everything on her shelves into a back sack. It was the same lip gloss she had flung at me only a few days before, not wanting to use it if I wasn't who she thought I was—who she expected me to be. I had put it back on her shelf a little while later. I hadn't wanted it either, not if it meant the end of our friendship.

"Are you sure?" I asked.

"Yeah, it looks better on you anyway. Besides, it's not like I won't be able to borrow it sometime, right?" There were tears in her eyes. She knew I was having doubts and she was struggling to hang on to me—struggling not to have to say goodbye.

"Right," I smiled, and took the lip gloss.

She stepped closer and gave me a hug. Like this morning's hug, before I ran the course, I could feel how much she still cared for me. However, this hug was also different—sadder—it felt like a goodbye, but I wasn't ready to say goodbye. I pulled back and smiled at her. "We've got all week to worry about what happens next. Right now, let's just enjoy today." I handed her one of the photos. "You should keep this one." It was a photo of us, celebrating our birthday two years ago. We were wearing big paper crowns that I had made and sharing a huge piece of cake I had smuggled out of the dining hall.

She started laughing as soon as she saw the photo. "Oh my stars, I remember I had the worst stomach ache after eating that cake."

"Well, it was the size of your head and you did eat most of it."

"Did not," she smiled, smacking my arm. "OK, maybe I did, but come on, it was so good!"

"It really was." We sat on her bed and flipped through the rest of the photos and talked, laughed, and even cried, just like old times.

"Hey guys, everyone's ready to head out to the dining hall," F97 called, interrupting our walk down memory lane. C and I looked around and realized that we were the last ones left in the room. "We're all gonna eat together one last time before the testing begins. You guys want to join us?"

"*Heck* yeah," we said at the exact same time, jumping up and grabbing our bags to follow him out.

C walked out ahead of me, and I turned back to the empty room—a room filled with so many memories, both good and bad, it just didn't feel right leaving without a proper goodbye. I flicked the switch on the wall and the lights went out. The pale blue glow of the curfew light above the door became visible in the dimmed room—the blue glow that said, 'It's safe to go out now.'

"Goodbye," I whispered, and then shut the door behind me.

17

We all stood outside the Selection Hall at precisely 13:00, as instructed. From the outside it looked like a large windowless warehouse. As far as I know, they only use the building for one week each year. None of us had ever been inside, but we had all heard the stories—the legends—most of which were most likely myths: large rooms where selection students are forced to fight each other to the death; endless hours of sitting in solitary; countless exams; excruciating medical tests; and classrooms with endless rows of desks and computer stations where students must complete test after test. I really didn't know what to believe anymore. I guess I was about to find out.

Naturally, the closer each class came to their Selection Week the more they were fascinated by the stories about what others had experienced there. Our class was no different, and rumors had been flying for weeks—months. It seemed everyone who entered the Selection Hall had a different experience there, and a different story to tell when, or if, they made it out. That's right, "if." It's no secret that not every student who goes through Selection Week actually makes it out. At least it didn't use to be. They call them sector defectors, but it is rumored that fewer than 5% of all sector defectors actually make it beyond the wall. The other 95%—well, they die. At least that's how the story goes. Maybe that's why there hasn't been a selection student sector defector in years. Typically if someone is going to defect, it happens after they've made the change. At least as a vampire or a lycanthrope you have a better chance of survival out in the wastelands.

Standing in front of our group were the members of the Selection Board: the sector members and Council representatives who would be administering and evaluating the tests throughout Selection Week. Among them were Professor Gunner, Professor Kade, Counselor Teagan, Councilman Ash, two men I didn't recognize, and a few others wearing medical uniforms.

"Welcome to Selection Week," Councilman Ash announced. "You have all completed the first phase of today's training, the selection course, and I was quite impressed with many of the scores. The rest of today will be spent preparing for the next four days. Once inside…" he motioned to the large metal door behind him. "…you will each be assigned a room. This room will be your living quarters for the remainder of your testing. Feel free to unpack what few belongings you brought with you, and then review the itinerary that you will find on the desk in your quarters. Everyone's itinerary will be different, based on your scoring over the past few years as well as the results of your counseling sessions with Counselor Teagan."

Great, I thought, *I haven't been able to resolve anything during my sessions. What could they possibly have learned about me?* I looked over at Counselor Teagan who was also staring in my direction. She smiled and nodded. Was I supposed to feel relieved? I didn't.

"Remember, when you walk out these doors at the end of the week, you will no longer be selection students. You will be sector members, with your chosen community here to support you and your new name to identify you. Select wisely what—*who*—you want your future self to be." His eyes fell on mine and I felt the importance of what he was saying settle on my shoulders like a steel weight.

The idea that in less than four days I was going to have to select between becoming a vampire or a lycanthrope for the rest of my life was scary, but what terrified me even more was my name selection. Was I going to follow my instincts—my visions—and go against the sector expectations and leave Selection Week as Zelina, or was I going to cave to the pressures and select an acceptable *'A'* indicator-approved name?

"Counselor Teagan, please show the students to their quarters," Professor Gunner continued, interrupting my thoughts as he pulled open the large door that led into the hall.

"Yes sir." Teagan walked through the doorway, motioning for us to follow. I was hesitant, but didn't want anyone to know it so I stepped up first and followed her in.

"A53," Professor Kade and Councilman Ash both said, nodding in my direction as I passed.

"Good afternoon, Councilman. Hello, Professor," I replied respectfully.

I heard Professor Kade greeting each student, in the same way, as they passed, but I could feel

Councilman Ash's eyes following me into the building and down the hall.

Inside, the walls were made of a foggy glass material. It seemed like you should be able to see through the walls, as if they were windows, but other than letting light shine through from behind the glass, the foggy, almost scuffed, coloring prevented that.

"As Councilman Ash said, you will want to unpack your belongings when you get into your room. Then, be sure to review the Selection Week packet located on your desk along with your computer tablet. In the packet you will find your itinerary, a selection form for indicating your injection selection, the login information for your first exam, a list of approved indicator-appropriate names, and additional literature.

"The exam and the selection form must be completed prior to your receiving dinner this evening. When you have completed the exam you will have the option to either submit it or review your answers. I suggest you review your answers to ensure their accuracy. For this exam you won't be timed, so take your time and concentrate. After you are fully satisfied with your work, be sure to select 'submit.'

"The completed selection form must be slipped through the slot in your door." She paused next to the first door, indicating the basket on the outside. "It will then fall into a basket like this. Once you have completed these two tasks, your dinner will be brought to your room."

U277 piped up, "We have to make our selection now—today?" She wasn't the only one surprised by the information.

"Yes, is that going to be a problem U277?"

I could see it written all over U's face. Yes, it was going to be a problem. "No ma'am. It won't be a problem," she answered.

I turned, glancing back at the rest of the class, and everyone seemed surprised. M smiled as our eyes met. I knew he wanted to know what my decision was going to be, but how could I tell him if I didn't know myself?

"It won't be a problem for *me* ma'am. I've known all my life where I fit in," burly R201 said proudly, and the rest of the students who were openly committed to becoming lycanthropes hooted and hollered their agreement.

Teagan raised her hands for silence. "All right. Yes, very well. I'm glad you will have no problems making your selection. However, for those of you who are still undecided, you will also find booklets on vampirism and lycanthropy in your packets. You should read both, fully, in order to evaluate and understand the positives and the negatives of each decision. There is also literature detailing the required test scores for each possible work placement within your chosen community. Be aware that the Council will select your work placement based not only on your choice of community, but also on your test scores, physical abilities, and the results of your medical exams. Knowing what is required of you for each position might help you to focus your energies if you have a particular position in mind. You will be given the opportunity on your selection form to indicate your desired position, but keep in mind that you may not receive your first choice."

She flipped through the papers on her clipboard then opened the first door. "H107, this is your room.

While your room is unoccupied, the door will remain unlocked so you can return from the gym, the clinic, and the cafeteria on our own. Each room has its own bathroom, but showers are located down the hall. You'll be given time each day, after your scheduled fights, to use those facilities. Once you enter your room the door will lock automatically. Please make sure you take all of your belongings with you. If you're going to unpack now is the time to do it." She held the door open only until H was inside. As he turned to look out, she shut the door and I could hear the lock slip into place. As we continued down the hall, I slowly edged to the back of the line and to M's side. One by one Teagan assigned our rooms. "W351"... "J102"...

M ducked his head and whispered, "I know you're still not sure, but—."

"I'm not, but I want to be with you."

"O154." "U277."

M took in a deep breath and let out a sigh of relief. "Then, unless you tell me differently, I will choose vampirism. I choose you."

"R201," Teagan continued.

Rooms were being assigned in what seemed like a random order, and pretty soon there were only a few of us left. Teagan opened the next door and something inside told me it was my turn. "A53, this is your room." She held the door open, just like she had done for the previous ten students, and as quickly as she had opened it she shut it behind me.

18

I stood there with the door closed and to my back, staring at my room. The ten by ten room felt more like a cell than any living space I had been assigned to in my life thus far. I didn't bother checking the door to see if it was locked. I knew it would be.

A single light hung from the ceiling, a small wooden desk sat in the corner with a chair slid underneath, and a matching twin-size bed with a simple headboard and basic blanket and pillow was directly in front of me. There was a door near the foot of the bed. *A closet?* I wondered. When I opened the door, I found a toilet and small sink. There were no mirrors in the bathroom or anywhere in the room, but I guess this week wasn't really going to be about how we look. This was the first room I'd ever had to myself, and even though it felt and looked like a prison cell I didn't really care because it was all mine. For the next four days anyway.

I didn't bother unpacking, except to put what little clothing I had brought into the desk drawer, my toiletries on the side of the sink, and to hang my necklace on the headboard of the bed—the necklace M had made for me, from a shoelace and some wire, to hold my flawless shimmering stone. I didn't see the point in unpacking everything. However, I did take out one picture—a selection class photo from earlier this year. It had been less than twelve months' time since the photo was taken, but we had all been through so much. In the photo we all seemed so young—so innocent—but we weren't, not anymore. I could only imagine what we would look like, sound like, and act like after this week was over. Would we still be friends or would we allow the politics of our selections to determine our behaviors and our beliefs, like every class before us? I guess maybe I had answered my own question.

The photo was in a nice wooden frame, so I set it on the desk. Other than the selection packet, computer tablet, and one sharpened pencil, the photo was the only thing there.

"I guess I'll read," I said to myself since there was no one else around to talk to. The silence seemed peaceful in that moment, but it had the potential to become deafeningly lonely. I picked up the packet, the tablet, and the pencil, and made myself comfortable on the bed—my bed.

I pulled the papers out of the large envelope, and right on top was the Itinerary.

SELECTION WEEK ITINERARY
~ C65A53 ~`

DAY 1
Selection Course – Timed
Selection Hall Initiation
Collection of Selection Form
Sector History Exam

DAY 2
Fighting Ring – Round One
Aptitude Test
Fighting Ring – Round Two
Personality Quiz

DAY 3
Medical Examination
Fighting Ring – Round Three
Intelligence Quotient (IQ) Exam
Fighting Ring – Round Four

DAY 4
Medical Examination
Fighting Ring – Round Five
Mental Health Assessment

DAY 5
Announcement of Selection, Work Placement, Name Choice, and Release

The next item in the packet was a list of approved names—names I was meant to select from.

APPROVED NAME SELECTION LIST
Indicator A
~ C65A53 ~

Abigail
Abbey
Abbi
Abbie
Abby
Abi

Aida
Aimee
Aisha
Alaina
Alana
Alee
Aleerah
Alina
Amelia
Amy
Annie
April
Autumn
Ava
Avery

My stars, how many different variations for the name Abbey can they come up with?

I read through the list at least ten times, but none of the names seemed right. All of the names seemed so plain, simple, boring. None of the names were mine. I can't explain how or why, it was just a gut feeling. Call it intuition. I knew that my name wasn't Alee, Autumn, or Abbi. It was Zelina, but I wasn't sure how or even if that was going to be possible.

I decided to save that decision for another day. According to my itinerary, I wouldn't have to announce my name selection until my release on the last day. *Thank the stars for the small gifts,* I thought.

Next were three booklets: one on vampirism one on lycanthropy, and one on the various work placements and the requirements for each. The last item in the packet was the selection form. I set the whole packet aside. I wasn't ready to make my selection, and figured I might as well start on the Sector History Exam first. They weren't going to feed me until they were both turned in anyway, so it didn't matter in which order they were completed.

I turned on the tablet, and used the login information from the packet to open up the exam. The exam consisted of one hundred-fifty multiple choice, true/false, and essay questions. I'm not sure how long it took me, because my internal monitor had been deactivated when I entered my room. Thinking back, other than knowing that I had gotten to the Selection Hall at 13:00, I had no idea what time it was or how long I had been there. Time seems almost non-existent when you don't have a clock or access to a window to see outside. My stomach grumbled, letting me know I was getting hungry, and I realized it must be later than I had thought.

After double checking my answers, just to be sure, I clicked on 'submit' and sat there staring at the screen. I'm not sure what I was waiting for—confirmation maybe. I stood up to stretch—my neck was hurting and my eyes were beginning to burn. I heard footsteps as someone walked past my door. "Hello?" I called out, but the footsteps didn't stop.

When I sat back down, I pulled out the selection form. *I wonder why these aren't electronic,* I thought.

SELECTION WEEK

Selection Form and Injection Authorization

~ C65A53 ~

Throughout the last seventeen years, your choices have made you the young woman you are today. This choice, not to be taken lightly, will determine the woman you are for the next seventeen years and all the years to follow. If you are unsure of your decision, we recommend you read through the provided materials completely. However, please keep in mind that you have already been given all the information necessary to make your selection.

Please enter your selection (vampirism or lycanthropy) on the line below:

____

Please indicate your three desired job choices or career paths below:

____

____

____

It used to be, before the sectors, and even in the early years as the sectors were being developed, that vampirism was spread through the exchange of blood between a vampire and a human. Even lycanthropy wasn't spread through an injection—it was spread through a bite or a scratch from the lycanthrope in animal form to a human. That's one of the main reasons why selection students, and human breeders, aren't allowed out after curfew: to protect them from "accidental" contact with one of the viruses. Of course, vampires can't contract lycanthropy, and vice versa.

Therefore, after you have gone through Selection Week there is no longer any need for a curfew.

The original Governing Council put scientists to work developing synthetic viruses because too many humans were dying after being infected directly from a vampire or lycanthrope host. It took years to develop successful injections, and even now five out of every hundred selection students die from failure to adapt to one of the two viruses. However, compared to the ninety-five percent rejection rate just one hundred years ago, our odds are pretty good.

I stared at my selection form. I didn't know what to select, but I didn't need to read the information booklets either. I wasn't going to learn anything I didn't already know. The real decision wasn't whether I wanted to be a vampire or a lycanthrope. The real question was whether I wanted to be a member of Sector C—or if I wanted to be released into the wastelands. True, the idea of being released into the wastelands and scavenging for survival didn't sound all that appealing, but at least I could stay human—at least I could stay…me.

The hardest part wasn't even making the decision. It would have been hard enough if it was just about me, but it wasn't anymore. My decision would affect M. He had decided to choose vampirism. He had decided to choose me.

The wall to the left of me went dark. *Did a light go out?* I wondered. I walked to the wall and pressed my ear to the glass, but I couldn't hear anything. Then the back wall went dark, and then, a little bit later, the one on my right. *Why is my overhead light still on?* I could still see the dim glow of the light in the hallway outside the front wall of my room, and I took comfort hoping that even after all of my other lights went out there would still be something to break up the darkness.

I didn't complete the Selection Form. Instead, I slipped the blank form into the provided envelope and sealed the envelope shut. *Maybe they won't check it tonight,* I thought as I slipped it through the slot in my door. *Maybe they'll just feed me and let me sleep once they see that I've turned it in.* A girl can hope right? *What's the worst thing that could happen?*

There was a knock on the door, and I jumped up from my bed. I must have fallen asleep, but my light was still on, so it must not have been for very long. "Hello?" I called out but my throat was dry and barely a sound came out. I crossed the room and pushed open the slot. "Hello?"

"Are you hungry?" It was Teagan.

Teagan is bringing my food? "Yes," I answered.

"Step back from the door, please." I did as I was told, and I could hear the lock turning before she pushed open the door and stepped into the room. She was carrying a small tray with a glass of water, a glass of milk, and a plate of eggs, sliced tomatoes, and toast.

"Breakfast?" I had never had breakfast for dinner, and the idea of eggs didn't sound all that appealing.

She glanced down at her monitor and then back up at me. "It's 05:30. They're only serving breakfast right now. Is there something else you were hoping for?"

"No, I just..." I did the math in my head, "...05:30? How can that be?" *Is it really possible that sixteen and a half hours had already passed since I got to the Selection Hall?*

"Time seems to move differently in here, A53. I can't really explain it, I think it has something to do with the—."

"Lack of clocks, windows, and natural lighting?"

"Exactly. You'll need to use your time wisely, or you'll get behind." She set the tray on my desk and turned and walked out, pulling the door shut behind her.

I hadn't even had dinner. I had no idea how long I had slept. How could it already be the beginning of day two?

19

I finished my breakfast and cleaned up, as best I could, in the cramped little bathroom closet with a washcloth I had packed. I wasn't sure when, or if, I would get a chance to use the showers. Before too long, there was a knock at my door.

"Hello?" I had committed my itinerary to memory and knew that I was scheduled for my first round on the fighting mat that morning, so I wasn't surprised when Professor Gunner opened the door.

"Good morning A53. How did you sleep?"

"Honestly, I'm not really sure. Do you know when I'll be able to use the shower?"

"I'll have someone show you where it is after your fight this morning. Unless you require the facilities first."

"No, I'm fine." To be honest, I wish I had said yes, but how do I tell my professor that I would prefer to shower before possibly seeing the guy I can't stop thinking about?

He escorted me down the hall and around the corner into a large open room. Some of my classmates were already there, gathered in small groups around two of the three fighting mats, and others were being escorted in just like I was.

"You'll be on Mat 3," he said, pointing across the room to a large blue mat. "You're paired with E82 this morning. It should be an easy round for you."

"Yes, sir." I continued in that direction, because I knew it's what he expected.

He didn't follow me to the mat, but that didn't surprise me. Professor Gunner was in charge of the physical testing, which included all the fights. So he had other students to attend to, not just me.

I sat next to the fighting mat for a few minutes as other members of the class were escorted in, one by one. I saw Professor Gunner point across the room at me, and C, E, J, and O crossed the room to sit with me.

"Oh my stars!" C had a black eye and a swollen lip. "C, what… What happened to you?"

"What do you think happened to me? I was fighting."

"But, when? Isn't this—?"

"I already went through round one yesterday. Earlier this morning I was paired with D77 for round two."

I scanned the room and saw D on the far side at Mat 1. As usual, he was standing there looking cocky—talking to M, T and W—probably about how tough he is for what he had done to C. "Why would they pair you with D? That's insane, he's twice your size and—."

"No he's not," she snapped. "He's thirty pounds heavier at best."

"Fine, maybe not twice but come on, he's known for being especially brutal on the mat. He fights dirty—that's why Gunner never let him fight any of the girls in class."

"You fought him."

"Yeah but—."

"And you beat him. Why is that any different? You think just because I'm not you—."

"I didn't say that. C—." *What is going on?* "Wait, did you say yesterday?"

"Yeah, why?"

"Did everyone else fight yesterday?" She shrugged her shoulders in that '*I really couldn't care*' way she does so often. "Hey guys," I said, getting E's, J's, and O's attention. "Did you three fight yesterday?"

"I did," J answered.

"Me too," said E.

"Not me." O said, smiling. "I don't even have mat time on my itinerary. Professor Gunner told me they don't have anyone to administer my medical exam right now, so I could either stay in my room or come here and watch. I decided to watch. My room's kind of boring."

No fighting on her itinerary? That has to be a mistake, I thought. "Did you ask him why you're not fighting this week?"

"Are you kidding? Of course not. I just took it as a blessing. Kill them with kindness, right? Besides, I hate fighting, I really don't see the point."

We just looked at her. What was she thinking? "Um, the point..." J interjected, "...is survival."

"Whatever." She rolled her eyes and sat down, ready for the show.

I leaned in close to C, not wanting O to hear. "You don't think they have other plans for her do you?"

"What, like donor? Of course. I mean look at her. I'm sure all the old Councilmen are eager to sink their teeth into—."

"C53!" Professor Gunner called from across the room, effectively cutting her off. "Mind your manners. We have visitors." He glanced up at the ceiling, where cameras were hanging, angled down perfectly to view each fighting mat, red lights blinking.

"Sorry sir," C answered. Then she jabbed me in the side, giving me her '*I told you so'* look.

I started stretching. Even though I was up against E, one of the weakest male students in our class, I wasn't about to get onto the mat without stretching. Especially since I hadn't slept in over twenty-four hours, at least not that I could remember. I turned to C who had already joined me. "So, I'm fighting E. That must mean you and J are together."

"Yup." She nodded. She was staring at J as though she were trying to burn a hole through J's head with the power of her mind.

"What? What's wrong?"

"Nothing, it's nothing. Things are just different in here, and besides I'm a little sore from this morning." She looked back at me. "So, you haven't fought at all then?"

"No. I submitted in my Sector History exam and I turned in my selection form, but that's all."

"Did you—?"

I knew what she was going to ask—did I pick the vampire or lycanthrope injection—but luckily I didn't have to answer. Professor Gunner interrupted her—again, just in time. "Most of you have already had a chance to fight either this morning or yesterday. However, if this is your first time on the Selection Hall fighting mats you and your partner will go second." I looked up at E who was pacing along the side of the mat. He didn't bother to look down at me. "Today's fight pairings are listed on the wall alongside each mat. If you don't know who you're paired with, check it now."

Students moved around, checking the list closest to their assigned mats, and then found spots around the edges of the mats, sitting next to their partners.

I leaned in and whispered to C, "Didn't you have to submit your Sector History exam and your selection form yesterday?"

"Of course—we all did. But that only took an hour or so."

"An hour?"

"Um yeah. It was only twenty questions A. Jeez, you must think I'm an idiot or something."

"No, I—."

"After the test I did round one on the mat, had dinner, and went to bed."

"Then you got up this morning, and did round two?"

"Yeah." C was looking at me like I was insane, and I was starting to agree with her.

"I was—just in my room this whole time," I said. "Teagan brought me breakfast and told me it was only 05:30. That couldn't have been more than twenty or thirty minutes before Professor Gunner came to get me. What time did you get up?"

"All I know is I had breakfast and then round two. No one told me what time it was, but then again I didn't ask. After my fight I took a shower and then they brought me back here."

"It just doesn't make sense that—."

"First group on your mats!" Professor Gunner called out and both C and J jumped up and ran to the weapons table on the other side of the mat. "And remember, you fight until someone goes down."

Until someone goes down? Is he crazy? I would have put money on the fact that fighting to the death had been a myth--not just a slight stretch of the truth. We always fight until someone gives up, not—. I raised my hand. "Professor Gunner, excuse me."

"Yes, A53. Did you have a question?"

"Um, yes. Did you say that we fight until someone goes down? What about—?"

"There are no rules here." He stopped me before I could finish my question. "You pick your weapon from the table, you get on the mat, and when the bell rings, you fight. The fight ends when only one person is standing." He just looked at me, almost daring me to ask another question, but I knew better. I kept quiet.

Both C and J were looking at me too. They knew the rules, or the fact that there was a distinct lack of rules. They had both been on the mat already. The bell rang, and the fight began. It wasn't like in class. Technique didn't matter here. When I looked over at E—E, the brainchild historian—he was as pale as a ghost, and didn't appear to be breathing. "Hey, you OK?" I asked, but I already knew the answer.

He didn't look at me when he answered—he just stared ahead watching C and J fight. "Yesterday was bad. I went down after only three minutes."

"Who did you fight?"

"U277."

Aside from pretty blonde-haired O154, U was the weakest of the females in our selection class. For E to lose to her had to have hurt his ego quite a bit, as well as his chance of a decent placement at the end of the week—not that fighting skills are all that necessary for someone who wants to work in the archives. But now, to be paired with me in his second fight, yeah, I could see why he looked scared.

"E, I'm—."

"Don't say it," he said, stopping me before I could apologize. "I don't want your pity."

"It's not pity. I mean, you've won fights before. I just don't understand what happened."

"In class, it's different. We fight, but not like this. I just couldn't make myself knock her out. I'd rather go down then do that to her."

"U? She can take it. She might not be the toughest in our class, but she can take a hit."

"I know, but it just didn't feel right. I know how I look. I know that I'm not seen as tough. Everyone thinks of me as all brains and no muscle. Everyone knows that, including me. I just—I just want to get through this week and make it out of here with some dignity left. If that's even possible." Then he did look at me. There were tears in his eyes, and what little dignity he still had slipped away.

C and J were rolling on the floor and as C rolled to the top I saw her fist connect with J's cheek. Blood splattered across the mat and J's head flew to the side. Her eyes drifted shut and didn't open back up. It wasn't until C stood, or tried to stand, that I noticed J wasn't the only one who was hurt. A stream of blood covered C's right eye, there were deep scratches along her neck, and the wooden stake J had grabbed from the weapons table was stuck in C's upper leg. It wasn't deep, but it was enough to send C to the floor. She landed on her knees and could barely hold herself up. I rushed to her side, but she just pushed me away. "NO!"

"But, I—."

"No, please."

"C, you've already won. Let me help you."

"No."

I backed away, kneeling on the side of the mat watching—ready to catch her if she did fall over. I didn't understand why she was refusing my help, why she was being so stubborn.

"Very nice C53," Professor Gunner called out. "That's a win. You may relax now."

As if his words had pushed an invisible button, C collapsed to the floor and every muscle in her body seemed to go slack.

The paramedics came and took both C and J off the mat and down the hall. They collected two other students from the other fighting mats as well. I wasn't sure if they were taking them to the sector hospital, a medical clinic here in the Selection Hall, or just back to their rooms. I prayed, for their sakes, it was the hospital but figured the best they would get was probably some peroxide, a bandage, and a pat on the back.

"Next fighters, take your places on the mats." Professor Gunner's voice carried through the hall, even without a microphone, now that almost half the class had left.

I stood there staring at the weapons selection on the table and watched as E made his selection. "A knife?" I asked. It wasn't what I would have picked. I mean, as far as I knew E was selecting vampirism, which meant the best weapon against him would be the wooden stake. If he had been selecting lycanthropy the weapons of choice would have been either the silver knife or the tranquilizer gun, which simulate the use of silver bullets. Although we have not yet announced our official selections yet, the selection board would be aware of what each student had selected. Because we are not only tested on our fighting abilities and whether we win or lose, our abilities to read our opponents are weighed in our final score. E, like everyone in our class, knew I had planned on selecting vampirism. Or at least I had up until recently. *Why didn't he select a stake?* I wondered.

"I just—I saw what the stake did to C, and I can't imagine using that on anyone."

"Oh." I was beginning to understand why knocking U out was so hard for him.

I stepped back from the table, without a weapon, and I stood on the mat. I watched his hands tremble around the handle of the knife. He was sweating and we hadn't even started. I didn't want the bell to go off, not because I was afraid for myself, but because I was afraid for him—for what I had to do to him.

Ding! The bell sounded throughout the room, and the other pairs jumped into action. I could hear them battling it out, but E didn't move. I took two steps forward, and as I swung I whispered, "I'm sorry." I hit him, with the heel of my hand, right under the chin, throwing him back. I didn't let him get too far before I spun and struck with a high side kick to the cheek. He went down, hard, landing on his side. He didn't get back up, and he didn't move when the paramedics rolled him onto the gurney. The blow to his chin had knocked a couple of his front teeth out, and his mouth was bleeding, but it was the kick that had knocked him out.

I just stood there watching as they carried him away.

20

I felt horrible about what I had done to E, but everyone else was treating me like I had done something amazing—something to be proud of.

"Oh my stars A, you knocked him out with one punch," O said, jumping up from where she had been sitting quietly, ready for the show.

"And a kick," I corrected her.

"It was amazing!" She was giddy—and it felt completely wrong.

"Yeah, I guess." I watched as the paramedics wheeled him out the door. "Is he going to be OK?" I asked.

No one answered me, but I hadn't really expected an answer.

I saw Professor Gunner walking toward me, and expected him to criticize me or make me do laps or something because I hadn't fought fair. "Well, well, well, A53. That was quite a fight."

"It wasn't really a fight sir. He—." I was going to say that he hadn't even tried to fight back, but Professor Gunner corrected me.

"Not a fight, are you kidding? The best fights never last long. He stepped onto the mat with a silver knife and you—you declined a weapon. He had the advantage, but you never gave him the chance to use it.

It took you less than five seconds before you had him on the mat." I couldn't tell if he was impressed or upset. "I can't wait to see how you perform against F97 later today."

"I'm fighting F? But he's—."

"One of the top male fighters in the class, and you *are* the top female fighter. Would you rather fight R201?"

"No sir." R was as big as they come. He was always working out, and although he wasn't very fast no one lasted more than a minute or two on the mat with him--and the ones who did only made it because they ran, instead of fighting back.

"Are you sure? Because I can make it happen if you want to."

I didn't answer, and eventually he walked away, saying, over his shoulder, "Very well."

The thought of getting on the mat with F instead of R didn't really make me feel any better. He might not have been as big, but what he lacked in size—he more than made up for it with skill. He knew every weapon available and could use each of them with pristine proficiency. He was fast too, and clever. He didn't move much when on the mat. He waited for you to come to him, then he'd pounce like a cat attacking a mouse. If I was going to fight F, I was going to need a plan.

"Wow, I wonder if I can come back for your next fight," O said, grabbing my arm as I made my way toward the hallway.

"Yeah, I don't know." I looked down at her. She was so giddy, and smiling like she didn't have a care in the world. "O, are you at all worried? I mean about not fighting this week. Don't you worry that there might be a reason they aren't having you fight?"

"No, not really. Selection Week is different for every student. You know that. Maybe they've just seen all the fighting they needed to see from me already. Besides, I want to go through the higher education program and train to be one of the nurses at the clinic. How much fighting can that possibly require?" She smiled and walked away, heading for Mat 1 where some of the other students were still waiting, with the same happy bounce in her step she always has.

I started to follow when, "Hey A!" M126 yelled from across the room. "Great fight. I saw the whole three seconds," he laughed, and smiled.

Oh… that smile. It had only been a day since I had seen him and already I was missing that smile. *Snap out of it A,* I scolded myself.

"Thanks. Hey who are you paired with?" I closed the gap between us, while still keeping a respectable, acceptable distance.

"N, but don't worry, I can take him." He laughed as N grabbed him from behind and threw him to the ground.

"Yeah, you think you can take me?" They were both laughing. The idea that one of them had to actually go down before the fight ended didn't seem to bother either of them.

Am I really the only one who has a problem with fighting until someone is unconscious? I thought it, but I didn't say it out loud. It just didn't seem real. Nothing had seemed real since I had stepped into my room the day before.

"O154, it's time for your medical exam." Teagan said, taking O's hand. "A53, why don't you head to the facilities and get cleaned up. They're just down that hall and on the left. Then, you'll need to head back to your room. Your lunch will be waiting, as will your aptitude test. You won't have long to complete it. Professor Gunner said he needs you back on the mat in less than two hours."

"Lunch, already?"

Looking down at her monitor Teagan shrugged. "It's almost 12:30. I would think you would be hungry by now."

12:30? There is no way I've been up seven hours already. I looked down at my own wrist, but my monitor was still deactivated, as I had known it would be—a tactic I was beginning to believe the Council used to keep the selection students disoriented during testing.

"Um, OK. This way?" I asked glancing down the long hall. She nodded and walked off, taking O down another hallway, to the medical clinic I assumed.

I found the bathroom and was finished showering in no time at all. There were plenty of towels and even clean clothing waiting in a locker marked with my name. I took my time, brushing my teeth and pulling my hair back, before making my way back to my room.

I took a left and then a right, but after a few more turns I realized I had no idea where my room actually was. I ended up wandering through what seemed like a maze of hallways. "OK, this can't be right." There were no signs on any of the doors and no one else around to ask.

Finally, I decided to just try one of the doors—locked. I tried the next one—locked, and the ones after that—all locked. “Hello? Hello, is anyone around?” No answer. I wasn’t really surprised. I turned around thinking I could just retrace my steps back to the fighting mats, but after what felt like an hour I still hadn’t found my way. I felt like a rat in a maze searching for the cheese that isn’t really there, and I started to wonder if this too was a test.

I closed my eyes, and thought about that first day, when Teagan was walking us through the halls to our rooms. It took a few minutes, but eventually I heard footsteps coming from down the hall. I turned to look but no one was there. I closed my eyes again and the footsteps got closer. Then she was there, in front of me. I could see her feet, long strides, and the clipboard she was holding. When I opened my eyes it was as if I was seeing the hallway through her eyes, and I knew where to go. I started walking, and within minutes I was standing in front of a door—my door. I turned the knob and pushed the door open to find that I was right, it was my room.

On my desk were a lunch tray, my computer tablet, and a small sheet of paper with my test login information. I picked up the tray and grabbed the tablet and login information and set everything up around me on the bed. I wasn’t sure how much time I had wasted wandering around the halls, so I knew I needed to get started right away. I quickly ate the sandwich and chips as my tablet loaded the test.

SELECTION WEEK

Aptitude Test

~ C65A53 ~

Aptitude - your natural ability to do something. This test will be timed. As you can see by your monitor, your time began when you entered your room. There is only one correct answer (true, false, or can't answer) for each of the following problems. Be sure to read each statement completely before answering. Once your time has lapsed your tablet will turn off and your exam will be automatically submitted. If your time ends prior to you completing the exam the incomplete test will be submitted. Questions that are not answered will count against your final score.

I looked down at my monitor and, sure enough, it had been re-activated. Only twenty-eight minutes remained, and the time was ticking away, one second at a time. I clicked through to the first question: *Statistical forecasting cannot be used for production and operations*.

"OK... True?" I quickly selected my answer and moved on through the next twenty-four questions. They covered everything from business to cultural issues, to health and fitness. I honestly couldn't tell you how I did, except to say that I finished the last question only moments before the tablet turned off and the door to my room opened.

"Has the tablet turned off?" Councilman Iris asked as she stepped in.

"It has." I tossed the tablet on the bed as I jumped up. "Councilmen Iris, I didn't know—."

"No, I am not usually involved in these events. Dealing with the housing and economic development issues for all of the sector students tends to keep me quite busy. However, I volunteered this year to oversee some of the testing."

I had known Councilman Iris for as long as I could remember. She is in charge of assigning housing and living space to all of the sector students from the time they are born until the time they get through Selection Week. She's also in charge of all the caregivers for the younger students, before they turn ten and are placed in a selection class. In all honesty, she is the closest thing any of us have to a mother. When we get hurt we go to her before the clinic, and when we just need to vent we go to her before the counselor. "I can't believe you're here." I'm not sure why it was affecting me so much, but I couldn't stop myself from jumping up and hugging her, hard.

"Is everything OK?" she asked, as she pulled back to see my face.

"Everything's fine," I lied. Everything wasn't fine. I still hadn't made my injection selection, I had no idea how I had done on my Selection History or my aptitude tests, I felt terrible about what I had done to E, and I definitely wasn't ready to go on the mat against F in less than an hour.

"A53, you seem tense." She sat me down and stroked my hair in the same loving way she had done a thousand times before. "I only wanted to check on you, not cause you anxiety."

"No, it's not you, honest."

"Then what is it? Are you worried about tonight? Because you don't have to be."

"Tonight?"

"Your injection." She said it as if I should have known already, but I didn't. Nowhere on my itinerary had it told me when the injection would come.

"But, I haven't even—." *They hadn't read my Selection Form and Injection Authorization yet.*

"You haven't what?"

Surely they will read it, maybe even discuss it with me before initiating the injection, right?

"Nothing, it's nothing." I quickly got up. *As if I didn't have enough to worry about already.* "I actually think I need to go. I mean, I'm supposed to be on the fighting mat soon." I tried the door, but it was locked. "Do you know if someone is coming to get me, or—?"

"I can take you." Iris stood and crossed to the door. As soon as she turned the knob, the door opened.

How—? But that was a question for another day.

When we got into the open gym she walked me to a mat, gave me a hug and wished me luck before she turned away. "You're not staying?" I asked, surprised at my disappointment.

"No, I'm not really a big fan of the fights…" she said. Then she smiled, an oddly sinister sort of grin, and added, "…at least not until after injections have been administered." Then she was gone.

"A, you ready for this?" I turned to see F standing on the side of the mat. F was tall and slender, but he was all muscle. *He looks bigger up close,* I realized. From the cuts up and down his arms and legs the swollen black eye, and still-damp curly hair, he looked as if he had just barely made it off the mat from his last fight, but there he was jumping up and down and bouncing from one leg to the other.

"I'm ready, are you?"

"What's that supposed to mean?"

"Nothing, you just look a little—."

"What, this?" He motioned to one of many cuts along his arm. "This is nothing. You should see Q—that is, if they ever let him out of the clinic." He threw his head back, laughing.

It seemed like the whole class was there, gathering around the mat, but as far as I could tell F and I were the only ones scheduled to fight. They had all come to see us—to see if I could hold my own or if F was going to send me to the clinic too. I wasn't sure which they were hoping for.

"A," C called, as she edged her way to my side of the mat. "Thank the stars I didn't miss it."

"Oh yeah, that's just great. I wouldn't want you to miss me being knocked unconscious and sent to the hospital or anything."

"Shut up," she pushed me back. "You know that's not going to happen. The way you took down E this morning—everyone's excited about this fight."

"I took E down so fast, not because I'm 'just that tough'—he didn't fight back."

"A, you got on the mat without a weapon. Tough or not, you got guts." Then she leaned in and whispered, "F hurt his left knee in his last fight, use it. Oh, and he's only been picking the stake, so if you get it first maybe you'll throw him off."

"Yeah, OK. He's only the most skilled weapons fighter in the class. I'm not so sure he's going to get unnerved just because he doesn't get the stake."

"Oh stop your whining. Just go make me proud!" Then she pulled away.

Professor Gunner walked up and pushed his way through the crowd. "OK, OK, back away from the mat. No one needs to be this close." I was standing closest to the weapons table, so when he said, "grab your weapons" I didn't even think twice before grabbing the wooden stake, leaving F there staring down at the table, deciding what to do next.

Hmmm. Maybe C was right. Maybe F really does prefer to fight with the stake rather than any other weapon.

21

The bell rang, and F quickly grabbed the silver knife from the table and tossed it back and forth in his hands. “Nice,” he said with a grin from ear to ear.

Nope, C was not correct.

Before I could even finish my thought he leapt toward me swinging. *OK, he doesn’t waste much time,* I thought. I ducked, but the knife still sliced through the side of my shoulder. It doesn’t matter how prepared you are or how many times it’s happened, it still hurts. I managed to keep a hold on the stake and struck his left knee as I was going down.

F collapsed, but it didn’t take him long to pull himself back up. “Ahhh,” he growled. He was mad. He lunged again, but this time not as fast. His knee was bleeding, and he wasn’t able to put all his weight on it without cringing.

C was right about one thing, if I wanted to take F down I would have to go after his weak spot. “What’s wrong F, got a little scratch?” But what she was wrong about was what that weakness was. F’s knee was only a physical weakness, he would push through the pain in order to win the fight. I had to attack him mentally, make him doubt his strength. “Surprised I was able to get close enough to make you bleed?” It took all I had to focus on not getting hit again, while trying to get under his skin.

"Do you have a death wish, A? You really think you can take me down?"

He attacked again, and I dropped to the floor, rolled to my right, and swept his legs out from underneath him. I jumped back up as he was going down. "Well, I don't know about a death wish, but I did just take you down." The whole class started laughing and cheering behind me.

F pushed himself up on one knee and then the other. Soon, he was standing but he wasn't moving that well anymore. "Yeah, I'd like to see you try that again," he laughed and his dark brown curls bounced in front of his eyes.

"Come on, A, you got this," I heard someone say from behind me. "He might be big, but you're faster. Use it."

I started to turn to see who it was, but then I felt it—him. Just as I was turning, he lunged and reached out to grab my shoulder. I tried to duck but he got me. The stake was in my left hand and the only move I had was to strike down and hard—I did. I could hear the ripping sound as the stake tore through his pants and then the muscle of his leg. His screams echoed in my ear as he pulled me to the floor.

I heard the knife hit the ground first but I couldn't tell where it landed. I was struggling, not because his grip was hurting me but because he landed right on top of me, and he was heavy. He was still awake, and still in the fight. His hands went straight to my throat as he started squeezing. He leaned in—close—and I could feel the stubble of his beard rub along my cheek and the heat of his breathe against my neck as he whispered, “Still think you’re tough?”

I couldn’t break free—he was too strong. I reached out with both arms, grabbing for anything I could find to help my situation. I had lost my grip on the stake when I fell, and I knew he didn’t have the knife anymore. Finally, I felt the cold metal and grabbed the blade of the knife a little too hard. I could feel the blood flowing down my hand as I lifted my arm off the floor. I heard gasps as people all around the mat just stared at us. We were both losing a lot of blood, but neither one of us was ready to lose this fight.

I was feeling lightheaded and woozy. I was about to pass out but just as the room was starting to go black I managed to bury the knife in his left side. F pulled back and I could see it in his eyes--the moment he realized what had just happened. He went down, letting go of his grip on my throat, and I managed to get a nice deep breath. I lay there on my back, praying he wouldn’t get back up—and he didn’t. Thank the stars for the small blessings. The paramedics moved in quickly, bandaging him up there on the mat. I rolled onto my side and managed to push myself up onto my knees. In order to have this fight count as a win for me I needed to at least be on my knees before they carried him away. Lucky for me, it was less than five minutes before they had him on the gurney and off the mat. I heard F mumbling something as they took him out the door, but I wasn’t sure what he had said. The paramedics didn’t even bother to check me over. That’s how bad of shape he was in.

My classmates didn’t move. They didn’t come to my side to check on me. They didn’t even say anything.

Sure, I had managed to pull myself up onto my knees, but standing wasn't going to happen—not without help. "C…" I tried to call her, but my voice wasn't working, "…I need—."

"You sure?" She asked as she quickly looked from me to the cameras above my mat.

"I…" I looked back to where Professor Gunner was standing—watching—waiting. "Professor Gunner, I've won this one, yes?"

"Yes. It's a win."

When I glanced back at C, "Please," was all I could manage to get out. I didn't care who was watching or what they thought of me asking for help.

She jumped onto the mat and grabbed me under my arms and pulled me up. She was quick to help me, even though she hadn't let me help her earlier. M quickly followed, and soon others joined in. They didn't say anything. I had just taken down one of the toughest guys in the class—there were no words. C and M helped me back to my room and one of the nurses came in and bandaged me up. They put a couple of stitches in my right shoulder where F had gotten me with the knife. The cut had been deeper than I thought. A few more stitches were placed in the palm of my hand where I had cut myself grabbing the knife on the wrong side. Other than that, I had broken one, maybe two ribs and I was covered with the usual bumps and bruises that go along with fighting. The nurse told me it would hurt to breath for a while, but there wasn't much she could do about my ribs. She gave me some pain medication, which seemed to help, and I fell right asleep.

Teagan came to see me—I'm not sure how long after the nurse had left—and explained I wouldn't be taking my personality quiz that night, but my brain didn't want to focus on what she was saying. "I like your perfume…"

"A53, you need to focus." She handed me something to drink and I guzzled it down. My throat was still tender from F choking me, but the warm liquid felt and tasted wonderful. "The Council has decided, after viewing your fight, that you need your rest," she said. "They feel that based on your actions and your decisions over the last two days, as well as your scores over the last few months, they are already able to determine what the results of the personality quiz would be."

"…it's so sweet. You smell like candy." I sat up and reached toward her, but she backed away.

She wasn't smiling and she didn't seem happy with what she was telling me, or maybe she was mad at me. "I'm not wearing any perfume." She lay me back down, took the empty cup, and tucked the blanket up around my shoulders. "The Council feels that the test is irrelevant and unnecessary."

Irrelevant? I thought to myself, *how can it be irrelevant?* I could feel myself fading in and out. Whatever the nurse had given me must have been strong. *Don't my results help determine my placement after Selection Week?*

"Try and get some rest. Tomorrow is a whole new day, and your body needs to adjust to the new changes you're going through." I heard the door shut as Teagan left, but I couldn't seem to open my eyes wide enough to see her go.

Changes, what changes? Then it hit me, and suddenly I was wide awake.

22

I sat there in the dark room unable to hear or see anything. I could still smell her sweet perfume, like cotton candy and vanilla. *"…your body needs to adjust to the new changes you're going through."* Teagan's words echoed in my mind. They could only mean one thing. My injection had already been administered. The Council had made my selection for me. Teagan had warned me it could happen, I guess I just didn't think it really would.

I couldn't remember getting the injection, but then again I had no idea how long I had been asleep since my last fight. I sat in the bed, too tired to get up but too awake to fall asleep. I'm not sure how long I sat there before the sleep started to take over.

I was getting sleepier by the second, and my body was starting to feel heavy. I managed to pull myself out of bed, not wanting to let the sleep pull me in. I hoped the room lights would turn on once I started moving around, but no—they weren't motion activated and there wasn't a switch on the wall either. *They must be on a timer, or controlled by…* I stared up, examining the dark ceiling all around me. I knew I had never noticed a camera in the room, but that didn't mean anything. Then I saw it. There was a small dimly lit blinking red light on the ceiling above the door. It had to be a surveillance camera.

"Hey," I waved to the blinking light. "Can you turn on the lights? Please." I didn't know if they could see me in the dark, let alone hear me, but I had to try. Nothing happened. The lights never came on.

Instead, I had to search my body by touch alone. I started with the injuries I knew I had—my hand and my shoulder—and they were both still bandaged and throbbing, but they weren't hurting as much as they had been. Then, feeling up and down my body I noticed a pulling sensation at the inside of my elbow. There was tape wrapped around my arm just below my elbow and under the tape was something that felt like cotton or gauze. I quickly started unwrapping the tape and threw it to the floor. The skin on the inside of my arm was tender, but I didn't't' feel any cuts or dried blood. It had to be the injection site.

I sat down on the bed and lay my head back. *It's done,* I thought. Even though I didn't know—I *knew*. At that moment, flowing through my body and melding—joining, bonding—with my blood was either the vampirism or lycanthropy virus, and I had no idea which one it was. My guess was vampirism—only because I knew that was what Councilman Blake had wanted.

I wasn't afraid—I wasn't in shock. I was angry.

I didn't remember falling back asleep—but I must have, because the next thing I remembered was waking up and finding the lights already on. I took my time getting out of bed, knowing most of my body parts, especially my ribs, were probably still going to be pretty sore from the fight the night before. I figured the pain meds had probably worn off, but when I stood up—I felt great! I felt better than great. Either the medication had lasted longer than I expected, or—.

Remembering what had happened the night before, and my realization about the injection, I quickly unwrapped my hand. The stitches were still there, but the skin looked completely healed around them. I didn't even want to look at my shoulder, but I had to. I unwrapped the bandage around my shoulder and upper arm, and wasn't surprised to see the stitches there surrounded by perfectly healthy skin as well.

I had not one single cut, scrape, scratch, bump or bruise. I reached toward the ceiling, stretching while taking in a deep breath. Even my broken ribs no longer hurt. It was as if the fights from the day before had never even happened.

I knew from all my classes that both vampires and lycanthropes heal at a much faster rate than humans. However, lycanthropes have to be in animal form in order to aid the healing process, and vampires have to feed. I didn't remember transforming into animal form the night before, but I didn't remember drinking blood either. Considering I had been under the influence of some pretty heavy drugs I was guessing either could have happened. I just wished I knew which.

I looked at the ceiling above my door, and there it was, the blinking red light I had noticed in the dark. *That has to be the smallest surveillance camera ever.* I waved at the camera, hoping someone would see me. "I need to talk to counselor Teagan." I said it over and over but no one came. Finally I gave up. They would have to come get me eventually.

There was a repeated, quiet rap at the door. Part of me didn't want to know who was on the other side, but the other part needed to know.

"Hello?"

"A53, are you dressed? Is it all right to come in?"

I didn't recognize her voice, but she sounded gentle—almost timid.

"Give me just a minute, please." I quickly pulled off yesterday's clothes and threw on a new pair of dark grey shorts and a light grey tank top. *I will not miss wearing grey after this week,* I thought, as I pulled my hair into a ponytail. "OK, you can come in."

The door opened, and a young girl walked in—a nurse. I didn't recognize her, so she wasn't from one of the selection classes in recent years, but she didn't look a day over fifteen. That couldn't be right, could it?

"You're really young."

"Is that a question?"

"No. Just an observation." *One of the benefits of vampirism*—I thought—*you don't age.* "Vampire, right?"

"Excuse me?" She quickly scanned through the chart she was holding. "Didn't you know—?"

"Not me, you." I stopped her before realizing that maybe I shouldn't have. *Had she been about to give me information about my injection? Had I just ruined my only chance of finding out what had happened to me last night?*

"Oh, right. Yes, I am a vampire." She was looking right at me, through me.

"Wait. Are you telling me that I'm—?"

"I'm sorry, I don't have the injection authorization forms here, and I don't have the authority to—."

"But, you know don't you? I mean, vampires and lycanthropes—they can sense each other. It's…" *What had I learned? Why is my head so fuzzy?* "…it's smell, right?"

"That's correct. Both vampires and lycanthropes have a keener sense of smell than humans. You'll learn to recognize the subtle differences in scent among the… cultures, as you… develop more." She set the chart on my desk. "Can you please take a seat on the bed? I need to do your medical examination before you eat breakfast."

"But I feel fine. I feel great actually."

"That's good, but I still need to examine you."

"How old are you?" I asked, but she didn't answer. "Can I at least ask how old you were when you were changed?"

"I was sixteen. It was three days before my seventeenth birthday. Now, if you'll please take a seat on the bed. I do have other students to examine this morning."

I did as she asked, "What's your name?" I needed to see that chart she as holding—I needed a way to distract her.

"Britt." She smiled, and her name seemed to somehow fit. "Have you made your name selection yet?"

"I—." In fact I hadn't even thought about it. I already knew my name—Zelina—but whether I was going to use it or not, that I didn't know. "No, no, I haven't really given it much thought."

"Well, you still have time I suppose."

I needed to find out what injection they had given me. Sure, I had my suspicions, but I didn't really want to let my imagination run wild. I hadn't signed my selection form and injection authorization—the least she could do was tell me who did. Otherwise, I would have to assume that I was right in thinking it was Councilman Blake. "Is this going to take long?" I asked as she wrapped a cuff around my arm to take my blood pressure.

"Only a few minutes. Please stand up and touch your toes." She ran her hand along my spine and her fingers were cold. "Now reach up toward the ceiling. Very good." She went back to the desk and wrote something down. "I'll need to take some blood, but you shouldn't feel anything." When she came back she was holding a long piece of rubber to tie around my arm and a needle with two tubes. You would think that, after everything I faced on the fighting mat, I wouldn't be afraid of needles, but they always make me anxious.

I closed my eyes and lay back on the bed, I didn't want to watch. "Afraid of blood?"

"No. Needles."

"Interesting." She took two tubes of blood before covering the puncture site with a bandage. "All right, you're all done," she said, as she started gathering her things together.

"Are you the one who gave me the injection last night?"

"No. I don't administer injections. I just do the medical exams."

"Can you tell me who did?"

"I'm sorry, I don't know. But, if you have concerns you can always talk to one of the counselors. I'm sure they would be happy to discuss your selection, and go over what changes you can expect."

"See, that's just it. I didn't make a selection."

"Of course you did. You turned in the form on the first day—everyone did." Britt sifted through her papers again. "I'm sorry, I don't have yours with me, but I know I saw it earlier today—otherwise, I wouldn't be conducting your post-injection exam yet." She turned to leave, and I noticed as she grabbed for the door-handle, she, like Teagan a while earlier, wasn't holding a key.

"I'm sorry." I stopped her before she left. "Can I ask you one more thing?"

"Is it about your injection?"

I contemplated arguing with her about the fact that I had not completed my form, but I thought better of it. "No."

"All right then." She stepped back inside and closed the door behind her. She stood at the door, clutching my medical chart to her chest. "What is it you wanted to know?"

"The door—it's locked, right? What I mean to say is, I tried it earlier and it was locked. But for you, well, it just opens. How does that work?"

"I…" She looked back over her shoulder as if deciding whether or not to answer my question. "…Yes, it is locked, but the locks throughout the selection hall don't require keys. Student quarters are locked only while students are inside. Offices and other rooms, like the clinic, are locked at all times. They remain locked until someone with the authority to enter is within close proximity to the chip inside the handle."

"How does the doorknob know? I mean that someone is authorized or not."

She lifted her wrist and she was wearing a thick black band—not a bracelet exactly, but I can't really think of another way to describe it. It seemed more utilitarian than decorative. "The chip in the door handle reads the chip in my identification band. This allows me access to the clinic, the medical laboratory, and the living quarters of the patients I am scheduled to treat."

"Oh." Not really sure what to do with that information, or why I really cared, I sat back down on my bed. "Thank you for not telling me to mind my own business. I just like to know how things work."

"Well, if that's all, I should be getting back to work."

"Of course." I tried to smile as she left, closing the door behind her—locking me back inside. As I leaned against the wall my stomach started to grumble and I realized how hungry I was.

23

Breakfast was less than appetizing, or maybe I wasn't as hungry as I had thought. My tray was still more than half full when Professor Gunner knocked at my door. "A53, are you ready?"

"Yes sir."

He opened the door, and I was standing—waiting. "Who do I get to fight this morning?"

He didn't step into the room. "Are you all right?" He had one hand on the door frame and the other on the door knob, as if he was ready to slam the door shut if needed.

"I'm fine. Just ready to get this over with." I moved to pass him, but he didn't move out of my way. "Yesterday it was F. I'm just wondering who I'm up against—. What is that smell?"

"What smell," he asked closing the door slightly between us.

"Nothing, never mind." A sweet almost honey-like smell wafted through the room. "Like I was saying, I was just wondering who you paired me with today, that's all."

"All right." He pushed the door open while watching me closely and then stepped aside. I marched out and led the way to the fighting mats as if I had known the way all the time. "You have two fights today. The first is against N152—."

"And the second?"

"You'll be fighting C53 this afternoon."

"C?" I stopped and turned to him. "I can't—." Why would he make me fight my best friend—my sister?

"You can and you will. She understands that these fights are necessary. I doubt she will have any issues with getting on the mat with you."

How could he know that? He couldn't. He doesn't know me, or C—he doesn't know any of us. "You don't know that," I said. He just watched me—unflinching.

"You will fight her, but don't think that today's fights will be as easy as yesterday's."

Easy? Are you kidding me?

"You are all—." He looked back over his shoulder and Professor Kade walked up.

"Professor Gunner," Kade interrupted. "I believe I was scheduled to get A53 this morning. Is there a reason you needed to see her?"

"No—no, just trying to help."

"Well, I don't think we need any help. I'll take her from here."

I had never seen Professors Kade and Gunner be anything but civil to each other. In fact, I had thought they were friends, but then again vampires and lycanthropes are rarely more than co-workers or acquaintances. Professor Gunner nodded, then headed down the hall, leaving Professor Kade and me alone.

"Um, is everything—?"

"Everything is fine. Professor Gunner is just scheduled to collect the..." He stopped himself, but I'm not sure why. He went silent—and perfectly still—like only the older vampires can.

"Professor Kade?"

"Shall we go then?"

"Um, OK." I followed him the rest of the way to the fighting hall. As we turned the corner I saw N152 standing there next to Mat 1, just waiting. I crossed the room and stood next to him. Tall, blonde, ever-serious N—no pre-fight joking around from him.

"Good morning," he said stiffly.

"Yes it is." I smiled but he didn't smile back. Well, N was always serious. I had always thought he takes *himself* a little too seriously. It was a little animalistic—animals don't smile, right?

"You know, I saw what you did to F yesterday."

"I figured everyone had seen that." I wasn't intentionally trying to mess with him. OK maybe I was, but that's all part of the game, right? If the Council is going to make me get on the mat with all of the toughest guys in the class at least I can have the mental advantage.

"Right. Well, I just wanted you to know that I don't plan to go down so easily." He was rallying behind his big words, but leaving open doors all over the place.

"That's OK, it doesn't need to be easy, as long as you go down." I didn't give him a chance to respond. I walked past him straight to the weapons table and something inside of me pushed me to pick up the silver knife—the same silver knife that F had selected to use against me the day before. I waited, listening for Professor Gunner's command. I touched my shoulder, remembering where it had sliced me—the feel of the skin being torn apart and the warm blood running down my arm—but there was no sign of the wound now. *Yes, that will do nicely,* I thought, as I turned to see N still standing there where I had left him.

There were two other groups paired up and standing at fighting Mats 2 and 3, but all the other students—those not getting ready to fight—were gathered around Mat 1. It seemed that we, or I, had drawn quite a crowd. "A, you think you can take him?"

"I—."

C smiled at me from the side of the mat. "He's nowhere near as big as F, or as strong. This should be easy for you."

"Look at him, he's just standing there. He doesn't even know what to do," D77 said from the back. When I looked back at N, they were right. He was just standing there watching me. He didn't look scared or even mad. He looked confused.

"First groups ready, grab your weapons," called Professor Gunner from somewhere in the middle of the room.

Without hesitation I reached back and grabbed the knife I knew was just behind me on the table. This time, I grabbed the handle and not the blade. Thank the stars for small blessings.

I glanced around and could see J102 and Q190 getting ready on Mat 2. Feisty little tomboy J had grabbed a gun and Q had grabbed a knife. We didn't use real guns, not on the mat or even throughout the sector—it was a tranquilizer gun. Only the guard uses real guns, and as far as I know that's only when they are patrolling outside the sector wall. J was the first person I had seen use one of the tranquilizer guns on the mat, aside from H a few weeks back during training. I always thought it was the coward's way out. The tranquilizer works on all humans, vampires, and lycanthropes. It's a way to subdue your victim but it isn't really fair fighting, at least not in my opinion. Then again, looking at J and Q standing side by side, I had to admit he is probably a hundred pounds of raw muscle bigger than she is. I can see why she felt the need to grab the gun.

On Mat 3, R201 and F97 were getting ready to fight. R stood there, like the rock—or mountain—he is, just flexing his muscles while F stretched, reaching his arm far over his head and then stretching down to touch his toes. I don't think R could bend like that to save his life. F still had a bandage wrapped around his torso, but other than that he seemed to be moving all right. They were friends and both were known for their vocal hatred of 'fangers'. Why they would pair them up I had no idea, it's not like they were ever going to fight each other out in the real world, but then again Professor Gunner had said they had paired me and C up for that afternoon.

"Take your positions," announced Professor Gunner—and the bell rang.

I had been so focused on everything else going on around me that I wasn't even aware that N was standing only two feet behind me. When I turned he swung hard and fast. His left fist met the side of my face so hard I spun around before going down. I wasn't out of the game yet though. I pulled myself up, and backed away. N was bouncing back and forth on his toes and his hands were up, blocking his face, just like we had been taught. *He's been practicing,* I realized.

I mirrored his movements, trying not to focus on the throbbing in my jaw, but instead trying to anticipate what he was going to do next. He struck with a left jab, and I ducked right then thrust the heel of my hand up and into the base of his nose. His eyes watered up instantly and I spun around out of his direct line of sight. He was faster than I had remembered from the last time I fought him.

He tried backing me into the corner, but he just came at me with left punches over and over. Finally, I was able to grab his arm and twist it down behind his back. "If you always attack with the left you leave yourself open to—." I froze.

Suddenly I was taken back to that night in the woods, with M. I could feel the tree pressing into my back as M's lips desperately, eagerly, searched mine. I could taste his kisses and smell the masculine scent of sweat and soap mixed together. Then I was standing, watching, as it all happened without me. I looked down and saw the cuts and bruises on my left hand as I peeked through the trees at M and someone who was somehow me. I backed away, but when I looked up N struck again. This time his fist caught my left side, right below my rib cage. I went down, but I still wasn't out. I swept my leg under him, and took him down with me.

"It was you!" I spit the words at N—the accusation. "Who told you to follow me? WHO?" I screamed.

His head hit the floor and he was once again confused, unsure of how he had gotten there. "What *are* you—?" I had lost the knife but was able to climb on top of him before he got up. I began punching him, over and over.

"Don't play dumb. You know what I'm talking about." I remembered Teagan telling me that Councilman Serenity had made accusations against me. "Was it her? Was it Councilman Seren—?"

The bell rang, and I felt someone pulling me off of him. When I turned, I saw that it was Professor Gunner. He lifted me off the mat and shoved me in the direction of the door. "Go. Now!" I looked down and saw N was lying there motionless, with blood running down his face and covering his eyes. "Back to your room." He stood up. "Someone take her back to her room. NOW!"

No one moved. Everyone was just staring at me, and I was just staring down at N. He hadn't been playing dumb, he had been unconscious. "Did I do that?"

"A, come on. We need to go." C was pulling me toward the door. I could see Councilmen Iris and Teagan standing near the door, whispering. When we got closer they each took one of my arms and led me out.

"Should I come—?"

"No, C53, we will take her from here. Please just tell the nurse to visit her room."

"But—."

"Thank you, C. After you speak with the nurse, you may join the rest of your class back here."

24

"A53, it's time to wake up now." It was Britt's voice, but I didn't remember falling asleep. "You need to sit up, I need you to drink this before your next fight."

"What is it?"

"Don't worry about that, just try to sit up and drink it."

"But—."

She lifted me up and sat me back against the wall. "I know you're tired. The sedative I gave you was pretty strong, but it should have already started to wear off."

"My body is so heavy. Everything feels so foggy."

"That's the medication. Please drink this."

She held the cup out just far enough that the straw reached my lips. It smelled—sweet. "What is it?"

"Just drink. It will help, I promise." I did as I was told, and in seconds the glass was empty, I heard the gurgle of air coming up through the nearly-empty straw, and I wanted more.

"Very good, you should be feeling better in no time."

She got up to leave, and without thinking I grabbed her arm, pleading, "Can I have more?"

"Not right now, but after your fight, OK?"

"All right. Thank you."

I watched her leave. As the door shut behind her I realized I was already feeling better. I stood up and made my way to the desk. My itinerary was there, right where I had left it, but next to it was another package with my name on the front. "What's this?" I opened the envelope and pulled out the single slip of paper inside. Log in information for my next exam. I picked up the tablet, logged in and the welcome page for my IQ exam appeared.

SELECTION WEEK

Intelligence Quotient (IQ) Exam

~ C65A53 ~

I couldn't believe it. *They can't be serious. They want me to take an IQ Exam after they used a tranquilizer on me? This is ridiculous.*

I went straight to my door and began knocking—banging. "Hello? Is anyone out there? I need to talk to someone please." I waited but no one came. Bam! Bam! "Hello? I know someone is out there. Whoever is listening, I need to... Please, just ask Counselor Teagan to come here. I need to talk to her."

I sat on the bed and waited. There was no way I was taking an IQ test when I couldn't even think straight. Finally there was a knock at the door. "A53, is it all right if I come in?" It wasn't Counselor Teagan—it was Nurse Britt again.

"Yes, you can come in."

"Thank you," she said, as she slowly opened the door. "The guards said you wanted to speak to someone. Is there something I can help you with?"

"I asked for Counselor Teagan,"

"Yes I know, but she isn't able to come right now. In fact, unless she is with me, she isn't permitted to be in your room from this point on."

"Why? Why can't I see her?"

"I believe you know why," she said in a very cryptic way.

"No." I shook my head. "I have no idea why I can't—." *Because I'm a vampire,* the thought struck me like a ball hitting a brick wall.

"It isn't safe right now. Until you are able to better control your—. Until your transformation is complete, it is just safer for me to be assisting you."

"Because you're a vampire too." It wasn't really a question but I was expecting a response. She gave me nothing. "Fine, don't tell me. You're lack of a response is answer enough."

"Whatever you needed to talk to Counselor Teagan about, you can say to me."

"You're a nurse, not my counselor."

"Yes, I am a nurse, but I'm also on the selection committee. I'm an advisor to the Council. So, you should feel free to—."

"An advisor to the Council?" I laughed. "Why would I—?"

"Fine, don't talk to me." She turned to leave but stopped before she reached the door. "You'll be fighting C53 this afternoon, so you haven't much time. I will walk you down to the mats when it is time."

"It isn't about my fight."

"Oh?"

Reluctantly, I handed her my tablet, already open to the IQ Exam. "I can't take this. Whatever you gave me, I don't feel right. I'm all foggy-headed and I can't seem to focus. I can't take a test right now."

"That's all right." She smiled as she typed something onto my tablet and put it back on my desk. "Don't worry about that right now. I've re-set the test. You can log back in later this evening when you are better able to focus." She sat me back down on the bed and pulled my chair up to sit across from me. "You know, after today you only have one more day here. Then, after tomorrow night, you will all be announced as sector residents. You've already been through a lot this week, I know, but you can make it through the rest of today and tomorrow. I know you can."

I didn't know how to respond, or if she even expected me too. I knew I could make it through. I just didn't know who I was going to be when I got out.

"We're allowing some of the students to eat dinner together after the next round of fights. If you would like to join them, I think it might be good for you."

Why the change of heart—why today? "That sounds great. Thank you."

She turned to leave, but she seemed hesitant. "I'll be back in an hour to get you." She looked at me, and I could tell she wanted to ask me something or tell me something, but she didn't. She just left.

I sat on the bed, thinking about my fight with N, and how Teagan and Iris had brought me back to my room. I was trying to remember what they had said, what they had been talking about as they helped me down the hall. I closed my eyes and focused on Teagan, the way she had been looking at me when Gunner pushed me off the mat—when C had walked me off toward the door.

'She's changing too fast, faster than any of the other students.' It was Teagan, and she had sounded scared.

'She'll be fine. We knew, with her advanced physical and mental abilities, there was a chance this would happen,' Iris had assured her. *'You said she's been having visions for a while now. She has powers I'm not even sure she knows how to use.'*

Powers? What powers is she talking about? Does she mean the visions, or something else? Why would Teagan have told her about the visions?

Teagan had helped me before Selection Week. We had been close, or as close as a selection student could get to any of the section residents. I had confided in her, and now I was beginning to wonder if I had placed my trust in the wrong person. I hadn't known at the time what my selection plans were going to be, and now—well, the Council had taken my choices away. My injection had been administered before I had a chance to decide for myself, and with that they had sealed my fate. I wondered what Teagan and Iris thought of my so-called choice, and who really knew what had happened.

I tried to push aside all the negative thoughts I had about being a vampire, and about not having been able to make my own choice. What I needed was a plan. I needed to know what was happening to me and what I was going to do about it. I focused on Britt—what she was doing right at that moment. She had just left my room, but where had she gone? I closed my eyes and focused on her—what she looked like, what she smelled like, and the sound of her voice.

"Explain it to me again."

"Yes, father."

Father? I looked down at my hands but they weren't my hands. When I looked back up, Councilman Blake was sitting at a desk in front of me. *Councilman Blake?*

"Sir, I—." A large mirror hung on the wall behind him, and there I was staring back at myself—at Britt. Councilman Blake is Britt's father? She/we continued. "Selection student A53 has displayed some, well, rather unusual behaviors this week. She almost broke the record during her selection course run, she tested exceptionally high on both her Sector History exam and her aptitude test. However, she refused to complete her selection form, which actually played in our favor."

Worked in their favor?

"She will make a fine addition to the vampire community. Whether or not she agrees, I do believe she will grow to understand and even appreciate what I have done for her."

My heart practically stopped in my chest. I had known—I had felt it, but hearing him say it made it real. *I'm a vampire.*

"Yes," Britt answered as if she had heard me.

"Excuse me?" Councilman Blake asked.

"Oh, nothing father. I only meant to say yes. As in yes sir. I'm sure with time she will appreciate the opportunity you have given her. However..."

"However?" his eyes peered through me/Britt.

"Well, you didn't allow her to complete her personality quiz, and I believe that information could have been very helpful in her overall assessment. Now, well, she is refusing to complete her IQ exam."

"Why is she refusing?"

"I'm not sure sir. I had to sedate her after her last fight. She says she isn't feeling well, that she can't focus, but I can tell that isn't altogether true."

"Sedate her? Why on earth would you do that? She is in the middle of her transformation. The last thing you should be doing is interfering with that."

"She almost killed another student, sir. N152 is still in the clinic. He hasn't woken up, and the doctor isn't sure if he is going to."

"Is he—?"

"He is one of theirs, but that shouldn't matter. I understand that she is performing exceptionally well on the mat, but if she can't learn to control her powers, we will never be able to control *her*."

"We?"

"I mean you, sir."

"And if you interfere, she may never become the vampire she is meant to be! We've discussed this. She was selected because she displays all the attributes we need: strength, courage, confidence, intuition—and yet she is still humble. She gives credit to others instead of taking it herself. She will be easy to sell as a leader, and yet easy to manipulate too. She will do our bidding, without even realizing—."

Easy to manipulate?

"Father, with all due respect, if she had killed N152 I'm not sure we would have been able to cover it up as a defection. There hasn't been a Selection Week defection in years. Besides, there were other students there as witnesses."

Cover it up? Are all selection student defectors really students who were killed on the mat?

"Then what do you suggest?"

"I'm not really sure, sir. It seems as if she is rejecting the transformation. I think that—."

"Rejecting the transformation? How is that even possible?"

"I don't know if it is, sir. It just seems like…" She swallowed then took a deep breath before continuing. "I'm sorry sir, I'm not sure."

"You're not sure? You're supposed to be the expert and you seem to be unsure about everything!"

"I've conducted all the normal tests, and her blood work appears to be in line. She has increased speed and awareness, although I'm not sure she realizes it yet. Her heart rate is considerably low—lower than I would have expected so soon—."

"All of that sounds perfectly normal. Better than normal in fact," Blake said.

"Yes sir. However, that isn't what bothers me. Even her moves on the mat are cunning and calculated—right on track—advanced even."

"Then what makes you assume she is rejecting the transformation? All of that seems to indicate that I was right in my selection. So, what is it that is bothering you?"

"There is something about the way she fights. She isn't hesitant, but there is an underlying compassion there. I don't think she wants to be fighting. Even when she had N152 pinned to the ground, she was relentless in her attack—but it wasn't animalistic or instinct like it should be at this stage. She wanted something from him—information—answers. It was her *human* nature guiding her."

"You don't think it is just a delay in the effects of the injection?"

"No sir, I don't." She cleared her throat, and I felt myself rub my temples as if I had a headache, but I didn't—Britt did. "I think that maybe—maybe we made a mistake selecting her."

"It cannot be a mistake!" He stood up abruptly, pushing the papers off his desk, and before I could blink he was standing there, two inches in front of me. "*You* said that she was the one. *You* said that you had studied them all and that she was the strongest, the most capable."

"Yes sir, she is, but—."

When had Britt been studying me? I couldn't remember even meeting her before Selection Week.

"This is the first time in over fifteen years that the lycanthropes have equaled our number in Selection Week. Seven students chose lycanthropy this year."

"Six sir."

"Excuse me?"

"Six students selected lycanthropy. However, because of the relationship between A53 and the boy, you made an exception, giving them one that they were not really entitled to."

"Right, yes, the boy. And, had we kept the boy and given her to them…" She was pacing now. "No, that wouldn't have worked either. They would have had the strongest of them all. She may not know it yet, but she will soon. Besides, the only way we can control *him* is if we have *her*. Together, they will be a very valuable tool for us."

"Sir, I'm not sure she would have chosen the lycanthropy injection. I'm not sure she was planning to choose either."

"What are you saying? If she didn't choose, she would have—."

"Become a castaway, sir. I might be wrong, but I'm just not sure she is loyal to the sector, much less to the Vampire Council."

"That doesn't matter now, does it? She will be loyal, once she understands what it means for the young man she so desperately loves."

Loves? M?

"We need her. We need her if we are to regain the power we are losing here in Sector C. Now, do your job. Get her on board. Prepare her for taking a position with the Council—or *you* prepare for the fact that if she doesn't, she won't be released! I think you understand how that might affect your position."

"Yes, father."

I was hyperventilating when I came out of the vision. *Not be released? What does that mean? They can't just keep me here can they?*

25

When Britt came back, I was ready. One way or another I was getting released in two days, with the rest of my class. What I would do after that, I still didn't know. I did know, however, that there was no way they were going to keep me locked up any longer than I had to be. If that meant I needed to play along and be the good little vampire they wanted me to be, then so be it.

"I've completed the IQ Exam," I said as she walked in.

"You have?"

"I thought about it again, and I understood the need. I was able to pull myself together and I finished it just a few minutes ago. It's been submitted already."

"That's—that's great. Thank you, A53."

"Of course. I only want to do the best I can here. I'm hoping to please the Council. I'm sorry about earlier." I couldn't tell if she was buying my act or not. "Councilman Blake talked to me about possibly taking a position working with or for the Council after Selection Week. I'm not exactly sure what he has in mind, but I think I might like to know more."

"You would?"

"Yes," I smiled. "Of course. It would be an honor to work with the Council. I can't imagine anyone turning that down."

She held the door open and I walked out, waiting for her to shut the door behind us. "That's great news. I'm sure he will be pleased to hear it."

We walked in silence for a few minutes. I'm sure she was processing the information and trying to figure out how she was going to report my change in behavior to him. I was processing, too—processing my next move that is.

"Are you ready for your fight?"

"I think so. I've always been stronger and better on the mat than C. I know it won't be easy--she *is* my best friend, after all--but this isn't about friendships, right?" *It's exactly what the Council wants me to do—separate my friendships from my duty as a selection student. Right now my responsibility is to fight and to win, no matter who they pair me up against.*

"That is correct." She smiled, and I knew I had her. "I think with that attitude you'll do just fine."

"Thank you."

When we turned the corner all of the mats were empty. "Where is everyone?"

"You won't be fighting C53 this afternoon."

"But, I thought—."

"Part of your testing during Selection Week is to see how you adapt to change. With the results of your last physical examination, and the blood work, we have decided that C53 is not a suitable opponent for you."

"We? Don't you mean the Council?"

She ignored my inference that she had little power or say in the matter, and moved right along with her explanation. "You will be completing your final round of fights this afternoon, and then tomorrow you will go through another medical examination, and your mental health assessment. Other than that, you are almost ready for release. You should be very proud."

"That sounds great." I was actually surprised, in a good way, for the first time since Selection Week had started. "Who will I be—?"

I didn't have to finish my question and there was no need for her to answer, because in the doorway behind her I saw Professor Gunner walking in with M126. My heart skipped a beat and M's smile took my breath away.

"Are you all right?" Britt asked, as she grabbed my hand. "You seem to be trembling."

"No—no, I'm fine." I wasn't afraid to fight M. I had been the one to help him get to where he was, after all. Before he started training with me he was one of the slowest and weakest male students in our class. Now—well, now he was someone to watch. What I was afraid of, however, was being so close to him. I had missed his smile, his scent, his voice, his touch. I wasn't sure what was going to happen if we got on the mat together.

"You didn't tell me I would be fighting A," I heard him say as he stopped short.

"Is that a problem?" Professor Gunner asked.

M and I stood there, staring at each other. He was nervous too, I could feel it. I closed my eyes, and I concentrated on him, everything about him, and suddenly I was there, in his body—in his mind. I whispered, *everything will be ok.*

"No sir, everything will be ok."

"Good, then let's get to it." Professor Gunner turned and started toward the mat.

I've missed you M, I whispered in his mind.

"I've miss—." He stopped himself, and I was thrown out of the vision, giggling.

"Is something funny?" Britt asked me, looking a little worried.

"No, no not at all. I was just thinking—."

M looked at me, and somehow he knew, and he wasn't scared. He just smiled.

"You miss what?" Professor Gunner was staring down at M—waiting.

"Oh, nothing sir. I misplaced my toothbrush. I'll need to get another one after dinner. That's all."

"Your toothbrush?" he questioned.

"Yes sir." Then looking back in my direction M added, "Shall we?"

Gunner just nodded and led the way.

"So, M and A back together again. It's just like old times," M said as he stepped onto the mat.

"Does that mean you expect to lose to me once again?" I laughed and he joined right in.

"We'll have to see about that. It seems I got a boost of energy and power with my injection. Not sure if you can take me now." He was bouncing around the mat like a basketball with no player. "What do you say, no weapons?"

"Agreed, if that's OK with Professor Gunner of course." We both turned toward Professor Gunner, who was standing with Britt at the edge of the mat. He nodded.

"I'm surprised no one came to see the fi—."

"It's a closed fight," Professor Gunner snapped, stopping me. "Now, if the two of you are done chit-chatting, shall we begin?"

The bell rang, and M lunged at me. He grabbed my arms at the biceps and his hands were hot on my skin.

Hot? Why is he so hot?

He whispered, so only I could hear him, “How did you do that? How did you—?”

I quickly reached up between his arms, and threw my arms out to the sides. I forced him to lose his grip on my arms as I grabbed his wrists and twisted them low in front of me. We were only inches apart and he struggled to get free. “Did you miss me?” I asked.

“I did.”

I let him pull away. We had trained for so long together that we knew each other’s moves. It was like a dance. He struck with a right jab and I ducked left. He kicked low and I jumped high. He circled around me, and managed to get his arms under my shoulders with his hands clasped behind my neck.

“Tell me how you did it.”

“Tell me why you changed your mind.”

“What do you mean?”

“About your injection. I thought—.” We were circling the mat.

“A, what are you talking about?”

“You’re— you’re a lycanthrope, I can tell because you smell so—sweet and tasty.” He stopped moving, his arms were around my shoulders and he held on, but not as tightly as he had been. I could feel the tears starting to well up in my eyes, and had to blink them away. He had made his decision, and it had nothing to do with me, and I needed to move on. “I mean, I was only wondering what animal you selected?”

I pretended to struggle in his grasp. "Do you even get to select your animal, or does the Council do that for you?"

"You have her, M126—finish her!" Professor Gunner was focused only on the fight, and not the conversation.

"A, What are you talking about? I selected vampirism."

"But—you couldn't have, you're—."

Then I remembered what Nurse Britt had said, *"...because of the relationship between her and the boy, you made an exception, giving them one they were not really entitled to."*

I'm not the only one!

I dropped to my knees, pulling him down with me, and threw my weight forward to the ground. He flew over me and landed with his back to the floor. Swinging my legs up and around, I landed on top of his chest with my hands around his throat. "You were saying, Professor?" I turned and smiled at Professor Gunner, who now looked extremely displeased. Then, leaning in I whispered so only M would hear, "I never made my selection, yet I'm a vampire. They ignored your selection, because of me. They've injected you with lycanthropy. I'm so sorry."

"What? No!"

"What's going on?" Professor Gunner started walking toward us. "M126, what are you doing? Get up! Finish this. Now."

M was still shaking his head, not wanting to believe what I had told him. "Fight me. M. You have to fight me."

"Very nice," Britt smiled, almost laughing. "It doesn't seem, Professor Gunner, that your little pet is very obedient."

"I'm not his pet," M barked. "It won't be that easy A." M said, as he struck at my arms, causing them to buckle. Then he thrust his pelvis upward, throwing me off of him. "Just go down, he whispered, I don't want to hurt you."

I spun and kicked at the same time, striking him hard in the left side, beneath the rib cage. He was thrown off balance, giving me just enough time to sweep the back of his legs causing him to buckle at the knees. He went down on all fours and I yanked his head back, by the hair and he cried out. "Why don't you take the fall? Everyone is expecting me to win anyway," I giggled in his ear, and I could feel his body relaxing under my grip.

"Don't do that, it isn't fair."

"Don't do what?"

A low growl came from somewhere deep in his chest. It was animalistic, I had never heard anything like it. "Don't giggle in my ear. It does something—."

"Wolf!" I said, just as I realized it was true.

He spun around on his knees, grabbed my waist and threw me across the mat. There was as much distance between us as the mat would allow and still my body was reacting to his. That rumbling, growling sound came again, but this time it was louder and fiercer. He sprung into the air, and just as he was coming down on me I dived to the right, but I wasn't fast enough. I could feel his nails—no, *claws,* as they dug into my left side.

When I looked back he was staring down at his hands in shock. I didn't waste a second before stepping in and jabbing the heel of my hand into the bridge of his nose. I grabbed his shoulders, to use as leverage, as I struck with my knee deep into his groin. He dropped to his knees and I finished him off with a swift roundhouse kick to the left side of his face. He wasn't unconscious, but he wasn't getting back up either.

I stepped off the mat, and was struck by a sudden burst of nausea. I threw up at Britt's feet, and the paramedics rushed to my side and started bandaging up the deep gashes he had left.

"I'm fine." I pushed them away. "Check on M, make sure he's OK, please." One of the paramedics stayed with me to stitch up my side, and the other went to tend to M as I had requested.

"I've never seen a student transform on the mat less than twenty-four hours after the injection, much less being controlled enough for a partial transformation," Britt said pointedly to Professor Gunner.

"I don't think it was a matter of control. If I had to guess, he had no idea what was happening." Professor Gunner turned to watch the paramedics finish wrapping me up.

"Will she be OK?"

"I can't say. I really don't know what effects the scratches will have on her, if any. Typically, vampires can't be affected by the lycanthropy virus, but she isn't a full-blooded vampire yet. If I had known his transformation was a possibility, I would never have allowed her to fight him."

"Really?" She asked, skeptically.

"This was not planned!" Professor Gunner snapped.

"Explain that to the Council, not to me." Britt quickly followed as the paramedics helped me toward the door. I looked back and saw M kneeling again, silently staring at his hands.

I'm OK, this wasn't your fault, I whispered in his mind. He looked up, and I could see—feel—the relief that washed over him.

26

I had survived my last fight of Selection Week, and they released me from the clinic with a good bill of health. They weren't sure how the gashes on my side managed to heal so quickly, but I wasn't going to question it. I told myself it was just another benefit of the vampirism injection. If I kept finding benefits, maybe I wouldn't be so bitter about the fact that I wasn't actually given the chance to make my own selection.

Britt had told me I was going to be able to have dinner with the other students, and I was excited to see M again. I wanted to make sure he was all right—that *we* were all right after our fight, but he wasn't there. In fact, none of the students who had selected lycanthropy were there.

I joined C, D77, E82, T240, U277, and W351 at the table. They brought us each a plate of chicken, corn, rice, and a salad on the side. It smelled fine, looked fine, and everyone seemed to be enjoying it, but it wasn't what I wanted—needed. I stared at the plate for what seemed like a lifetime before one of the servers noticed.

"Is everything OK?"

"Yes. No—I'm sorry, this just doesn't seem entirely appetizing. Is there any way I can get a steak, rare, please?"

"Um… I will have to—."

"Here, A53, drink this," Britt interrupted. It was the same sweet, smooth drink I remembered her giving me earlier that day, and I drank it down so fast that I didn't realize that everyone at the table was staring at me. "Is that better?" she asked.

I dabbed my mouth with my napkin and nodded. "Yes, thank you."

"Did you need anything else?"

I thought about it, and although the drink had helped, there was still a burning hunger, deep in my stomach that it hadn't eliminated. "I would, if it's all right, still like the steak."

"Of course," she smiled, and nodded to the server who quickly ran back to the kitchen. "Try and get some rest tonight…" she said, looking around the table at the others, "…all of you." Then, without turning back, she quickly left the dining hall.

"Well, well, well, A. I've never seen you demand what you want like that," C said, slapping me on the back.

"I didn't—." I was going to say that I hadn't demanded anything, but she was right. I wasn't the type to ask for something that hadn't been offered. Why I wanted the steak and not the chicken was something I couldn't explain. I just knew my body wanted it—craved it—the taste, or maybe the protein.

"Hey, where is everyone else?" I asked, as we all went back to eating and chatting.

"You mean the animals?" D asked, laughing. "I'm sure they've got them caged up somewhere. Trying to housetrain them, no doubt."

Everyone laughed, as if his joke had been so very funny, and not in the least been offensive.

"They're keeping us separated. They said it's for our own protection, but I think they're just worried we'll be the only ones who make it out alive at the end of the week," C announced. Again everyone erupted into laughter, but I just didn't see what was so funny. They were still our classmates. Why did a difference in injection selections have to separate us so much?

We spent the rest of dinner talking about what we had been doing over the last couple of days—who we had fought and the different tests and medical exams they had put us through.

"That reminds me," C said. "What happened to our fight? I thought we were supposed to go head to head earlier this afternoon."

"Yeah, we—."

"Maybe they thought A was going to be the only one to make it out alive!" T240 said, mirroring C's words from earlier, and once again getting everyone riled up. Everyone except E. He didn't as much as look at me. I knew he was still upset about our five-second fight, and I didn't want to make it any worse by trying to talk to him about it.

"Ha-Ha, very funny." C didn't find it funny at all. "Seriously, what happened? They made me fight U277 instead, and well, no offense U, but that didn't go so well..." I looked over at U, who was trying to cover her black eye, and ignoring C as best she could. "...at least not for U."

"They made me fight M."

"What?" C asked, glaring at me from across the table.

Everyone was, once again, staring at me. It seemed I commanded a lot of attention these days, which wasn't something I wanted. "Why would they do that? Everyone knows they don't let the lycanthropes and the vampires on the mat together until after the transformations have been completed. There's no way the two of you—unless—."

Saved by the bell, so to speak. "A53, I need to speak with you for a moment please." It was Professor Kade, and he had interrupted just in time. Not that I was afraid to answer the unspoken question, I just didn't know what I would have said.

"Yes sir." I got up, leaving my tray and half-eaten steak behind, and everyone watched me go. I could hear them whispering as I walked across the room. "What is it, sir," I asked, when we got to the hallway.

"I just wanted to see if you're feeling all right. Nurse Britt came to see me. She had a few concerns. She said that you asked for steak this evening."

Why would my asking for steak be any concern to Nurse Britt? I wondered.

"I did, but it's not like I haven't had steak before."

"No, no, of course not. It's just that—well, your medical exams are indicating that you are much farther along in your change than expected in less than twenty-four hours." Professor Kade was watching me carefully, but I couldn't tell if he wanted me to respond or not. "After the injuries you suffered in your fight against M126, well, we were worried you may be having some side effects."

"Side effects, sir?"

"It's probably nothing. A lycanthrope can't infect a vampire. It's just that your body hasn't completed your transition, not fully anyway. Like I said, it's probably nothing. You seem fine, and I'm sure your exam tomorrow will confirm that."

"What would my choice of foods have to do with—?"

"Nurse Britt was just under the impression that you shouldn't be craving…" He started over. "You see, when you didn't want the chicken, she thought it might just be because your body wasn't craving normal foods any longer."

Normal foods? "Wait, you mean—what do you mean? What should I be—blood? Is that what that drink was? Did she give me—?"

"We're vampires A53. It is no secret that we drink blood, and you'd best get used to it quickly. Pretty soon, that is all you will need—all you will want."

"Right. I know. It's just that—I wasn't expecting—. Sir, I didn't fill out my selection form and injection authorization. So, I wasn't exactly prepared for—."

"You what?!"

"I didn't fill—."

"I heard what you said," he said in a low voice, cutting me off. "If you didn't complete it, then who did?"

I peeked into the doorway of the dining hall. Everyone had gone back to eating. "I have my suspicions, sir. I believe it may have been Councilman Blake, but I don't have proof."

"This goes against everything the Council believes in. Sector C was founded on the idea of free will, and the right to select the life we want. If what you are saying is true—." He got really quiet—that absolute stillness of the seasoned vampire.

Finally, he asked, "If you *had* chosen, which injection would you have selected?"

"Does it matter?"

"To me, it does."

"I'm still not sure, sir. I see the benefits of both, but I also see the negatives of both. I'm just not sure I would have—."

Professor Kade grabbed my arm and pulled me farther down the hall and into a small office. "Before you say anything else, you must select your words wisely. You mustn't speak so freely—so rashly in a public place. The walls have ears here, just as they always have throughout the sector. If it is because the Council suspected you might defect, they may have made the choice for you in order to persuade you to stay. You must decide, and quickly, where your loyalties lie, or you could be in serious danger."

"Danger?" *What had I done to deserve all of this? All I wanted—all I had ever wanted was to make it through Selection Week, and to decide for myself where I went from there.* "Sir, I have decided. They may have made my selection against my will, but there is no point in fighting it now."

"Very well. I think that is a wise decision." As he opened the office door to guide me out I spotted a black band, like the one Nurse Britt had been wearing, on a shelf near the door. As I followed Professor Kade out, I grabbed the band, and slipped it into my pocket just before he stopped and turned back toward me. "You should get some rest. Do you need me to show you the way back to your room?

"I can find my way, sir."

"Alright," he nodded.

I headed down the hall and left him standing in the doorway watching me walk away.

When I turned the corner and could no longer feel him watching me, I leaned against the wall and sat down. Everything was changing too quickly. I needed someone to talk to, but they wouldn't let me talk to Teagan, because she was a lycanthrope. For the same reason, I knew they wouldn't let me talk to Councilman Iris, so there was no point in even asking. I couldn't talk to C—she would never understand what I was going through. The one person, the only person, I wanted to talk to was M, but there was no way they were going to let me get close to him, unless—.

I looked up and down the hallway. No one was coming so I sat back, closed my eyes and focused on M. On his sweet, tempting scent, his strong hands, smoky grey eyes, and that amazing smile. Then, just as I had hoped, I was there—sitting in his room. I looked down, and his dinner tray was on his lap. *"M, can you hear me?"* I asked, but he didn't answer. *"M, it's me, A. I need to talk to you."*

"A? Where are you? How are—?"

"That isn't important." I cut him off. I knew I didn't have long before someone walked around the corner and found me suspiciously sitting in the hallway. *"I need to see you."*

"But, how?"

"I need you to show me where your room is."

"I don't understand."

"Just think about your room. Think about the last time you walked from the dining hall to your room." He

did it, just like I asked. I felt him close his eyes. Then, as if I was standing in the dining hall, I could see the tables all around me. He started walking and as he went down the hall, I could feel him passing me. I got up off the floor and followed him through the hall until I was standing outside one of the selection student rooms. Sure enough, on the door was a plaque that read 126. It had to be M126's room—though I didn't remember there being a plaque on the door of my own room. *Could I really have missed that?* I wondered.

I pulled myself out of the vision, and behind the door I heard his low voice. "A? Are you still there?"

I tried the door, but it was locked. Then I remembered the black band. Quickly, I took it from my pocket and slipped it onto my wrist, then tried the door again. This time, it opened. "M?"

"A?" I quickly shut the door behind me, and M was right there in front of me.

"How did you—?"

"Shhh. There's a camera, directly above the door. If I'm right, it's angled at your bed. Can you cover it or get it down?"

"They'll know."

"Yeah. But, probably not right away."

He pulled his chair over and reached up to the small blinking light and pulled the device off the ceiling. "That has to be the smallest camera I've ever seen."

27

"I missed you, M. I needed to know that you were all right." I closed the space between us and wrapped my arms around his neck.

"I don't understand. How did you find me? How were you in my head?" He pulled me to his bed and sat me down. "A, what you did just now, what you did earlier, before our fight, it's not even possible."

How do you explain the impossible to someone else when you don't understand it yourself? "I know." I held his hand. "Please don't be afraid. I—." When he smiled it took my breath away, but just at that moment I caught a whiff of his scent—sweet and musky all at the same time. "You smell—wow."

"Why thank you," he laughed, and smiled again. "You don't smell half bad yourself. Almost good enough to ea—. Wait, you smell—A, I'm not sure it's safe for you to be in here."

I slowly stood up and backed away from him. My eyes never left his. "M, I'm not afraid of you. You won't hurt me."

"Then why are you backing up?"

"I'm not, I—." But I was.

"A, there is a reason they keep the vampires and the lycanthropes separated until the transformations are complete. I'm not sure I can control—."

"You can, I know you can." I took a couple of steps closer. "Believe me, I know how hard it is. I want, so badly, to taste—." I swallowed back my hunger, and took another step closer. "We can do this. We can fight this."

"Why?"

"Why?"

"Yeah, why? Why do you want to fight it? Why should we fight these feelings—these urges?" he insisted. He stood up and closed the space between us just a little more.

"Because what I feel for you, inside, is so much more than the cravings the vampire virus is making me feel. I—I think I—."

He grabbed my arm and yanked me into his body—hard. He was getting stronger, I could feel it in his grip. His lips were on mine before I could finish my sentence and I forgot about everything.

I couldn't seem to get close enough to him, and he seemed to be having the same problem. I could feel his hands digging at my back, pulling me closer, tighter. I ran my fingers through his hair and breathed in the smell of him—the taste of him—with every breath, every kiss. His body was reacting to my touch and mine to his.

He pulled me down beside him on the edge of the bed. I moved to straddle his lap. "A. I—I can't." He pulled away, yet held me tighter at the same time. Suddenly, a sharp pain tore through my shoulder. I gasped for breath as his hand pulled away and I saw his blood-stained claws. "What have I done?" he whispered. He pushed me off of him, shoving me toward the door. “A, you have to go. You have to go before—.”

“I told you, I’m not afraid of you. You won’t hurt me. You can’t.” I knew the scratch had been bad, by the amount of blood on his hands, but my shoulder didn’t hurt anymore. I turned my back to him, and lifted my shirt. “I’m OK.” My shirt was ruined but the skin across my shoulder had already started to heal.

M didn’t say anything, he just stood there watching as my body finished mending itself back together.

“You see? You aren’t going to hurt me.”

Bang-bang-bang, there was a loud rapping at the door. “M126, what was that noise?” It was Teagan. “Are you all right?” She sounded concerned and scared.

“I—I’m fine.”

“Are you sure? I got a call from security saying there was a problem with the surveillance camera in your room.”

“Surveillance camera?” I kissed his nose. “Oh, that must be this little thing that fell off the ceiling while I was doing… fingertip pull-ups on the doorframe.”

I couldn’t help but smirk. He just winked at me and whispered, “Don’t worry. I got this.”

“So, you’re sure you’re OK?”

“Yes, I’m sure. I was just getting in bed.” He pulled me close and smiled down at me and I melted into those grey eyes. “Everything’s OK.” I wasn’t sure if he was talking to Teagan or me, but I couldn’t agree more. Everything was OK.

“Well, I’m going to have to send someone in to re-install the camera, but I suppose they can do that in the morning.”

"That would be great. Thanks."

We stood there, just holding each other, waiting to make sure she was gone. "I'll need to borrow a t-shirt." Mine was shredded and I couldn't chance someone seeing it as I made my way back to my room.

As I slipped his shirt over my head I took a deep breath, breathing in the scent of his cologne and soap mixed together. It was heavenly. "Like what you smell?" he smirked as I poked my head through the neck hole.

"Maybe."

"Maybe, huh?" He stepped closer but didn't touch me. "It *looked* like you liked it."

"I might have liked it, a little." M leaned down and gave me the softest kiss I had ever had. Not that I had much to compare it too, seeing as he was the only guy who had ever kissed me.

"You should go."

"Yeah."

"I think I might be—."

I knew what he was going to say, because I felt it too. So, I quickly put my finger on his lips. "Don't. Not yet." He just looked at me, and I could feel his question as if it were my own. "After tomorrow, we get released. Let's just see how things go. Then, if you still feel the same way, you can tell me. OK?"

"OK."

I edged out the door and into the hallway, and made my way quickly through the maze of halls until I reached my door. When I opened the door, I was surprised to find Councilman Blake, Nurse Britt, and Professor Kade sitting in my room, waiting for me. Hands behind my back, I quickly pulled off the black band and slipped it back into my pocket.

28

"Would you like to explain where you've been?" Councilman Blake asked, before I could even shut the door behind me.

"I was—." *What am I doing?*

"She was in my office," Professor Kade said.

"Your office? You told us you sent her back to her room over an hour ago, when you came to see me."

"No, if you recall, I told you that I had just spoken to her. I never said I sent her back to her room." He glanced my way, and I knew he was trying to tell me something but I didn't know what. "I asked her to do some—filing for me. Isn't that right A53?"

Filing? What is he talking about?

"Um, yes. Yes sir. It's all taken care of. I'm sorry that it took me so long. I—I had a hard time figuring out your system."

"Of course, I understand."

"Why did you bring us here if she was still in your office? Why not just take us there?"

"That's my fault, sir." I interrupted. "Like I said, I had a hard time figuring out his filing system. I'm sure he didn't think it would take me so long." I grabbed at the bottom of my—M's—shirt. I was sure they could tell it was too big for me. Did they notice his scent? "So, what did you—what can I do for you?"

Councilman Blake was holding a file similar to the one he had on his desk the day I had gone to see him only a week ago, but this one was thicker. "Your file," he said, waving it at me. "I have found watching you over these past few days to be rather interesting."

"Interesting sir?"

He stood, and Nurse Britt quickly joined him at his side. Watching them together I could actually see a resemblance. But, if he really was her father and she had been turned at the age of sixteen, that would mean he had turned her himself. I knew he was one of the oldest vampires in Sector C, but wouldn't that make her one of the oldest too?

"I believe you knew you would perform exceptionally, both physically and mentally, but what you couldn't possibly have known was how your body would react to your injection. None of us could have anticipated that. How has it affected you, if I might ask?"

"Fine."

"Just fine? You haven't experienced any side effects?"

"No sir."

"Good." He flipped through the file. "It has come to my attention that you were under the impression that you didn't complete your selection and injection authorization form. Is that correct?"

If I say yes, he will know that I know he did it, but if I say no, he will know that I'm lying. I turned to Professor Kade for help.

"Councilman Blake, I may have misunderstood what she was trying to tell me," he said.

"Misunderstood?"

"Perhaps." Professor Kade looked at me and I could see in his eyes that he finally understood. He believed Councilman Blake had been the one to complete my form.

"Is that what has happened?" Councilman Blake turned to me. "Has Professor Kade misunderstood?"

"I… Yes sir."

"You have no complaints about your injection then?"

"Other than my fear of needles?" I laughed. "No. No, I have no complaints sir."

"Professor Kade, could you give me a moment alone with the child please?"

Professor Kade hesitated, but he finally nodded. "Yes sir." He crossed the room, with Nurse Britt following along behind them. That left me standing there alone, with Councilman Blake.

Councilman Blake closed the distance between us and did what I can only describe as smelling me. "You smell like…" He sniffed the air around me again, "…wolf." Cocking his head to the side he glared at me through squinted eyes. He looked me over, the way a predator looks at his next meal just before killing it. "Nurse Britt was concerned that the injuries you sustained during your last fight might have had an effect on you, but—."

"No sir, I'm fine." I spun around. "See, everything is fine. No pain or anything. My side is already healed." I lifted the side of my shirt for him to see. His hands were cold on my skin as he ran his fingers across where M had scratched me during the fight.

"Remarkable." He was studying my skin as if it was a piece of art.

"Nope, just skin. Nothing too exciting." I crossed to the door. "If there's nothing else, I'd really like to get some rest before tomorrow."

"Of course. Although I should have nurse Britt come back in and take those stiches out. Considering you've already healed around them, you might be more comfortable if she removes them."

"Couldn't it wait until morning? I'm pretty tired."

"If that's what you wish." He started to leave, but turned back. "Just one more thing. Have you given any thought to our previous conversation?"

"Yes. If you still want me, I would like to accept a position with the Council." He smiled, nodded, and left. He didn't bother to tell me what I could expect, what type of job it would be, or even what it would mean to work for the Council. I guess that was something I would have to find out in time.

I sat down on my bed, finally alone, and took a deep breath. *Wow, what a day*. Had I known the day would end like this, I would have woken up earlier just so I could try to rush through the day and get to M's arms again.

I closed my eyes. "M?" I whispered out loud. "If you can hear me—."

"I know."

I fell asleep with M's t-shirt wrapped tightly around my body, and the scent of him filling my head.

29

"Rise and shine."

I rolled over in bed to find Britt standing over me. "What? What time is it?" I quickly reached back to snag my necklace from the headboard before she could see it, but it wasn't there.

Oh Crap, I thought. *Where could it have gone?* As she turned to place her things on my desk, I quickly looked down checking under the bed.

"Late. It's already ten o'clock. The rest of your class has already had breakfast, finished their physicals, and are warming up in the gym getting ready for their final rounds of fighting."

"How long did I sleep?"

"I'm not sure. It was pretty late when we left you last night, but I don't know what time you finally fell asleep. How could I possibly know that?" She smiled.

Why did she smile?

"Understandably, your body needed the sleep, so we didn't wake you earlier. However, now I need you to get up. I need to complete your medical exam, remove the stiches from your side, and get you ready for your last fight."

"My last fight?" I stood up and stretched, trying to comprehend what she was saying. "I thought my fight with M yesterday was my last fight."

"It was. At least, it was your last fight with another selection student." She sat me back down, "Please lift up the side of your shirt so I can get to the stiches." I did as she asked, and she proceeded to snip and tug at the stiches one by one. After they were all out she cleaned the area with alcohol then wrapped a blood pressure cuff around my arm. "The Council has decided that, before release, they would like to see you on the mat one more time."

"By the Council, you mean Councilman Blake, right?"

"I'm sorry?"

"When is this going to end? Why do they keep changing everything?"

She took the cuff off my arm, and swabbed the vein on the top of my hand. I couldn't look. I don't like needles, and with all the poking she had been doing lately I felt like a pincushion. "Don't worry, this isn't going to hurt."

"Yeah, easy for you to say," I laughed, because who doesn't laugh in the face of danger.

She took two tubes of blood, swabbed the back of my mouth with a long Q-tip, and then examined my teeth. "Very nice, it seems your fangs are already starting to show."

"What?" I reached up and felt the roof of my mouth with my finger. Sure enough, two small nubs of what would soon be fangs had already started to grow. Vampire fangs aren't like normal teeth, or even those of a lycanthrope, which extend and grow during their transformation and then retract when they return to human form.

Vampire fangs grow behind the traditional row of human teeth, and retract or fold back to the roof of the mouth when we're not feeding. Think of them like the fangs of a snake. That's how they described them in class anyway. Similar to a snake's fangs, vampire fangs are sharp, long, and hollow. They are connected to a small sac, which produces a poisonous venom. The sac develops over time, somewhere in our nasal cavity. The venom won't kill a human, but it will temporarily paralyze them so we can feed. Some vampires—the really strong ones—can even use mind control on their victims, to make it so they don't even remember the attack. At least that's what I've been told. However, unlike a snake that can regrow fangs if they break or fall out, vampires only produce one set. If we lose our fangs, we aren't able to grow another set.

Britt stood me up and was standing behind me running her hand along my spine. "Now, bend and touch your toes." I did as I was told. "You knew the testing during Selection Week would be hard."

"Yeah, but—ouch. What was that?"

"I need to test your healing speed."

"My healing speed? So, what—you cut me?"

"I did."

OK, this doesn't seem odd to anyone but me?

"Yeah, I'm not really OK with that. I don't like being used as a pincushion and I especially don't like being used for you to practice your cutting skills on." I quickly pulled my shirt back down and sat down on the bed.

"You're all healed you know. Faster than any vampire I've ever seen, and I've been around for quite a while." She opened the door. "I'll give you five minutes to get dressed. You'll have breakfast in the dining hall and then you need to get to the gym. You can shower after the fight. And A, don't look so worried, you're almost done."

"Easy for you to say," I said again.

I had known that Selection Week was going to be hard, but I had had no idea how hard. They don't prepare you for all of the mental games they play. They don't prepare you for all of the physical challenges you face. They just don't prepare you.

Nurse Britt was nothing if not timely. Five minutes to her seemed more like two to me. She opened the door without even knocking. "Time to eat." Luckily I was dressed. I had a big breakfast: two glasses of blood—yes, blood—sausage, eggs, and potatoes. After I finished it all I wasn't sure I'd be able to move, but Britt announced. "Time to get going." I was beginning to wonder if she was planning to follow me around all day.

When she led me into the gym, I saw that my whole class was there, along with Professor Gunner, Professor Kade, Counselor Teagan, three of the paramedics, and all eight of the Sector C Council members. Unlike the setup for previous fights, there were chairs set up around one of the mats. The officials were seated in the front row, and the others filled in the seats behind them. I couldn't remember the last time I had seen all of these officials in the same room together, except during the final Selection Week ceremonies from previous years. I knew they had monthly Council meetings, and sector resident meetings, but I wasn't even sure all of the Council members attended those. This all seemed so formal—important—and intimidating.

I stopped at the door, stunned by what I was seeing. I think I was in shock. *Have they all come to see me? Surely there has to be another reason they're all here.*

"Are you all right?" I looked up and Britt was staring at me. "A53, are you all right?"

I shook my head, but my mouth defied me when finally, I answered, "Yes, I'm fine."

"Good, we should go in now."

"Wait…" I looked at the waiting crowd and saw C waving from her spot next to the mat. "…I know I'm not supposed to, but—but is there any way I could talk to Counselor Teagan before I go in?"

"You…" Britt opened her mouth to say something but then started over. "…I don't see why not. You seem to be in control."

"I am. Really," I said, maybe a little too eagerly.

"I was hoping to get your blood work back before the fight anyway. Maybe this will give me time to run back to the lab and check on it. Stay here for a moment, please."

She left me standing there in the doorway, and headed over to where Councilman Blake and Sector C leader Remy were sitting. I couldn't hear what she whispered to them, but they were both watching me closely. I smiled, trying to act casual, but I think the sweat pouring down my face gave me away. I was nervous. Something didn't feel right, but I couldn't put my finger on it.

Finally, Britt came back, with Teagan in tow. "You have five minutes," Britt said. "I'm going to run to the lab for your blood work, but when I get back we will proceed. Do you understand?"

"Yes. Thank you," I said, eager to have a few minutes alone with Counselor Teagan.

Britt left, and when she was around the corner I pulled Teagan into the hallway. "A53, this is highly irregular," she began. "Why did you—?"

"You were right." Her warnings had played over in my mind a thousand times since I had realized they had administered my injection without my signed authorization.

'They could decide, no matter your scores, to place you as a breeder, a donor, or they could choose your injection classification… no matter your selection of choice,' she had warned me. *'Punishments are not meant to please the wrongdoer, they are meant to teach you a lesson.'*

"About what?" she asked.

"The Council is punishing me. I didn't make my selection, I never filled out the form. But, here I stand—."

"A vampire, but not by choice." She finished my thoughts and I saw on her face what it meant. I saw the reality sink in. "I'm so sorry A53. I was hoping this wouldn't happen to you. I was hoping—."

"That it would turn out differently for me than it did for you?"

"Yes. I'm so sorry."

"It doesn't matter now. I can't change it, so now I have to learn to live with it." I heard footsteps coming from the hall behind me, but when I turned, no one was there.

"Then what did you want from me. Why did you insist on talking to me?"

"You're still my counselor and you once told me to trust you. Can I still trust you?" She nodded, but I could see fear in her eyes. "What's happening now? What do they have planned for me?"

She swallowed hard, and I could feel, no *hear*, her heart rate speeding up—the thumping sound as her blood rushed through her veins echoed in my ears. "They are putting you on the mat with the outcast, with—."

"With Micah."

"Yes." A tear slipped down her cheek. "They want you to kill him as a sign of your loyalty to the sector and to your community."

"As a sign that I will be faithful to the vampires, you mean."

"Yes."

"I've never—. I can't kill—."

"You have to." She wiped her eyes, took a couple of deep breaths, and looked me straight in the eyes. "You must accept this is for your own safety, and he will understand you are only doing what must be done."

He will understand? What does that even mean?

"I can't—." I started to object.

"You must," she insisted. "There's one more thing." She held her hand out. "You might want to keep this in a safe place. Hanging it on your headboard where anyone can see it could get you into trouble." She was holding my necklace—the one with the wire charm cradling the unusual stone I had found.

"How did you—?"

"I took it the other day, when Councilman Iris and I brought you to your room," she answered, before I could finish.

The other day? How had I not noticed until this morning? I wondered. "But why?" I asked. "It's just a rock."

"This is not *just* a rock, but I believe you already know that." She was looking at me with her intense frozen gaze. "Or maybe you don't. You really don't know?"

"Know what?"

"We don't have much time for me to explain, so you'll just have to take me at my word."

"All right."

"This isn't just a rock. It's called a vision stone. They are very rare, and they are said to only show themselves to individuals who possess the power, or openness to the reception, of visions."

"If that's true, and it was meant for me, then how did you know what it was?" I asked.

"I'm… well, I don't have visions now, but when I was younger I did."

"Why didn't you tell me before? When I first told you about my visions."

"I wasn't sure how much you already knew, and I couldn't risk exposing myself."

"What happened? Why don't you have them anymore?"

"I'm not sure. They stopped after I was turned." She dropped the necklace into my hand. "But honestly, I'm glad. The Council doesn't look too kindly on seers."

"Seers?"

"Yes, clairvoyants, psychics, oracles. They used to be called fortune-tellers in the old world. Now we call them seers. They are the ones who have visions, or premonitions," she explained.

"What's the difference between a vision and a premonition?"

"Visions are things that have happened in the past or are currently happening. Premonitions are events that will happen in the future."

"Oh."

"Like I said, I would keep that hidden if I were you." She turned to leave. "Put it on, but make sure it stays hidden."

I slid the necklace over my head and tucked it into my shirt. "Why didn't you tell? Why did you protect me?"

She stopped, with her back still to me. "If I had told them I found a vision stone in your room, I wouldn't just have been exposing you—I would have been exposing myself as well. Vision stones are only recognizable by those with the gift of foresight. Even if I don't have visions anymore, I did at one time. That alone would be enough to make the Council exile me from the sector. Everything I did to get here would have all been for nothing if I got exiled now." When she looked back I could see the fear in her eyes. "Do you understand now how serious this is?"

"I do."

"Good."

"It's time to go." Britt interrupted, her heels clicking on the tile floor to the rhythm of her steps. "Back inside, ladies."

Teagan took her seat on the side of the mat. Britt led me to the center of the mat, and then crossed to where Sector Leader Remy was seated and handed him the file—my file.

Remy thumbed through the file and then, snapping it closed, he handed it to Blake who did the same before handing it to Councilman Ash who was sitting next to him. Ash took only a second's glance at the paper inside the cover of the file and then looked up at me. "Oh this is interesting, very interesting." He glanced to his right and I saw M sitting there, his eyes for me only. I didn't even notice when Ash turned his attention back to me until he started talking again. "You continue to intrigue me, child."

"That isn't my intention sir."

He laughed, but it wasn't the kind of laugh you have when you find something funny. It was a sinister, calculated laugh. "Your intention or not, I do look forward to seeing what you can do today."

30

Sector Leader Remy stood and joined me on the mat. "It is a rare treat when one of our selection students so eagerly volunteers to demonstrate her abilities on the mat for us."

"But I—." Had he not cut me off, I would have told him that I hadn't volunteered, that I wanted nothing to do with what was about to happen, but he didn't give me that chance.

He addressed the audience. "You have all performed so well this week. You have accepted your transformations as was to be expected, and you will all make wonderful additions to Sector C as full residents once your transformations are complete. Later today, you will finish your final round of tests. Depending on your individualized schedules, that might be your mental health assessment, your final medical examination, your IQ test, or your Aptitude test. Whatever the case might be, it will be your final requirement as a selection student." Sighs of relief were heard throughout the room. Yet, I felt no relief.

"Yes, yes, it has been a long week, but rest assured, you are almost finished. In the morning, you will all be announced and introduced to the sector community as residents. You will also receive your new housing placement and be assigned to a mentor to assist with your transition."

"Do we get to pick our own mentor?" someone called out. I didn't bother looking to see who it was—it was D, of course, never afraid to ignore convention. All my attention was focused on what was coming—the fight I was about to have.

"No, you won't." Remy said sternly, before continuing. "For those of you entering the vampire community, your mentor will not only be there to guide you through the first few weeks as you learn to control your cravings and to teach you the laws that govern vampires within our sector, but they will also welcome you into their home to stay until your cravings are under control and you can be trusted to live on your own. Similarly each lycanthrope will be assigned a mentor to prepare and guide you through the first moon cycle. You will be assigned your own living quarters, but you will be required to spend your evenings, during the three days of the full-moon cycle, in a secure facility designed for newly turned lycanthropes. This will only be required through your first few transformations—until you have managed to control your..." He scanned the room as he searched for the right world "...animalistic urges."

As if on cue, Q and R started growling, which made half of the class laugh, hoot, and holler.

I just stood there. *Are they all blind? How can none of them realize what's really going on?* Then my eyes met M's, and he was just staring up at me. He knew, and in that moment I also knew, that we were thinking the same thing.

"Tonight, if you haven't done so already, take time to think about who you want to be—who you want the sector to see you as. Your name announcement is not only a right but a privilege. You only get to select your name once, so make sure you select wisely."

Zelina—Zelina—Zelina. The name repeated itself in my mind like a broken record. Remy looked at me, as if he knew something. *He couldn't have known what I was thinking, right?*

He turned his back to the rest of the class, and focused only on me. "The weapons table is to your right." He nodded in that direction without actually looking. "Make your selection, and return to the center of the mat."

I crossed to the table, trying not to look at my classmates. I could feel M's eyes on me, but I knew if I looked at him he would see how afraid I really was. If Teagan was right, then the Council planned for me to kill Micah, right there in front of everyone. I stood at the table, looking down at the weapons I had to choose from: a knife, a dagger, a wooden stake, an ax, and a gun—not a tranquilizer gun, but a real gun. I picked it up, and quickly set it back down. It felt too heavy in my hands—probably the silver bullets. I knew the second I picked it up that I would never use it.

I knew that Micah was a lycanthrope. Teagan had told me that back in Sector M he had made it through Selection Week with great scores, and was later assigned as her assistant, after he was injured during his advanced education program. I just didn't know what type of lycanthrope he was. The stake is the best choice for fighting a vampire, and given the chance I was sure Micah would take it. Silver is especially successful against lycanthropes, and so the gun, the knives, the daggers, and even the ax would work. I picked up each one, spending a little time balancing them in my hands. I could have fought with any one of them, since we had trained on all of them, and others, in class.

In the end, I selected the stake. I didn't want him to use it against me and I knew I could heal most wounds caused by the other weapons, as long as he didn't take my head off with the ax. The stake wouldn't kill him, at least not as easily, but then again, as far as the Council knew, I didn't know who, or what, they were putting me on the mat with.

I made my way back to the center of the mat, holding the stake with both hands in front of me, and waited. I saw Teagan, those large brown eyes wondering *why*—questioning my weapon choice. I allowed myself a moment to look at each of my classmates. Pretty little blonde-haired O154 was sitting in the front row, alone, directly in front of the Council. I wasn't sure why they had singled her out, but she seemed happy there. I guess if she was happy, I should be happy for her.

The other students were divided, vampires to the left of the Council and lycanthropes to the right. It was so clear to me, suddenly, as I stood before them. The Council had intentionally created the divide between the lycanthropes and the vampires. They perpetuated the hate by purposefully segregating us from each other, and no one seemed to see any problem with that. Well, I saw one, and in that moment I made a promise to myself—a promise to find a way to do something about it.

I smiled at M, but he didn't smile back. I closed my eyes. *'Don't be afraid. I'm not.'* When I opened my eyes again he was smiling.

"Are you ready?" Remy asked me from his seat.

"I am."

He nodded to two guards who were standing near a door in the back of the room. I hadn't even noticed the guards before, but that didn't mean they hadn't been there. "Bring in the castaway!" My classmates immediately started turning to see who was coming. I heard mumbling and gasps of shock—maybe fear.

"Did he say castaway?" I heard the shock in C's voice.

"This has to be a joke." I heard J's disbelief. But the room quickly went silent when Micah walked in behind the two guards.

"Oh my stars, A." I heard C whisper, as she gazed up at me.

"It's OK. I'm OK." I whispered back. I took a deep breath to settle my nerves. I was actually feeling a lot calmer than I had expected, calmer than I had felt only moments before.

The guards shoved Micah into the center of the mat with me, and he fell to his knees. I reached out to help him up and he smiled. He actually smiled.

"It's you. Do you remember me?" he asked. He took my hand, and I didn't have time to answer him before I was thrown into a vision—Micah's vision. I/Micah—was kneeling on the mat as I/A plunged the stake deep into his chest. I could feel the pain as if it were happening to me, I/Micah, and then I felt—grateful—*relief*.

Not a vision, a premonition, I thought, remembering Teagan's explanation of the difference. Me staking Micah through the chest—that hadn't happened yet. It was a future event, and therefore not a vision. *But I've never had a premonition before.*

The next thing he showed me, and I can only describe it that way, was another premonition. I was standing in the center of a crowd—vampires and lycanthropes together, intermingled—and they were cheering. When I turned, a woman with beautiful long red hair smiled at me. *'Don't give up. You have to fight this. You have to keep fighting,'* she said. *'I won't give up on you.'* She was squeezing my hand so hard it pulled me out of the premonition and I was staring down at Micah, who was still holding my hand—*squeezing* my hand.

In that moment I realized what Teagan had meant. Micah did understand. He had already known this was going to happen. He had seen the future. He had seen me kill him. That's why he had come to Sector C. He wasn't looking for Teagan, he was looking for me. For whatever reason, I was meant to kill him and he was OK with it. So I had to be OK with it too.

31

I knew how the fight would end—I had seen it—but I didn't know how long it would last or how much fighting back Micah would do. Surely he had to fight back. We stood there, on opposite sides of the mat, and waited for the bell to ring. When it did, he didn't move.

The guards shoved him toward me—striking his back with an electric wand. The wands are used by the sector's external security guards during their border patrols beyond the sector wall. I had never seen anyone use one in person. Micah fell to the floor, shaking from the shock.

"Stop!" I yelled. "How can you expect him to fight if he can't even stand?"

"He is a castaway, he is not meant to win." Councilman Ash said from his seat next to Remy.

"No? Well, then I refuse to fight. I won't fight unless he has an equal advantage. It isn't fair. You didn't even give him a weapon and now you're torturing him? It isn't moral."

"Hmmm, modesty and now morality," Ash said. "What will you do next?"

"I can't tell you what I will do, but I can tell you what I won't—."

"HUSH!" Blake rose to his feet. "You will not speak to a member of this Council in that tone. Do you understand me?"

I just stared at him. I wasn't budging. If they didn't stop torturing Micah, then I wouldn't fight.

"I will take your silence as understanding." He turned to the guards. "The girl wants a fair fight. You can release him." They pulled back their wands and stepped off the mat. "If it is a fair fight you wish for, then you should arm him as you are armed."

I glanced back at the weapons table, where I had selected the only stake, and now saw a pile of stakes available for the choosing. I looked back at Blake and he nodded. I took the ten short steps, which felt like a mile, and grabbed another stake off of the table. When I made it back to Micah's side I knelt down and handed him the stake.

"I can't," he whispered.

"You have to. I won't fight you any other way."

"But—."

"I know," I smiled. "No matter the outcome, I won't fight you unless it's fair." I knew that giving him a weapon, especially the one weapon specifically designed to kill vampires, put me in even more danger, but I had to do it.

The bell rang again, and this time he lunged at me. There was ferocity in the way he moved, a hunger for survival, even though the wands must have slowed him down. I could only imagine what he would have been like before. I was easily able to dodge his attacks, one after the other. He went left I went right. He jumped I ducked. It was more like choreography than a fight, and it was breathtaking in the way that a warrior finds beauty in the quiet moments of an intense battle.

Then it all changed. One second he was there with me as a human, looking like anyone else in the room. Then, he was reaching, not moving just reaching out with his hands. He fell forward and I watched the muscles along his arms, back, and legs—expanding. His bones seemed to be rearranging themselves throughout his body, and his mouth, as he screamed, stretched outwards. Teeth—no, fangs—started to form— two on top and two on the bottom.

My body wanted to run, but I couldn't move. I could hear screaming coming from the others in the room, my classmates, but I couldn't turn to look at them.

His clothing ripped away from his body as his muscles grew around his new form, golden fur spilling out of his skin all around his body. His screams turned into a low rumble—a roar—and he stood there on all fours, staring across the mat at me. His human eyes looked foreign in the enormous body of a lion, but human still.

He was massive compared to my small frame. I knew if he got hold of me, I would have no chance of surviving, and still I wasn't afraid. I heard a low, deep rumbling—a growl. I didn't look around to see where it was coming from. I wasn't going to take my eyes off of the lion in front of me. Then I heard it again—felt it coming from within my chest and up my throat. "Grrrrrrrr." The beast I didn't even know I had inside snarled at the lion, who roared back.

I could feel my muscles reacting—stretching—but nothing happened. There was no explosion of fur.

No shifting of bones and muscles. I was just a girl, standing face to face with a beast.

We both knew how the fight would end—how it had to end—and he sprang into the air directly at me. I lifted my stake with both hands and buried it deep into the chest of the lion. He dropped to the floor, and his body slowly transformed back into the human he had been, kneeling on the mat before me. Both he and I were covered in what I could only describe as mucus. It must have been a side effect of the rapid transformation. I made a mental note to ask someone about that later. I was still holding the stake as I fell to my knees before him. "Thank you," he whispered, so softly I wasn't sure if he had actually said it or if I had imagined it. Then he fell back, pulling the stake out of my grip, and he didn't get back up.

The room was silent around me as I stood up. When I looked back my classmates were gone—all except for M, who sat there staring wide-eyed and stunned. They had all fled at some point during the fight. I could only imagine it had been when Micah had transformed into the lion. If I had had the chance, I probably would have fled too. The Council members were still sitting there, silently, watching and waiting to see what I would do next.

"If there is nothing else you need from me, I'd like to take a shower." I didn't wait for them to respond before I left the mat and made my way out the door.

32

I took a long hot shower, and no one bothered me. I don't think anyone knew what to say to me, or maybe they were just afraid. After my shower I grabbed dinner from the dining hall and took it back to my room. I couldn't believe Selection Week was almost over. All I had to do was finished my Mental Health Assessment, another multiple choice test that I found waiting for me when I got back to my room, and then I was done.

Tomorrow morning I, and all of my classmates, would go through the release ceremony. I had seen this ceremony a few times over the years because everyone in the sector is invited, sector residents and selection students of all ages. It's a pretty big deal. The selection committee is there to present each of the students as sector residents and to announce what position each student will be given within the community. The release ceremony is also where we, as newly announced sector residents, announce our chosen names. That was the only part of the ceremony I wasn't looking forward to.

What to expect after that, I had no idea. Selection students and sector residents don't really mingle. We live on different sides of the sector and are pretty much restricted to our quadrants. That is, unless we are assigned a position as a caregiver, an instructor, a counselor, or a position within the clinic. However, I had heard rumors. If what I've heard is true, the newly turned vampires and lycanthropes will be separated, unable to interact until we have gained full control of our powers. For me, that would mean controlling the hungers of a newborn vampire.

We had studied the changes associated with both the vampirism and lycanthropy injections in our anatomy classes. For the first week after the injections are administered, our bodies would begin to adjust to the virus in different ways. For vampires it would mean a significant decrease in resting heart rate, reduced appetite for human food, reduced need for sleep, the physical changes associated with the development of fangs and venom sacs, and, of course, a craving for blood. Human blood is what sustains the vampires, and what I was least looking forward to.

For the lycanthropes the changes would include an increased appetite and the need for more protein, increased need for sleep—especially after physical transformations—and, of course, the muscular and skeletal changes associated with the actual transformations. Although I wasn't looking forward to drinking human blood, I was relieved I wouldn't have to go through the painful physical changes associated with the lycanthropy transformations, especially after what I watched Micah go through as he changed into his lion form. Growing fangs hardly seemed to compare.

Knock-knock-knock

"Hello?" The knocking sounded like it was coming from my door, but the lights in my room had already been turned out. I wasn't expecting any visitors. "Hello?" I asked again as I crossed to the door.

Knock-Knock-Knock

I heard it again, but this time I could tell that it wasn't coming from the door, it was coming from the wall at the foot of my bed. I pressed my ear to the wall and called out, "Who's there?"

"A, is that you?"

"Yes..." I couldn't recognize the muffled voice through the wall. "Who are you?"

"It's Teagan. I needed to talk to you. How are you feeling? Are you OK?"

"I'm fine, or I will be."

"You did well today. You fought well. Micah would have been proud."

"Micah's dead," I snapped. Killing Micah, although for some necessary reason, wasn't something I wanted to do. I hope someday I will understand why—why they made me do it—why he was OK with it.

"He is, you're right, but you're still alive." She was quiet for a few moments, and I pressed my hand to the wall, and she did the same. I could see the faint outline of her hand through the foggy glass. "A, I'm glad you're OK, but you need to be careful. I tried to see you after dinner. I wanted to warn you..." The outline of her hand disappeared and I heard screaming, then she was gone.

Warn me? Warn me about what?

I waited, but she didn't return. "Teagan? Teagan? Warn me about what? What's happening? Are you—?" The door to my room slammed open, crashing back against the wall.

"Go quick, get her now!" It was Britt's voice, but she was clothed from head to toe in some sort of medical uniform.

Two large guards followed her in. "But—she's awake. You said she would be—."

"NOW!"

They lunged. I tried to avoid them, but they were too fast for me and coming from both directions. In that cramped little room, I had nowhere to go. I struggled in their arms as they carried me out the door and down the hall. I would have screamed, but one of the men had his hand over my mouth. I tried to bite down, but it did no good.

"Get her inside and put her on the table across from the boy."

On the table? The boy? I looked around, but they were restricting my movements. *I have to fight back. I have to get away,* I thought.

"Over there. Strap her down," Britt instructed them, and I felt the cold metal table beneath me. "I don't need her struggling while I'm working on her."

"I won't. I—." I tried to tell her that I wouldn't struggle, but she wasn't in the mood to listen.

"Keep her quiet."

Britt was standing at a sink, washing her hands. *Why is she washing her hands, what is she doing?*

"She's secure," one of the guards said, cinching the last strap tightly across my chest.

"Good. Now, we must move quickly so we can get them back to their rooms before any of the instructors take notice that they are missing." She stepped up to the side of the table holding a tray with three syringes, and stroked my hair back off of my face. "This will only hurt…a little…but don't worry, you won't remember a thing."

"Waaaiitt," I mumbled from around the gag in my mouth. I was breathing heavily and trying to calm down my ever-increasing heart rate. "Peeezz."

She looked at me, and slowly began to pull the cloth out of my mouth. "You're not going to scream are you?" I shook my head vigorously and she pulled the gag out the rest of the way. "What?"

"Just, please, tell me what you're doing."

"It doesn't matter."

"It does! It matters to *me*." She started to put the gag back. "Wait, wait. You already said I wouldn't remember. What is the harm in telling me now?" I was hoping she could see the logic. Whatever she was going to do to me she was going to do, I couldn't stop her, but at least I could know what it was. Whether I remembered or not didn't matter in that moment.

"Fine." She looked up at the two guards standing near the door, waiting for her orders. "Give us some privacy." They didn't move. "NOW!" They turned and walked out, shutting the door behind them. "I guess it doesn't matter if you know or not. Earlier today, your blood work came back positive for both vampirism and lycanthropy. This is unheard of, at least in sector C, and as far as we are aware, anywhere. Of course this news has upset the Council. They wish to know how it happened, and if you are in fact capable of both the transformation and the immortality of a vampire as well as the shift from human to animal form of the lycanthrope."

"But, how would you test—?"

"You don't want to know. Besides, after we're done, you won't remember a thing. It's best not to even know."

"Who's the boy?" Anything to stall her.

"What?"

"You said, 'put her on the table across from the boy.' Who? Who is he?" She stepped aside, just enough for me to turn my head to see M lying on another table about four feet away. He was strapped down, but it was unnecessary because he was unconscious. At least I was hoping he was only unconscious. "Is he—?"

"Alive? Yes. I'm not a monster, A53, I'm just a nurse and I'm following orders. It isn't my intention to hurt anyone, but it is important for us to understand what is happening to you, and how this boy—."

"M, his name is M126."

"Yes, right. It is important for us to understand how M126 was able to infect you."

"And you need him for that?"

"I need you both. Now, it is getting late." She slipped the gag back over my mouth. "We should continue."

I didn't struggle, there was no use. I lay there watching M's eyelids flutter about, and knew he was dreaming. I just hoped his dreams were better than mine had been over the last several months. Then, everything went dark.

She was right about one thing, I don't remember what happened next. I remember feeling the pinch as she injected something into the vein on my neck and then—.

33

Knock—Knock—Knock.

I woke up, alone in my room, to the sound of someone knocking on my door. When I stood up I had a terrible headache, a stabbing pain in my neck, and the faint memory of being carried off into the night. "Hello?"

"A53, it's Professor Kade, I'm going to open the door now."

I was still in the clothes I had slept in, and as I reached up I could feel that my hair was in complete disarray. The door opened before I had a chance to fix it.

"I wanted to stop by and apologize for—." He rushed to my side. "What's happened to your neck?"

"My neck? I think I just slept on it wrong. Wait, how did you know it was hurting?"

"You—?" He reached out and touched the side of my neck and a shock went through my body, forcing me to my knees.

"Are you all right?" he asked, but then he grabbed me under my arms, threw me over his shoulder, and started out the door with me. Down the hall he kicked open the door to the clinic. "Nurse Britt. Nurse Britt, come quickly."

"No! Not the clinic," I begged, but he wasn't listening.

"Nurse Britt!" He put me down, and I was able to stand on my own.

She ran around the corner but stopped dead in her tracks when she saw me. "Wh—what, what's happened to her?"

"I'm not sure. I found her like this in her room just now," Professor Kade explained.

'After we're done, you won't remember a thing…you won't remember a thing…you won't remember a thing.'

"I don't understand," Britt said calmly, but I could smell the sweat already forming.

Vampires don't typically sweat—she must be seriously nervous, I thought.

"It looks like an infection. I'll need to—I should draw some blood. We'll need to find out what's causing the infection so that I can treat it. Can you help her to the table, please?"

"No, wait, no!" I pulled out of Professor Kade's grip, and backed up to the door making sure Britt didn't come any closer.

'This will only hurt…a little...' Britt's voice echoed in my mind.

Was I dreaming? Is this a vision? What's happening? Then suddenly I remembered seeing M, strapped to the table in the dark room. I could feel the straps tighten across my chest and legs. It wasn't a dream—it wasn't a vision—it was a memory.

"No, wait, I'm fine." I looked back and forth from Professor Kade to Britt. "I swear, I'm fine." I turned to my left and came face to face with my reflection. The left side of my neck was red and swollen.

"A53, you can't go through the release ceremony looking like—."

"I know." I stopped him because it didn't matter what he was about to say. He was right, and I wasn't fine. I knew it and so did Britt. It also didn't matter that she was the one who had done this to me, since she was probably the only one who could fix it. "Professor Kade, would you mind giving me some privacy with Nurse Britt?" The only way I was going to find out what had happened to M was to deal with her one on one. "I'm sure she needs to examine me, and it would be easier—."

"Of course." He moved to open the door. "Take your time. When you're done you can get cleaned up and showered. Breakfast will be waiting in your room. Everyone is going to be meeting for the ceremony at a quarter after eleven. Someone will come get you shortly before then."

"Professor Kade," I stopped him before he could leave.

"Yes?"

"You came to my room this morning. Was there something you needed?"

"Oh, that. Well, considering the circumstances, I think it can wait." He turned and left, leaving me in Britt's hands in the small exam room.

I turned to Britt who was standing quietly on the other side of the room. "What did you do?"

"Nothing, what do you me—?"

"Don't play games with me. I know you had them drag me out of my room last night. I know you tied me up and played pincushion on my neck. I even remember why. What I don't know is what was in those needles, or why my throat now feels like it's on fire and my neck looks like—like I've contracted some rare plague. So, I'll ask you again, what did you do?"

"The burning in your throat is normal. It's hunger. I can get you some blo—."

"I don't want blood. I want answers!"

"I know, it's just that—. You weren't supposed to—."

"Remember. Yeah, I know, but here we are. Come to think of it, you know what else I remember—I remember M126 strapped to the table across from me. What did you do to him? Where is he? Is he OK?"

"I—."

"I want to see him. NOW!"

She quickly crossed the room and picked up a phone.

"Don't try anything funny. You've seen me on the fighting mat—you can't take me down all by yourself," I warned her before she dialed.

"Hello, yes, this is Nurse Britt in the clinic. Can you please send M126 to my office? No, everything is fine. Yes. Thank you." She hung up and smiled. "See, everything is fine."

"Right. I think I'll decide for myself thank you."

"Would you like me to—?" She reached out to touch my neck, but I moved away.

"To what?"

"Just to look at your neck. I believe you had a reaction to—to the—."

"To the what? What did you drug me with? What was in those needles?" She didn't answer. "Would you rather I call Professor Kade back in here and tell him what happened last night?"

"No. No, I'll—I'll explain." She gathered some gauze and a jar of what looked like clear jelly. She held up the jar. "It's just an ointment, an antibiotic, to help the infection. Typically, I would let you heal it on your own. Vampires aren't usually affected by infections. However, there are a few that lycanthropes can contract." She cleaned my neck, and every touch burned. "The first injection was a tranquilizer. It wasn't strong, but it was enough to make you sleep." She began applying the ointment to my neck and it was cold.

"I saw three needles. What was in the other two?" I asked, as she rubbed on the cool ointment.

"One was M126's blood. I needed to know how it would affect you, in a higher concentration—if it would increase your tendencies toward lycanthropy or if the vampire virus would fight it off." She walked away, grabbing something out of the cooler across the room. She held it out to me. "Here, drink this. I believe you're just having an allergic reaction to the tranquilizer. Drinking fresh blood will help flush out your system, and speed your healing process."

I took it, not because she told me to, but because I knew I needed it. "And the last one?"

"The Council, based on your performance—and your reaction to M126's blood—."

"What?"

"The Council has selected you. You have been chosen—."

I was on the verge of throwing something. If she didn't just spit it out soon, I just might throw her across the room. "Oh my stars, chosen for what? What was in the other needle? What did you inject me with?"

"The blood of a werelion."

"A werelion? Who—whose blood was it?"

"Counselor Teagan's."

"Counselor Teagan, but—." Then it hit me. I remembered her whispering to me through the wall, trying to warn me. "What did you do to her?

"Nothing!" she snapped. "She is fine. I told you last night, it isn't my intention to hurt anyone. I'm only—."

"Following orders, right. I remember." I headed to the door with every intention of leaving, but just as I reached for the handle it turned and in walked M. "Oh my stars, M, you're all right!" I grabbed him, wrapping my arms around his neck, and held on tight. "I was so worried. I was so scared. I thought—I didn't know what to—."

He quickly pulled away, looking from me to Nurse Britt. I could tell he had no idea what I was rambling about. "Um, A, is everything OK?" He looked up, turning to Britt, not waiting for me to answer. "I was told you needed to see me."

"Right, yes. I just needed to get one last blood sample before you're cleared for release."

"Oh, OK, yeah sure." He jumped up on the table and started rolling up his sleeve.

Does he really not remember? How can he not remember? "M, are you OK?"

He laughed. "I think I'm the one who should be asking you that. What was all that? And, what's going on with your neck?"

"It was…" Britt was staring me down, "…nothing. Sorry, just excited about the release ceremony I guess."

"And your neck?"

"Um, yeah this is nothing. Just a minor infection. Right Nurse Britt?" I smiled at her and she just smiled back.

"That's right. Just a minor infection." Britt finished taking M's blood and I walked him to the door.

"You know, I'm excited too, but—." He nodded his head toward Britt and I knew what he was thinking, *no PDA in front of the sector residents,* and he was right. Hell, we could have gotten kicked out of the sector for our behavior over the last few weeks. The last thing we needed was to be so open in public right before the release ceremony. It was already nine-thirty. In less than two hours things would be different for us—at least I hoped they would.

Still not thinking clearly, or cautiously, I asked. "Save me a seat at the ceremony, OK?"

"I would—you know I would—but they're not going to let us sit together. They can't." He reminded me once again of the ridiculous wall the Council builds between the vampires and the lycanthropes. I'll never understand why it has to be that way.

"Right, yeah. I almost forgot." He grabbed my shoulder, and squeezed a silent goodbye before nodding and heading back down the hall to his room.

Then again, if Britt is right, I'm half lycanthrope. Why can't I sit wherever I want?

"Why did you need M's blood?" I asked, as soon as I turned back to Britt.

"What do you mean?"

"Last night, why did he have to be here? You keep a sample of all of our blood on hand in the clinic, don't you?"

"Yes, but—."

"Then, why did he have to be here? Unless…" *They wouldn't, would they?* "Unless it wasn't just me you've decided to test on."

"I don't know what you—."

"Did you inject M with my blood too?" She didn't answer. "Did you inject M with my blood?"

"I—." Droplets of sweat were forming around her hairline. "I was only—."

"Don't tell me you were only following orders. Does he know?"

"No, and you mustn't say anything."

"He has a right to know. You can't make me keep that from him. I won't."

"Please, you have to give me time. I've only just gotten more blood to test. We don't even know if he's been infected."

"Fine, but you find out and do it quickly. If he's infected you better tell him before the release ceremony, or I will."

"I will. I promise." Her hands were shaking as she took the vial of blood to a small machine on the desk along the wall. "It will take about thirty minutes to run the test."

"I'll wait." I jumped up on the table and held out my arm, palm up. "Go on, take more blood, I know you want to."

"But—."

"I already know my blood test is positive for the vampire virus and the lycanthropy virus. M infected me with wolf. You've infected me with lion. So, figure out what I am because as much as the Council *wants* to know, I think *I* have a right to know."

34

It was exactly eleven thirty when the Selection Board walked into the hall, led by none other than sector leader Remy himself. “Good morning students,” he announced, as he walked in. “I am honored to be here with you all today and to be the first to welcome you to Sector C, not as selection students but as sector residents.”

We were all gathered together, standing around, not really knowing what to expect or what we were supposed to do.

“The release ceremony is a sacred tradition, one we have followed since the very beginning of the selection program. You have all seen the ceremony, but today you participate. Today you are the focus. You are the honored guests. Once you step on the stage, once you have been assigned your position within our society, once you have selected your name, you become the person you will forever be.” I swear he was looking right at me. “Make wise choices, and know that your Council stands behind you. We are here to guide you as you take this next step.” Then he turned away, adding, “All of you.”

Everyone started clapping, but I couldn’t. I couldn’t move. *What had he meant? Was he talking to me? Was it a warning?*

At twelve o'clock they lined us up, youngest to oldest. I could tell that H107 was nervous to be in the front of the line, but he stood tall and put on a brave face. I was all the way at the back, as the first born. Being the first born of a selection class is said to be an honor, a privilege, but I'm not sure what it ever really got me.

We filed out the main doors of the Selection Hall and down the steps. A large stage had been erected in the yard just outside, and rows and rows of chairs had already been filled by sector residents and up-and-coming selection students. They guided us into the first two rows, and everyone cheered for us. The Council and selection committee sat together on the stage, and Remy stood at the podium, ready to address the waiting crowd.

It's funny, in that moment I wasn't thinking about the ceremony or the crowd or even what would happen next. In that moment, I was thinking, *Wow, if ever there was a time to cross the wall either into or out of the sector, this is it.* With so many of the sector residents in attendance, there wouldn't be anyone to catch a castaway trying to get in, or a sector resident trying to get out. Then again, I didn't see too many guards standing around—maybe they aren't invited to the ceremony.

"Good afternoon," Remy said in greeting, and the crowd started cheering again. "Welcome to the selection ceremony for our newest sector residents. I am so excited to be able to personally introduce them and to be here as they receive their rightful place among our family."

Family? I had never heard anyone refer to the sector as a family. Community, sure, but family seemed too familiar a word for a sector that, although they pretend to be united, is in reality very much divided.

"C66H107" Remy called out, and H stood up, walked to the side of the stage and up the steps. "H107, the youngest of the selection class, joined his fellow selection students late in life. He showed great promise both physically and mentally, and the Council made the decision to advance him."

Students from the selection class just behind ours started to cheer. "WooHoo, go H!" "We're so proud of you!" and other cheers could be heard from his younger friends.

Remy held up his hands, and the crowd went silent. "It is my great honor to welcome you, as a lycanthrope, a werelion, and a sector resident, here today." They shook hands, and Counselor Teagan stood up and stepped forward.

"You have been selected," Remy said, "as selection counselor in training."

"What?"

"You are a bright young man." Teagan said standing between Remy and H. "You are strong in mind and body, and you have a heart that knows pain and challenge. The Council feels, and I agree, that you will make a wonderful counselor and guide for the up and coming selection students."

"I—I don't know what to say. Thank you." H didn't smile, but anyone could see that he was pleased.

Teagan smiled, big enough for the both of them. "You will start your training, as my apprentice. Eventually you will take on a class of your own."

"Thank you, so much," he said before Teagan returned to her seat. As I watched H, his chin just a little higher than usual, he nodded at me and whispered, "Thank you." I just smiled back. It was his accomplishment, not mine. I just helped give him a little push.

"There is only one thing remaining," Remy announced. "Have you chosen your name?"

"I have, sir." Remy handed him the microphone and he accepted it with shaking hands. "Hudson. My name is Hudson." The crowd cheered, and called out his name: *Hudson. Hudson. Hudson.* It didn't matter that he was a lycanthrope—everyone was excited. Hudson crossed the stage, walked down the steps, and found his way back to his seat. He seemed to be standing a little taller, more confidently, or maybe it was just the relief of finally being done.

The ceremony seemed to last forever, as each student took their turn on stage to be welcomed, given their positions, and to announce their name.

C65W351 was next to step onto the stage. Remy announced W as a vampire, and the vampires in the crowd cheered. Then he was given his position, service worker, and the crowd went silent. He hadn't scored well, and service worker was the least desired position, aside from donor or breeder. W, the coaster. I looked around at T, but she seemed unconcerned. When he announced his name, Wyatt, it almost didn't matter, but I still cheered.

"C65U277." Remy called, and U stood tall as she crossed the stage. "U277, has chosen vampirism." Again the vampires cheered. "She has performed wonderfully this past week and has been selected to work as a caregiver in our birthing center." I could see U's face light up when he said caregiver. Working with the younger students had always been something she enjoyed. Caregiver was an honor. It was one of the advanced education positions, and she would not only be assigned as a caregiver, but she would assist in births as well as learn basic pediatric medical procedures.

"You will study under Councilman Iris, but will be assigned a mentor within the vampire community."

"Yes sir," she nodded.

"Have you chosen your name?"

U smiled again, turned to the crowd and announced, "My name is Uma." Everyone clapped.

"Welcome, Uma."

No one was surprised when C65T240 was introduced as a vampire and given a position working with the events and recreations committee. She had always been the "it girl" and she loved being the center of attention and telling everyone else what to do. As a sector events coordinator she knew her work load would be minimal and keep her in the social spotlight. She happily announced her name, Tamsin, and took her seat to watch the rest of us.

R201 and Q190 were the next two students to be announced. They were both introduced as lycanthropes, and the lycanthropes side of the crowd cheered. It wasn't surprising that they were both assigned to security positions. They were two of the strongest students, and they were also the only two werebears in the selection class. Riker and Quinn were the names they chose and, somehow, the names seemed fitting.

I don't think I was the only one on the edge of my seat when Remy called O154 to the stage. "C65O154." All of us had noticed that she hadn't participated in the Selection Week fights, and she was the only one who didn't seem changed by an injection. "There is always one student who stands out among the rest. One student who possesses an unwavering humanity that can't be denied. This year, that student was O154." The crowd didn't cheer—they didn't even breathe. We all knew what he was telling us, even if she didn't. "Have you picked a name, child?"

O looked as scared and confused as I had ever seen her. "I—I have. Opal, sir."

"Then Opal it is. As beautiful as the stone itself." Then he turned to the crowd. "I would like you to welcome Opal, sector resident and the newest Sector C breeder." The crowd was as silent as the night as Opal looked blankly at the crowd—at the sea of faces.

"But I—."

Remy started to clap, forcing the rest of us to clap with him. Opal just stood there, frozen in time, as reality sank in. Silent tears started to escape her eyes, and Counselor Teagan stepped up from behind her, to help her off the stage and back to her seat.

A feeling of uneasiness began to grow within the crowd on both sides as the ceremony moved on.

"C65N152." Remy called out.

N had always been close with Opal, and his shock and disappointment at her placement was written all over his face as he stepped on stage. "As a selection student, N152 proved himself loyal to his classmates and his Council. In many ways."

As a spy! A traitor, I thought, watching the erect blonde figure stride confidently toward the stage.

"His testing began well before Selection Week even started."

Of course it had. He was the Council's little pawn, spying on me and gathering evidence against M and me.

"N152 will join the many werefoxes of our community. His cunning skills have proven him worthy of a position within the internal security division. He will be working under Councilman Serenity, on the lycanthrope security team."

Of course he will. It was so fitting. Mr. Serious. He raised a hand to straighten the already-perfect short blonde hair.

Cheers came from the lycanthrope side of the crowd, and I watched as Councilman Serenity's lips curled up into a wicked grin. "Have you chosen your name?" Remy asked.

N nodded and took the microphone. "I wish to be called Nash."

"Then Nash you will be called." Remy motioned him off the stage and back to his seat.

M was next. I think I stopped breathing as I watched him step on stage. I already knew he was a lycanthrope—a wolf to be exact. I already knew he was near the top of his class, and therefore he should be placed in one of the better positions. What I didn't know, and what came as a surprise, was what position they would give him. "...Council Liaison. You will work directly with the Lycanthrope members of the Council as a liaison and councilman in training." M seemed surprised too. We had both known we might be not only punished, but banned from the sector, for our previous actions. So, for him to be placed in a position of such honor could only mean one of two things. They either were so impressed with him that they were willing to overlook his errors, or they wanted to keep him close—to watch him. I was betting on the latter.

"Have you chosen your name?"

"I have." He looked at me, our eyes met, and I finally was able to breathe again. "My name—is Merick." He smiled, *oh that smile*, and then, head high and shoulders straight he returned to his seat.

J102 had always been *one of the boys*. She was the daredevil of the class, always willing to try anything at least once. She was good on the fighting mat, mainly because she never gave up. She didn't care about looks, even though she was beautiful with her long dark brown hair and her chocolate brown eyes, but she didn't care about cuts and bruises. Her main focus over the years had been on physical, rather than mental, strength. So, when it was announced that she would be joining the weretigers of Sector C and that she was assigned as one of the first females on the external security team none of us, her selection classmates, were surprised. Of course, others throughout the sector seemed shocked and even appalled that such a "girly girl" had received such an assignment, but we, her classmates, understood completely.

"Jade," she loudly announced. "You can call me Jade." Everyone cheered, and I saw F97's face light up as he watched her standing so proudly on stage. They had something, or they would—I could see it as clearly as I could my own feelings for M—for Merick. I wondered why I hadn't seen it before.

"C65F97." Remy announced. "C65F97," he announced again.

Now it was F's turn, but he was still mesmerized by Jade's jaunty quickstep back toward her seat. E82 elbowed him, whispering, "F, that's you!"

"Oh, yeah, right." F jumped up, tearing his gaze away from Jade. "Yes sir, sorry sir," he said, as he hurried up to the stage.

"C65F97, a lycanthrope—a weretiger—is strong and focused on the fighting mat. He will make a good leader, if we can get him to focus outside of the mat." The audience laughed.

"I'm sorry sir."

"No apologies necessary. You have been selected to join the builders of our community. They not only build and restore our community when necessary, they also do work outside of the sector, working to salvage whatever possible from the wastelands."

"The Builders? But you just said I'm a good fighter. Why am I not being assigned to—?"

"Are you questioning the decision of the Council?"

"No sir, I just thought—. I was hoping to be—." He looked over at Jade who was staring back in disbelief.

"He was hoping to be security," D77, ever the jokester, yelled out. "I always knew he didn't have what it takes," he laughed.

"Shut up *Pretty Boy*," F yelled from the stage.

"Make me!" D said standing up, preparing to fight.

"This is not the time, or the place," Remy announced. "Take your seat." D77 did as he was told, but the smile never left his face.

"He's right," F said, turning to Remy. "I had hoped to be a member of the external security team sir, but I understand that you have your reasons." He looked down, defeated. His hopes had been crushed.

"Do not be discouraged. You have yet to understand the importance of your new role, but you will."

"Yes sir."

"Have you chosen your name?" Remy asked.

"Forrest sir, although I'm not so sure it's fitting now."

"Forrest, to symbolize growth and progress. Yes, I believe it is quite fitting. Forrest it is! Everyone, I would like you to meet, Forrest!" The crowd cheered but it didn't seem to affect Forrest. He didn't look up again as he went back to his seat.

As everyone suspected, E82, the smartest student in our selection class, was assigned to the position of Archivist. It was an advanced education position. Not only would he be working as the apprentice to the current archives keeper, he would assist the professors in educating up and coming selection students in the histories. He was ecstatic, and it was written all over his face. He chose Earnest as his name, which seemed to fit since he always had been the most sincere and honest of all of us.

Next up was D77, and as he headed for the stage Forrest tripped him, sending him face first to the ground. Gasps of shock filled the crowd, but D quickly got up, yanked Forrest out of his seat, and threw him to the ground. “Watch yourself,” he warned, then he turned and climbed the steps to the center of the stage. The two of them just couldn’t seem to avoid any opportunity for ‘in-your-face’ confrontations.

“C65D77,” Remy began, “you are a strong vampire and will be an asset to our community. However, you often allow your emotions to lead you when you should be listening to your mind. It will do you well to join the sector builders.”

“The builders? With F—with Forrest?” The crowd went silent, and D and Forrest exchanged looks of hate—disgust.

“What name have you selected?” D didn’t answer. “What name have you selected?” Remy asked again, demanding D’s attention.

“Darius sir.”

“A strong name, it will suit you well.”

“Thank you sir.” Darius crossed the stage and took his seat--speechless, for once in his life.

I had high hopes for C, mainly because she was my best friend, but deep down I knew she had never really applied herself. I was hoping our instructors had seen her potential and that she had given her all during her Selection Week exams. So when Remy called her to the stage and announced that, like Wyatt, she would be joining the ranks of service worker I was disappointed but not entirely surprised. I don’t even think she was all that surprised.

“Have you selected your name?” Remy asked.

“Ciara, sir.” She said it with a smile, but not the vibrant, excited, ready-to-play smile I was so used to seeing. No, she seemed older somehow, more reserved, maybe even a little defeated.

I knew that Councilman Remy would be calling my name next and suddenly I felt nervous—almost sick to my stomach.

"We have only one student remaining, but I want to take a minute to reflect on those sector students we have just met—to congratulate all of the new sector residents."

What is he doing? Why isn't he calling my name? I looked around at my classmates. Merick looked just as confused as I felt, and even Ciara, although still thinking about her own placement, looked up at me with worry in her eyes.

"Our sector is stronger now, because of our new members. We grow stronger every year as new blood—young blood—enters our community. I extend a warm welcome to each and every one of you, as you are now full sector residents, with all the privileges and responsibilities that come with that honor. Take your jobs seriously and learn from your mentors, because one day you will be the leaders we look to."

Nurse Britt quietly stepped on stage, passing an envelope to Teagan. Then the note was passed, one by one, down the line through the selection committee and up to Remy who quietly stood at the podium waiting. He opened the envelope as the audience stared in silence and I—. Well, I waited too. I wasn't thinking, I wasn't moving, and I wasn't even breathing.

"C65A53, please come to the stage."

That's me, oh my stars, that's me. Please come to the stage? Right, go to the stage. I tried, I really did, but I couldn't move. My heart pounded in my chest and every ounce of my being wanted to get up and run away from the stage—away from the crowd—just away. I just knew this was the moment I had been dreading—this was the moment the Council had chosen to announce my punishment.

"C65A53," he called again. This time I was able to stand. I took a deep breath then walked slowly toward the steps. I took the first step up, focusing on not falling, and then continued up and across the stage. My hands were shaking as I stood there in front of not only my class but the majority of the Sector C population—those who had chosen to attend the ceremony anyway.

He didn't speak to me; he didn't even look at me. Instead, he turned to the audience and began. "As the first born among her class, A53 has proven herself a leader. She excels both mentally and physically far beyond what we could ever have imagined. With her run time of thirty-nine minutes and seven seconds she nearly beat the record, missing only by seven seconds." I glanced back at Councilman Ash, who was grinning—happy that he could still claim the record. "During Selection Week she ranked at the top of the charts on the fighting mat. As the first selection student ever to battle a castaway…" He paused as the crowd gasped with shock. "…she displayed complete control and confidence. Her exam scores prove her to be worthy of any position available throughout the sector." The crowd cheered, and I was finally able to breath. Maybe I wasn't going to be punished after all.

35

Then it happened. Remy held up the envelope, for everyone to see. "But this—this is something I cannot explain. This is something that causes me pause." He slowly pulled out the single sheet of paper and everyone seemed to be holding their breath, myself included. Then, he began to read.

Medical Report and Lab Test Results
~ C65A53 ~

Day 2 (Evening) – The patient was injected with the vampire virus.

(The vampires in the crowd cheered, but it didn't last long. Remy quickly silenced them as he continued to read.)

Day 3 (Morning) – Blood work shows the vampire virus is active. The patient displays early signs of bloodlust, significantly reduced heart rate, as well as increased speed and awareness.

Day 3 (Evening) – The patient was exposed to the lycanthropy virus (wolf), but there are no signs of current side effects. It seems the active vampire virus is fighting off the new infection.

Day 4 (Morning) – Blood work shows signs of both the active vampire virus as well as an active lycanthropy virus. The patient demonstrates increased healing speed, beyond what is normal for a vampire. It is my opinion that this is a side effect of the lycanthropy virus.

Day 4 (Evening) – We have injected the patent with more of the lycanthrope (wolf) blood to see if the vampire virus will fight off the infection, or if the patient is capable of sustaining both. We have also injected the patient with an active werelion virus. We will assess the effects in the morning.

(I had known all of this already, but hearing the crowd's mumbles of disbelief and shock made it seem even more real.)

Day 5 – Patient is carrying active viruses for vampirism, werewolf, and werelion. She poses a danger to all sector residents and it is recommended that she be banished from the sector.

The crowd was silent. Their whispers had stopped and all eyes were on me. Remy was silent. The Council was silent. It felt like the world had gone still, that I was moving in slow motion. I turned back and saw Teagan, wide-eyed and open mouthed. She whispered, "I'm so sorry," but I couldn't hear her.

Then I turned back to my classmates, my friends, and everyone was just staring at me. Merick was the only one who didn't look scared. *Why? Why isn't he scared? What did I do to deserve this?*

"I—." I turned to Remy and started to explain myself, but there were just no words. How was I supposed to explain what had happened, what I was, when I myself had no clue.

"The Council…" He stopped me. "…Takes this very seriously, as should all of you."

Murmurs began to fill the crowd. “What is she?” “Banish her!” “How is it even possible?” “This can’t be happening.”

I could feel their stares, their disgust, and their judgment as if it were a weight upon my shoulders. I was different, and because of it, I knew that, given the chance, they would all gladly throw me out into the wastelands and forget all about me.

“Stop!” I shouted. “I have done nothing to you. You all look at me like I’m a beast, a monster. But, what am I that you are not?” I snatched the slip of paper out of Councilman Remy’s hand and held it up. “I’m a vampire! Not by choice but because someone…” I looked back at Councilman Blake. “…someone decided that should be my fate.” Then I turned back to the crowd. “I am a wolf, not by choice but by circumstance.” I smiled at Merick. I knew it wasn’t his fault and I wanted him to know I wasn’t upset or angry with him. “I am a lion, not by choice, but because the Council decided to use me as their experiment--and not only me, I might add. If you think I was the only one, or even the first then you are naive.” I dropped the paper. “I haven’t even shifted. You’re all scared, and I get that, I’m scared too, but we don’t even know if the wolf or the lion inside of me will ever be more than just a feeling—an instinct.” I scanned the crowd, and no one was moving. No one was talking. “Who among you can say they are not vampire or lycanthrope? Who among you can say they are not beast?” I stepped forward to the edge of the stage. “Let any one of you who can say you are without beast within you be the first to throw a stone and cast me out.”

No one moved. No one spoke.

Councilman Remy bent down and picked up the paper, the medical report that would determine my fate, and did something I never would have expected—he ripped it in half. "The Council, although concerned, has chosen to disregard the advice from our medical personnel. We will allow A53 to remain here in Sector C." Gasps of shock and mumbles of disapproval filled the air, but it didn't stop him. "A53 has proven her worth, and until she proves otherwise she will be given the same opportunities as all sector residents. She has been assigned to work with the Council, as Council liaison and councilman in training, for the Vampire Council members." He turned to me and I think I was still in shock. In my role I would be working closely with Merick, and I didn't know what to say. "Have you selected your name?"

"I—." *Oh crap!* "Zelina, sir." *Oh crap!* It had come out before I could stop myself.

"Did she say *Zelina*?" I heard someone yell from the audience.

Remy just stared down at me. I could see his throat move up and down as he swallowed back his reaction. He clenched his teeth, closed his eyes, and took a deep breath before turning back to the audience. "Let us all welcome—Zelina—to our community. As the first vampire-lycanthrope I am sure she will have much to teach us in the months and years to come." He stepped back and walked off the stage without another word. I stood there, with everyone watching me, for what felt like forever until, slowly, people began to leave.

When the last of the crowd had left, only Merick and I remained. I sat down where I was, in the center of the stage, and he came to sit beside me. "You never do anything small do you?" he asked with a smile.

Oh that smile.

"Go big or go home, that's what I always say."

36

It had been a week since our release ceremony. We had all been assigned new living quarters, each of us placed with a mentor or guide who would help us through our transition. At such point that they felt we were ready; we would each be moved into our own private living space, among the other sector residents.

I hadn't seen my friends all week. In fact, I hadn't seen the outside of Britt's apartment all week. Which also meant I had also gone a full week without talking to Merick, but he was never far from my thoughts. I had tried a couple of times to reach him, through my visions, but it didn't work. I wasn't sure if it was just the physical distance between us or if there was another reason. I chose to believe it was just the distance.

My new life—my new job—would start in the morning. Against Britt's persistent claims that I wasn't ready to start working, the Council decided to let me try. I had been told to report to the Council offices to meet with Remy himself first thing in the morning. Although I didn't want Britt to be right, I really wasn't sure how I was supposed to focus at work, when all I could think about was eating—feeding.

I was living with Nurse Britt, because she had been assigned as my mentor. I'm not sure if it was to punish me or her, or just another way for Councilman Blake to keep an eye on me. To say it was an uncomfortable living arrangement would have been putting it mildly. I didn't trust her, she wouldn't let me out of the apartment, and she was constantly forcing bottled blood on me. It tasted stale, but she assured me it was just like the real thing. I had a feeling she was lying.

"You need to drink it."

"Seriously, I can't drink another bottle of that stuff. When are you going to let me feed, the way you do, the way all the vampires in Sector C feed?" I asked. I was starting to become impatient.

"Sector C vampires do drink bottled blood."

"Yes, but not as their only source of nutrition."

"You really want to feed? You think you're ready to join the others in the dining hall?"

"I don't know if I'm ready or not, but unless you let me try, I'll never know, will I?" Looking back, I think that might have been the worst thing I could have said—because I wasn't anywhere near prepared for what came next.

Britt got permission from the Council to let me join her for dinner. We paused just inside the door to the dining hall and a sweet honey scent I had never noticed before smacked me in the face. "What is that… smell?" I looked around, but I didn't see anyone eating anything sweet that could have matched the smell. "It's so—." I started walking toward one of the tables, but Britt quickly grabbed my arm.

"You don't need to go over there, not just yet."

"But, I just want—."

"Yeah, I know what you want. I just don't think *you* do." I guess she could see my confusion because even though I don't think she wanted to, she explained. "That smell—almost too sweet, right?"

"No, not too sweet at all. It smells perfect, delicious, like—."

"Yeah, that's your friends you're smelling. So, unless you want them for dinner, I suggest we go upstairs."

"My—?"

"Lycanthropes—they smell sweet to us. You'll get used to it as you get older, but yeah, it can be hard at first."

"Oh, I—." I looked around the room. *Had I really just been tempted to eat the people around me? Crap!*

I saw a few of my classmates eating in the dining hall. Riker and Quinn were sitting with a few of the other sector security guards. *That's odd,* I thought to myself, *I wonder if they've already started training.*

Forrest and Jade were sitting together at a table in the far corner, whispering and laughing. I couldn't help smiling. I guess he had gotten over his disappointment at being assigned to the sector's building committee.

Even N—Nash—was there. He was eating at one of the side tables, alone, and he didn't look happy. Part of me felt bad for him—knowing that he was struggling to deal with Opal's fate—but then I remembered he had been the Council's little pawn. How bad could I really feel for him? Now, with him working on the internal security team, who knows if he wasn't being paid to watch me right now? At least I could take comfort in the fact that, as a lycanthrope, he wasn't allowed upstairs in the vampire dining room.

I followed Britt up the long staircase to the upper level of the dining hall. I had heard stories about what happens up there, but as a sector student you never really know what to believe. The walls were black, and there were red curtains hanging all around the room. There were tables along the walls, sectioned off with curtains for private dining. There were also large banquet tables in the center of the room, for group dining.

When we walked in, there was already a group of about ten people, gathered around one of the center tables. Lying on top of the table was a donor. She looked older than most of the people in Sector C, which meant that she was probably in her forties or fifties. Most donors don't live that long. Most donors are either turned, or killed, by the time they reach their late thirties. She had long red hair and stunning blue eyes that seemed to stare right through me as I passed by.

I wonder what's so special about her, I thought. There had to be a reason they had kept her around for so long.

She wasn't struggling or trying to get away. In fact, she almost seemed peaceful on the table. I can't say I knew her—I'm sure I had never met her—but something about her seemed so familiar. I couldn't tell who was around her, because all of them had their heads down, quietly feeding from her neck, arms, and legs. Then I she looked right at me, and I 'heard' the thought. *"Don't give up. You have to keep fighting. I won't give up on you."*

"What?" I moved toward her but Britt grabbed my arm.

"Would you like to join them?" Britt asked.

When I looked back the woman was just staring up at the ceiling, as if lost in a fog, and I replied, "No."

"A private table it is then." She led me past a number of curtained-off tables, and through the slits between the curtains I saw vampires—feeding. We finally sat down at a table at the far end of the room—and waited.

"Where are all the others?" I asked.

"The others?"

"Yes. My classmates. I mean, some of the Lycanthropes were downstairs in the main dining hall. What about Ciara, Darius, Earnest? Why aren't they up here?"

"They're not ready," she smirked. "But you are, right?"

"I—."

"Lycanthropes join the sector community right after Selection Week is concluded. They even start their jobs. Their lives change very little, until the first full moon cycle. Vampires are different. It often takes weeks, sometime months, for a vampire to be ready to begin working and join society."

"Weeks? Months? But—." I looked around and suddenly I realized that maybe Britt had been right. Maybe I wasn't ready.

It didn't take long for our *donor* to join us at the table. "Shall I lie down, or would you like me to sit between you?"

Britt turned to me and stared. "It's up to you."

"I—." *Lie down or sit between us?* "I guess, just sit between us," I answered.

He nodded, closed the curtain around our table, and slid into the booth between us. I half expected him to undress, but was thankful when he didn't. He just rolled up his sleeves and extended an arm to each of us. I took his arm, trying not to look too obvious, but to be honest, I had no idea what I was supposed to do next.

When I first started feeding on bottled blood it was just like drinking had always been. Over the past few days, my fangs had begun to emerge whenever I drank. The process is actually quite painful—I wasn't expecting that. But, the problem I was facing, sitting there in the booth, was that I didn't know how to make my fangs come down without first tasting the blood. "Um—."

"Is this your first time?" he asked. I just nodded and looked away. "Don't be embarrassed. Everyone has to do it for the first time once." He smiled, and it was a good smile—not as nice as Merick's, but still pleasant. "I'm impressed."

"Why?" I asked.

"You're the first selection student of your class, to come in and feed."

Maybe I'm not ready. Maybe I'm not ready. Maybe I'm not ready.

"Usually it's weeks, even months, before we see any of the new sector residents. I'm honored I could be here, for your first time."

Weeks. Months. Maybe I'm not ready. I'm not ready. I wanted to get up and leave, but I couldn't.

I glanced over at Britt and she was watching me cautiously.

I didn't know what to say, and was happy when Britt interrupted so I didn't have to. "Yes, it's such an honor. Now, can we get on with it?"

"I'm sorry," he said, as he lifted his other hand to show me what looked like a metal fingernail on his index finger. Then, he quickly slashed across his wrist and blood started to drip from the cut. "That should help."

Britt was smirking at me, and then she smiled a big smile, showing fang just before grabbing his wrist and biting down. I followed suit, and as soon as the blood touched my tongue my own fangs emerged. "Pretty soon, just the thought of blood will cause your fangs to extend," he said as I drank.

"Zelina, stop! Stop!" The next thing I knew Britt was yanking on my arm, pulling me off of him—the nameless donor. Without even knowing it, I had forced him to the floor and had proceeded to drain him. "You have to stop!"

When I finally took a breath he wasn't moving. "Oh my stars." I jumped up and backed away. The smell of blood was all around me and my throat was burning.

"He's alive." Britt said, crouching down with her ear pressed to his chest. "It's faint, but I can still hear his heartbeat."

"What have I done?"

"Still think you're ready to feed with the rest of us?"

37

Beep...Beep...Beep...Beep

"Turn that alarm off, please!" Britt yelled from the other room.

"Sorry." I rolled over in bed—five o'clock. I had gotten lazy over the last week. I had set an alarm, on my tablet, knowing that if I didn't I wasn't going to wake up on time. Usually I just wake up, instinctively, but not being allowed out of the apartment for over a week, there wasn't much I could do but sleep in and relax. Unfortunately, that also meant there wasn't much I could do in terms of training. That was all going to change today. Today, my new job was starting and with it my new life. I had promised myself I would get out of bed and go run the course before I had to head to work for the first time ever. I was practically bubbling with excitement.

It still felt weird wearing all black instead of grey, but I liked it. My pale skin seemed even more porcelain against the sharp contrast of the black. My hazel eyes seem to somehow darken to a chocolate brown, the pupils and the irises seeming to almost blend together. It was eerie, but also somehow fitting, for a vampire anyway.

I pulled my hair up into a ponytail before heading out the door. *Hmmm, maybe I need to start styling it more, now that I'm no longer just a student.* It was just a passing thought.

"Grab a bottle before you go," Britt called from her bedroom.

I grabbed a sports bottle filled with blood out of the refrigerator and left. As I jogged down the road I took a sip, and it just confirmed what I had already known—bottled blood is nowhere near as good as when it comes directly from the source. However, after last night, I was going to stay away from the dining hall for a while. So, bottled blood would have to do. Britt had made me promise to carry a bottle with me, from now on, any time I left the apartment. I felt like a child with a sippy-cup, but I guess it was better than attacking and draining an unsuspecting sector resident just because they smelled good.

I wasn't living as close to the course as I had been—it was about a half-mile jog—but the trip was a good warm-up. As soon as I crossed the tree line at the start of the course I smelled it—honey mixed with the fresh clean scent of soap. "Merick? M?" I looked around, but I didn't see anyone. "Is that you?" Still no answer.

I continued down the path and the smell got stronger. Stopping by a large oak tree I closed my eyes, and focused. I focused on that sweet smell, his beautiful smile, and those strong hands of his. Suddenly, in my mind, I was leaping, jumping up and pulling myself onto the 10-foot warp wall.

"What the—?" I could hear his voice in my head and I couldn't help but laugh. "A?"

"Stay there." I took off running. When I made it to the warp wall Merick was sitting at the top, just relaxing—waiting.

He laughed when he saw me coming and I stumbled on a rock. I never stumble, especially when I'm on the course. I may not know how to dance, but I'm pretty athletic. "I still don't understand how you do that," Merick smiled.

"I don't know, I just—." I stopped talking, I stopped moving. I just stopped.

"...that's your friends you're smelling. So, unless you want them for dinner, I suggest we go..." Britt's warning from last night played through my mind and I quickly took a long drink from my bottle.

"A, what's wrong?"

I heard Merick jump down from the wall and I quickly backed away from him. "No, wait. You can't—."

"A, what is it?"

"I—I almost ate Riker and Quinn last night." It came out like word vomit—too fast, and not at all how I had heard it in my head.

"You almost what?"

"No, I didn't, but I could have." *This is coming out all wrong.* "I mean—."

"Hey." He stepped closer. "Hey, you're safe with me, remember? I'm not going to hurt you."

"It's not me I'm worried about, it's you. What if I—?"

"You won't. Besides, if you had eaten Riker and Quinn, would it really have been the end of the world? I mean, they are both kind of unpleasant to be around."

"Unpleasant?"

He laughed, and I laughed, and the tension was gone, at least for a second, but that sweet scent wasn't.

"Merick—."

"M."

"What?"

"Please, I want you to call me M. Everybody else calls me Merick now, but—." He took my hand, and instantly I could feel my body warming up at his touch. "I really want you to call me M."

"OK." I couldn't help but smile, even though I was fighting every nerve in my body from pushing me forward into his arms—closer to that smell. My throat was burning. I took another quick drink from my sports bottle, but it didn't help. "M, it's just that you smell—you smell so—."

"I smell? That's kind of rude," he laughed, and I loved that he was trying to ease the tension, but it wasn't working.

"No. That's not what I meant. You smell great, really great, too great in fact."

"Wow, three greats in one complement. That's pretty great."

"Damn it, M. I'm trying to tell you something."

"I already know and I don't care." I looked up and he took another step closer, closing what little gap there was still between us. "You're a vampire, A. I know what that means. I know that right now all you can think about is how I smell and what I must taste like."

He wasn't wrong.

"But that doesn't mean we can't still—. I like you and I know you like me too. I'm not sure how it will work, but I know it can." I started to interrupt him, but he stopped me with a finger over my lips. "And, I know that you're not going to eat me. So stop worrying. We will figure it out." He kissed the tip of my nose and my knees went weak. "OK?"

"OK."

"Besides, you're not only a vampire." He pulled away and started running down the path past the wall to the one-rope bridge that crossed the river. "Show me what that wolf inside of you can do."

I ran after him, and he was right, I wasn't only a vampire. I was part wolf and part lion. I didn't really know or understand what that meant, but I did know that over the last week I had been suppressing those parts of me—Britt had been suppressing those parts of me. Letting them out now felt somehow freeing. It's hard to describe the feeling of having three distinct parts of yourself, but when I started running, I could feel the wolf and the lion getting excited. It was as if they were finally able to stretch their legs out, and they liked it. I felt like I was floating, as if they were just carrying me along for the ride.

By the time M and I made it up the 20-foot vertical rope ladder we just stopped and lay across the 20-foot horizontal rope bridge as if it were a huge hammock.

"Can I ask you something?" Merick said.

"Of course."

"Why Zelina?"

"What do you mean why?"

"Why'd you pick it? Why didn't you go with one of the approved 'A' indicator names?"

"I don't know. I read the list a dozen times, but none of them were right." I rolled over and he was lying there, two feet away, staring up at the clouds. "Besides,

I've known my name for a while now. I think it just took making it through Selection Week for me to finally admit it to myself."

"You mean, you planned to select Zelina before Selection Week?" Merick asked as he rolled toward me.

"No, it wasn't a plan. It was more a feeling. Zelina just feels right. I guess I like the taste of it in my mouth." I rolled back and the ropes shifted and bounced under our weight. I closed my eyes, and as I did I could feel Merick's—M's--hand slowly wrap around mine. We didn't stay there long--we both had to get to work--but it was nice while it lasted.

Crossing the finish line we went our separate ways. "Tomorrow?" He called back over his shoulder.

"Same time."

"Same place."

I made it back to Britt's apartment in time to shower and change before work. I had to meet Councilor Remy and I was actually starting to feel nervous. He had the opportunity to banish me, on Britt's recommendation, no less, but he decided to keep me. Granted, he made me live with her, probably so she could keep me under control, or maybe that was Councilman Blake's plan. Either way, I had been allowed to stay, so I was thankful.

When I got to his office, Remy wasn't in yet. "You can have a seat in his office and wait if you would like." His assistant was a petite woman with shoulder length brown hair and chiseled cheekbones. "I'm Calliope, but you can call me Clara—it's easier to say."

"Do you prefer Calliope?" I asked.

"I do."

"Then that is what I will call you. It's a beautiful name."

"Thank you." Calliope smiled and I noticed a faint scar that ran up the left side of her face. It was subtle, but shocking too. "You look thirsty. There's some bottled blood in the wet bar. You can help yourself. Or if you prefer, I can send in a donor."

"NO! I—I mean, no thank you. A donor won't be necessary. Thank you." She was staring at me as if she knew. I couldn't help wondering, but I was pretty sure that by then everyone knew about my accident at the dining hall. *Why would she even offer me a donor in the first place? Was she trying to embarrass me?*

"Then the wet bar it is." She smiled and I turned away.

The wet bar?

I walked into Remy's office and stood there in awe. It was a large room, immaculately decorated. There were hardwood floors, large windows with elaborate heavy curtains, and a large wooden desk with bookshelves behind it. At the other end of the room there was a large conference table with leather seats around it and, of course, just as Calliope had said, a wet bar on the far wall. I crossed to the wet bar and grabbed a bottle of blood and a glass. As I was pouring myself a drink I heard the door shut behind me.

"I'm glad you've made yourself comfortable."

I turned and Remy was standing less than five feet from me. "Oh, I—." I put the glass and bottle down. "I was only—. Calliope said that it would be all right if I helped myself to a—."

"Of course." He stepped around me, finished pouring my glass, and poured one for himself. Handing me the drink, he asked, "Shall we sit down?"

"OK." I followed him to the desk, but instead of walking around it he took a seat next to mine.

"As a liaison to the Vampire Council, you will be working very closely with both Vampire and Lycanthrope Council members as well as the sector residents. Your hours will be long and your duties—." He took a sip of his drink. "Your duties will be extensive."

"I understand."

"No, you don't, but you will. It has been a long time since we have chosen a liaison. Typically we don't trust someone so new—so young—with access to as much information as you will be privy to. But there is something about you, we all agree, that gives us pause—that has made us take notice. You aren't like the others, and I believe that if trained—if guided—you will do great things."

"Thank you sir."

"Don't thank me yet. Your training hasn't begun. Let us see how you are feeling in a week…in a month…in a year. Then, you can thank me if you still wish."

I wasn't sure how to take that, and he didn't give me a chance to respond before he stood up and walked out of the office. "I—."

Calliope walked in. "Remy had to step out, but he said to get you settled in." She turned. "You can follow me."

"I—OK." I quickly followed her down the hall. At the end of the hall there was a large metal door with a barred window, about one foot square, right at eye level. “Where are we going?”

“You’ll be working in the neutral quarters.”

“The neutral quarters?” I asked.

“Unbiased. Impartial. Objective. Unprejudiced. Equitable.”

“I know what neutral means. I’m just wondering what you mean by *the neutral quarters*.”

She turned slowly, she was probably an inch or two shorter than me, but she stood tall and somehow seemed to take up more room in the hallway. “Once you’ve been around a bit longer you’ll understand how the Council works. But, for now, just remember this—out there in front of the sector residents everything is peachy, all sunshine and roses—the Council is one big happy family. In here, well, this is where the real work happens. The Vampire Council and the Lycanthrope Council are in fact two separate entities, and they don’t always get along. The animals have a different way of seeing things, but we keep them in line. Remy is still the sector leader after all.”

“Still no glass in this window, Calliope!” someone called from behind the doors.

“I haven’t forgotten,” she smiled. “Behind this door is what we call the neutral zone, or the neutral quarters. You and the lycanthrope liaison will work here, together, guarded, of course, for your protection.”

The lycanthrope liaison? She means M. I couldn’t help but smile.

“Is something funny?”

“No, no, nothing's funny.”

“All right.” She was eyeing me up and down. “Whenever the Council members have information to exchange, other than in our regular meetings, it will go through the two of you. Whenever we have information, informal of course, to disperse through the community, it will go through the two of you. That will start after you have completed your training and have learned all of the sector rules and regulations of course. You will act as the eyes and the ears of the Council as well." She turned back to the door and inserted a large metal skeleton key. "Would you like to see your office?" She laughed as she pushed the door open. The metal screeched and screamed as it rubbed against the concrete floor.

38

There were two guards, one vampire and one lycanthrope, sitting in the small ten foot hallway behind the door. They were sandwiched between two identical metal doors—the one we had just entered, and the other at the opposite end of the hallway. Midway down the hallway was a third door—this one a simple, regular, wooden one. “So, is that—?” I pointed to the other metal door at the far end of the hallway.

“The Lycanthrope Council offices? Yes.” Calliope answered, before I could finish. “Good morning, William. Good morning, Haden.” William was the vampire and Haden the lycanthrope. I could tell, not only because of where they had positioned themselves in the hallway, but also from their smells. Haden, although he tried to cover it with a strong musky cologne, smelled sweet…tasty. “This is Zelina. She has been assigned as the new Vampire Council liaison.” I smiled and nodded. I wasn’t sure if I was supposed to say anything or just observe.

Haden stood, offering his hand, and I took it. “That’s too bad. I thought you were bringing her in as a little snack.” He pulled me close, wrapping me in his strong arms, and then he sniffed my hair. “I missed breakfast this morning.”

"Let go of her Haden. I don't have time for your games this morning." He let me go and both he and William laughed. "They're harmless really. Just a couple of overgrown kids. William and Haden have been friends since they were little."

"But, Haden's a—."

"Yes I know." She shook her head. "I don't understand it either, but if it came down to it they would choose their family over their friendship. I'm sure of it." She was staring at William, and there was something more there--a challenge, or maybe a plea--but I wasn't sure exactly.

"Their family?" I asked.

"Of course. William would stand with the vampires—with me. Haden would stand with the werewolves and other lycanthropes. Isn't that right William?"

"You know I love you Calliope. You don't need me to say it every time you come in."

"That's not—."

"Yes it is. Now, take the girl in before Haden really does decide to have her for a snack."

She obviously wasn't afraid of them because she turned her back to them, completely dismissing them both and ignoring William's comment. "Through this door..." she said as she was reaching for the handle of the wooden door, "...is your office. You'll share it with—."

"M. I mean, Merick."

"That's right."

"I... I remember hearing his assignment, during the release ceremony." I could feel both Haden and

William staring at me from behind. "We were friends before Selection Week. We trained together, that's all."

"Uh huh. OK. Well, since you're such close friends I guess I don't have to worry about you draining him, like you almost did to your donor last night, or the two of you killing each other, like the last set of liaisons."

"Did they really—?"

"Yes." Calliope didn't expand on her answer or tell me why or how it had happened as I was hoping. She simply said yes, and then pushed open the door to the office. It wasn't at all what I had expected. No, it wasn't as nice as Remy's office had been, but it wasn't the prison cell I was expecting after seeing the large metal doors and the two intimidating security guards, one of whom might actually enjoy eating me for a snack.

The room was about ten feet deep and twenty feet wide. There was a round table with four chairs in the center of the room, a couch along the back wall under the window, bookshelves lining the walls on either side of the door, and two desks on opposite sides of the room. Merick was sitting behind his desk with his head in a stack of files, reading, but he looked up as soon as I walked in. "A… I mean, Zelina. How are you?"

"Good, thank you." *Awkward!* "Oh, this is Calliope. Have you met?"

"No." He stood up and started toward us. "Hi, I'm Merick." He extended his hand, but she didn't take it.

"I guess I don't have to introduce you two," Calliope said. "This is your desk over here, Zelina." She guided me, with her hand on my shoulder, over to the desk opposite M's. "I've taken the liberty of printing copies of all the Council regulations. You'll need to become familiar with them, very familiar, but these documents don't leave the Council offices. After you feel comfortable with all of these let me know and I'll bring you the sector residents' files."

"Sector residents' files?"

"Yes, it is your job, and his," she said nodding to M, "to get to know the sector residents. Part of that will be done by attending events, as the Council liaisons, and by just being involved in your communities. The other part will be by knowing, in detail, everything about our sector and who resides here. I told you that you would have access to some confidential information. You must not share what you learn here outside of these walls. Do you understand?"

"Yes, of course."

"Good." She glanced over her shoulder at M, who was quietly watching, then looked back at me. "Did you bring some bottled blood with you today?"

"I have a bottle in my bag."

"Just one?" I nodded. "Well, that won't do. There is a small refrigerator behind your desk. It is fully stocked, but make sure you keep it stocked. We wouldn't want you getting hungry and feeding off young Merick here. It wouldn't look good."

"Right. Of course. I should have thought about that. I'm sorry." I could see M smirking as I glanced over her shoulder.

"Very well." She turned to leave, but before pulling the door closed behind her she smiled. "If you need anything, anything at all, William and Haden are here to assist you." As she pulled the door shut I heard them laughing in the hall. Then the latch clicked into place and there was only silence filling the space between Merick and me.

He was standing next to the table in the center of the room as he watched the door shut. I couldn't help but notice how the muscles along his shoulders seemed to relax once she was gone. "What time did you get here?" I asked.

He turned and our eyes met. "At eight o'clock. I took a tour of the building a few days ago. Other than that, Councilman Cruz has had me in here reading sector regulations all week." He nodded back toward his desk. "I thought once Selection Week was over we'd be done with the homework, but it seems we have more than ever."

"Yeah, it would seem so." I looked down at the stack of files on my own desk. "So, you've been working already?"

"Yeah, most of the lycanthropes were put right to work, the day after the release ceremony. I guess there isn't much to our transition period, at least not until the first full moon cycle." He started toward my desk. "I was wondering when you were gonna start. They told me it might take you a while. William said he didn't think you'd start for a few weeks if not longer. Then, when I saw you on the course I wanted to ask, but I didn't want to seem like I was rushing you or anything."

"Rushing me?"

"You know, pushing you to be ready faster than you should be. Besides, you did say you almost ate—."

"Can we please not talk about that?"

"Of course. Sorry."

"Don't be." I looked down at the stack of files on my desk. "I wonder if your files are the same as mine."

"What do you mean?"

"I don't know. I'm sure it's nothing. It just seems like—."

"Like the vampires and lycanthropes aren't quiet on the same page?"

"Yeah."

"Yeah, I noticed that too."

"I mean, even Calliope said the Vampire Council and the Lycanthrope Council are two separate entities. I'm wondering how different they really are. Want to compare notes?" I asked. He just smiled and went back to his desk to grab his stack of Council regulations. I did the same and we both took seats at the center table and started reading.

39

It took a while. We read through sector regulations covering housing assignments, security measures, town hall meetings, and resident activities. We even read the regulations concerning breeding rights and how the Council determines how many babies are allowed to survive each year, and how selection students are chosen as breeders.

"I hate to say it, but O does kind of fit the profile of a breeder," Merick said.

"What do you mean?"

"Look here," he scooted his chair as close to mine as possible, and we both leaned in over the file to read.

The scent of him washed over me, and I quickly downed the last of the bottle of blood I had open on the table next to me. "Hungry?" he asked.

"No, just—." I swallowed. He smelled so good. "Maybe a little, but I'll be fine."

> ***Breeder Selection - Sector C***
>
> *One Breeder will be selected from each selection class. Breeders must be intelligent, testing high in a majority of their courses, with a proven ability to use common sense in stressful situations. Breeders must be of the nonviolent nature. Students with a propensity toward*

fighting or athletics should not be selected for the breeder program.

Breeders must be naturally healthy eaters and physically fit. Any student being considered for the position of breeder must pass a series of medical examinations, starting in their fifteenth year of life.

"Wait, do you really think they have been testing O, as a possible breeder, since she was fifteen?" I asked.

"I don't know. Maybe they've been testing us all. She's just the lucky one who actually got selected."

"The lucky one?"

"I'm kidding A. Opal got the raw end of the deal. Her—. Her life has already ended, she just doesn't know it yet."

Morbid thoughts from Merick, I smiled to myself. "What do you mean?"

"Just keep reading."

Assignments within the breeder program will last eight years or through the birth of six children, whichever comes first.

If a breeder fails to conceive within the first twelve months of their assignment, or if they have two failed pregnancies, the Council can select to prematurely terminate the breeder's assignment.

Breeders who have completed their eight-year term, given birth to six healthy babies, or whose assignments have been prematurely terminated, will be given the option of becoming a donor or defecting to live in the wastelands as a castaway.

"Oh my stars. Does that mean—?"

"Yeah, she has eight years left here in Sector C, if she's lucky," Merick answered.

"But, how can they do that? Does she know? Do you think she knows?"

"I don't know. Probably not."

We sat there in silence, because, really, what was left to say? We had grown up with O, Opal, all our lives and to think that we knew her fate, and it wasn't good, before she knew it herself—just didn't feel right.

A loud banging on the door pulled us out of our daze. "You two going to come out anytime in the near future or what?" Haden called from behind the door.

"What's his problem?" Merick asked as he started toward the door.

"Who knows, maybe he forgot to pack his puppy treats today." The second it came out of my mouth I regretted it. Merick stopped mid-step and just turned and stared at me. "I didn't mean it. I mean, I don't think of you—I mean of lycanthropes—."

He started laughing and I felt a weight lifting off of me. "Don't sweat it A. I think that's the first time I've ever heard you actually tell a joke. Not bad for your first try."

"Shut up, you know I'm funny." He turned back and opened the door. "I am," I called after him. "I'm very funny!"

Haden and William stepped into the office, passing Merick and making their way to the table. "So, you two almost done in here?" William asked, as he thumbed through the files on the table then grabbed my empty blood bottles, throwing them in the trash.

"I guess." I looked across the room at Merick. "We're just reading, like we were told to."

"Yeah, but it's almost seven o'clock."

"Seven o'clock already?" I turned back, looking out the window, and sure enough it was already getting dark outside. "How did we not notice—?"

Haden laughed. "Yeah, I can smell—I mean see—how you could get so distracted—*'reading'*—that you didn't even notice the sun going down. I mean, what with such a small window and all."

Smartass, I thought. No, our window wasn't small, it took up the majority of the back wall, but he didn't have the right to imply that we were doing anything other than our job.

"Haden over there hasn't eaten today, and we don't get to leave until you two leave. So, unless you want to *be* dinner, you might want to wrap things up in here." William smiled, and then turned to leave, grabbing Haden's arm as he crossed to the door.

The door shut behind them and Merick and I just stood there staring at each other. "We haven't done anything wrong." "He's just being a jerk." We both started talking at the same time.

"You know," Merick started again, "we aren't students anymore. We have the right to spend time with whoever we want. So—."

"So, tomorrow morning, on the course?"

"I was thinking tonight—dinner."

"Oh." *Dinner with Merick? How would that work?* I had no idea. "I don't know. I mean, I've only been to the dining hall once since, you know, and as you also know, that didn't go so well. Besides, now that you're a—, and I'm a—."

"A, it doesn't have to be so complicated. We won't go to the dining hall. We'll go somewhere else. Just leave it to me, OK?" I didn't answer, because I wasn't sure how I felt about it. On second thought, I did know—I was nervous and scared and excited all at the same time.

"It's almost seven, and Britt wants me back at the apartment no later than nine o'clock. She says that until I can control my thirst the sector curfew still applies to me."

"Then we better hurry," he said, as he grabbed my hand and pulled me toward the door. However, he quickly let go when he saw William standing in the doorway watching us.

"You'll need to exit through your own Council offices." William held the door to the Vampire Council offices open for me, and Haden did the same for Merick.

"Of course," Merick said. "I'll just see you outside." He nodded to me then turned and made his way down the hall with Haden quick to follow.

"You'll get yourself in trouble with that one." William said as he led me down the hall and through the Vampire Council offices to the main door.

"I'm sorry?"

"Nothing, it's none of my business." William pushed the main door open, and waved me out. "Have a good night. I'll see you in the morning."

"Right, OK." I started down the stairs, but something didn't feel right. "William, why did the last—?" I had started to ask why the last two liaisons had killed each other, but William was already gone.

40

"Psst... A, come on." Merick was standing at the corner of the building waving at me when I turned and headed back down the stairs.

"How did you get out here so fast?" I asked.

"I have my ways," he laughed. "Come on." I followed him through town, and down some roads I didn't recognize.

"Where are we?"

"This is the lycanthrope section." He pointed as he talked, but I was too busy scanning the dark alleys we were passing to notice what he was showing me. "The werebears live over in those buildings, the tigers and the lions are down that street, and the wolves live over here, by the park." When I turned back he was pointing up at a window on the second floor of one of the complexes, "...do you see it?"

"What?" I must have zoned out for a second.

"My room." He took my hand and pulled me into him. Turning me so his chest was to my back he pointed up at the window again. "Right there, the third window on the second floor, that's my room."

"Oh. Is that where we're going?"

"No, are you kidding? I don't think they would be too happy if I brought a vampire home for dinner."

"Oh, yeah, right. Of course. I don't know what I was thinking."

Merick laughed as he pulled me the other way, across the street and into the park.

We walked down a path that led off into the woods. Just past the tree line there was a clearing with picnic tables, park benches, and a small lake. "Wow, it's so pretty out here. I never even knew this lake was here."

"Yeah, it's not on the sector maps because the Lycanthrope Council had it made about fifty years ago. It's lycanthrope territory, so I guess they didn't feel the need to inform the Vampire Council."

"How do you—?"

"Lycanthropes aren't all that secretive with each other. They brought us all here the night of the release ceremony. We had dinner together, and the elders told us stories about the sector, the Council, even the war of 2082. Pretty crazy stuff too, stuff that professor Kade never talked about in class."

"So, what are we doing here? Are you sure it's OK for me to be here?" I asked, looking around to make sure no one was watching.

"You're part lycanthrope, A. You deserve to be here just as much as any of us do. You deserve to know the histories too."

"Yeah, you might think so, but I doubt anyone else does. I saw the way everyone looked at me when Remy told them what I was."

M took my hand and led me a little farther down the path. On the ground, next to one of the picnic tables, was a blanket and basket. "What's this?" I asked.

"Dinner," he said smiling.

Oh that smile. I wondered if he knew what it did to me.

We sat down, and out of the basket he pulled two bottles of blood. "I wasn't sure how hungry you would be." Then he pulled out a large steak—rare--a baked potato, corn, baked beans, and dinner rolls.

"Wow, that's a lot of food."

"Oh yeah," he said, "and if you want some—."

"I think I'm good…" I lifted my bottled blood as if toasting, "…but thanks."

We sat there in the dark, enjoying our dinner and the company. It felt like we were the only two people in the world. "How did you do it? You were at work all day too, so how did you manage all of this?"

"I told you, I have my ways."

I had finished my second bottle, and was still feeling hungry. My throat was burning and my fangs hadn't retracted, which wasn't usual for me. I kept my hand over my mouth, I didn't want to scare him away. "Maybe I will have a bite, if that's OK."

"Of course." He held up a piece of steak, on his fork, to my mouth. "Go ahead."

The steak practically melted in my mouth--it was good—better than good, and I wanted more. Looking back I'm not really sure how it happened, but the next thing I knew I was sitting on M's lap, he had dropped his fork, and I had his face in my hands. The sweet, tasty scent of him filled the air all around me. "How is it that I didn't notice how good you smell, earlier today?"

"You didn't?"

"OK, maybe I did, but I was able to… I mean I didn't… Why is it different now?"

"I—I don't know." His hands covered mine. He wasn't struggling or trying to get away, but he did manage to take my hands off of his face and moved them around his waist giving himself the physical advantage, should something go wrong.

I stared into his silver grey eyes and could hear his racing heartbeat. "I—I'm still hungry."

"Then eat the rest of my steak."

"I don't think that's what I want." I knew that wasn't what I wanted, but how was I supposed to tell him that I would rather bite into his neck than the juicy steak he was eating?

"A, you're part wolf—part lion. You can't keep suppressing that part of you. Try feeding your wolf instead of your blood lust."

"I—."

"Yes you can."

It wasn't easy, but he was right. I finished off his steak and two of the rolls before my fangs finally retracted, and I was feeling better. "Wow, for a girl you can really eat."

"Hey." I smacked his arm. "You better watch it, I'm still tougher than you."

He grabbed my arms, turned, and flung me to the ground, landing on top of me. "You think so?" His legs were straddling my waist and he leaned in so close I could almost taste him. "Want to test that theory?"

"I—." He kissed me and everything was perfect. At least until I bit him. I didn't mean to, but I was swept away by his smell—by the feel of his lips on mine. Before I could stop myself my fangs had extended and I could taste his sweet, thick blood on my tongue.

"Mmmm." He moaned under his breath. "A…Zelina, I—."

Zelina, stop! Stop! You have to stop! Again Britt's voice filled my mind and pulled me back to reality.

"Oh no!" I scurried out from under him. "What have I done?" He was lying on the ground, not moving. "M? M, are you OK? Please say you're OK." He rolled over and smiled up at me and I sank to my knees crying. I could have killed him, I almost had.

The sound of cicadas filled the air and a cool breeze started to pick up. I looked down at my monitor and was surprised to see that it was already a quarter to nine. "I have to go." I grabbed my shoes, which I didn't remember taking off, and quickly pulled them back on.

"You really have to go?" He asked.

"I do. If I'm not back before nine, Britt will have a search party out to find me. I'm not so sure how the Council would feel if they found me here, with you, like this."

He grabbed my arm before I could turn to walk away. "Wait." He leaned in and gave me one more kiss, soft and slow, then let go.

I turned and took off running back down the path, trying not to think about what had just happened.

"Where have you been?" Britt said as I walked in.

"What? It's not even—."

"Is that blood?" she asked, stopping me mid-step, mid-sentence.

I turned to look in the mirror near the foyer entrance. She was right, there was a spot of dried blood on the corner of my mouth—Merick's blood, but I couldn't tell her that. "I—it's not what you think."

41

I could hear the yelling all the way from my room, even with the door shut. "What was so urgent that you called me away from my hunt?" It was Councilman Blake—I could tell by the calm yet menacing way he spoke to her, as if every word was a warning and a threat.

"I'm—I'm sorry father. I just—."

"Stop apologizing and answer my question."

"Yes sir. It's the girl. She—."

"She has a name."

"Yes, Zelina, a name unfitting for a firstborn child." Britt practically spit the words at him.

"Her *name* is of no consequence to you!" Blake said, clearly holding back his anger. "You have had issues with her since Selection Week. I was hoping that having her stay with you would help her transition and help you to figure out what she is. But it doesn't seem possible for you to see her as anything but a danger. What issue do you have with her this time?"

"Blood--she came home covered in it."

That's a lie, I thought, but I wasn't yet ready to explain what had happened between Merick and me, so I just sat quietly in my room, listening.

"Covered in it?"

She didn't answer for a few seconds, and when she did she sounded less sure of herself than I had ever heard her. "I mean, her face. Her mouth, it was around her mouth. She fed—that is all that matters. When I took her to the dining hall, she almost killed the donor. She isn't ready to be feeding *with* supervision, let alone without."

"Whose blood?"

"What? I don't know. She reeks of wolf and lion constantly. It's hard enough for me to determine what *species* the blood belonged too much less *whose* it was."

"You are around blood all day long. It is your job to recognize the scent of all sector members and be able to track their blood."

What does he mean 'track their blood?' I wondered.

I could hear Blake moving around the room. "Are you telling me now that you are incapable of doing your job?"

"No," Britt answered.

"If you couldn't tell what *species*, let alone who the blood belonged to, then perhaps it could have been bottled—." He was suddenly calmer.

"No!" she demanded.

"Are you sure these feelings aren't just jealousy?"

"No, father, I'm not jealous of her. What reason would I have? I told you she was dangerous, and I was right. I warned you and the Council what would happen if you let her stay."

"Who are you to question the decision of the Council?"

"I don't have to answer to you."

"Excuse me?"

"I only mean, I understand that you are my father and my maker, but it was Remy who assigned me to watch her. He alone asked for my opinion and I gave it. I came to you because you are my father and because I respect you, but I stand behind my recommendation. She isn't—."

I hadn't intended to take over her body, I only wanted to see what was going on. I was hoping to watch from a dark corner, as a fly on the wall, but instead I was there standing in front of Blake as if I had always been there.

"She isn't what?" he demanded.

"She isn't—."

Do something. Fix this. I thought desperately.

"She isn't a threat," I blurted out.

"But you just said—."

"I was wrong. You're my father. I should have listened to you. It was an accident, I'm sure of it. She didn't mean to feed on..." *Don't say his name, don't say his name.* "...the boy. It won't happen again. I won't let it."

I could feel Blake's eyes burning through me as I stood there. "The boy? I thought you didn't know whose blood it was."

"I don't. That was a mistake. I only meant that she didn't mean to feed... without supervision. She won't do it again. I won't allow it."

I was certain he knew it was me, but he didn't say it. "I trust you can keep her in line?"

"Yes sir, of course. It was probably just bottled blood anyway, like you said."

"Very well, I don't think we need to report it then—."

"No, of course not. I'm sorry to have bothered you."

"You are my daughter; it is never a bother." He started to the door, but he paused and turned back. "Zelina?"

"Yes? I mean, did you need to see her?"

"No, no. I think I have everything I came for."

He left and I could feel Britt fighting me, pushing me out of her head, but she seemed confused. I didn't think she knew it was me, or even what was happening. When I opened my eyes I was sitting on my bed with the vision stone gripped tightly between my hands. "Zelina," Britt screamed, as she slammed the bedroom door open, bouncing it off of the wall. "If I ever find out that you've been feeding without my permission I will *personally* see to it that you're escorted out of the sector and handed over to the castaways. I'm sure someone as pretty as you won't have a problem finding some savage to take care of you. Do I make myself clear?" I nodded, but she wasn't satisfied. "I said, do I make myself clear?"

"Yes, ma'am."

"Good, now get some sleep. Somehow, you're going to have to find a way to get through work tomorrow without attacking anyone."

"I didn't attack anyone. It wasn't like that."

"I don't care what it was like. Just make sure it doesn't happen again, or the next time you feed, you'll be explaining yourself to the Council, not to me."

I heard her angry footsteps as she walked down the hall and out the front door. It was well after curfew, not that it applied to her, but I couldn't help but wonder what happened out there in the dark when only the vampires and lycanthropes roamed the streets.

Still holding the vision stone, I thought about peeking in on Britt one more time before bed, but I knew I was pushing my luck. Eventually, she would figure out what I had been doing, and she wasn't going to be pleased. Instead, I thought about C—Ciara. I hadn't seen her in over a week and, if I were to be honest with myself, things hadn't really been the same between us for longer than that. She was stubborn, and had strong beliefs about how vampires and lycanthropes were supposed to behave. She was fully on board with the *vamp initiative*, and she was ready to fight for whatever the Vampire Council wanted—even if she had no idea what that meant.

It wasn't hard to get into her mind. I had known her all my life, and as soon as I thought about her I was there, sitting in a quiet room—alone. I could tell that it was dark but I didn't have any trouble seeing—just another perk of being a vampire. "What is this place?" I asked myself, but she must have heard me because she answered.

"A, is that you?"

"Where are you, Ciara? Why are you just sitting in the dark?"

"I can't see you—where are you?" Ciara asked, frantically scanning the room. As she looked around, I could see the bare walls, empty shelves, and an empty closet with the door hanging off the hinges. "A?"

I could feel her heart racing, and panic rising inside of her. "C, try to calm down. I just wanted to talk."

"You can't be here. You shouldn't be here." She was pulling away, I could feel it.

"Where? Where are you Ciara?"

I couldn't keep her from pulling away. I tried to hold on, but she forced me out of her mind and back into my own reality. I opened my eyes to my empty bedroom. I couldn't tell where C had been, and not knowing who her mentor was I wasn't sure how to find out.

The resident files. I remembered Calliope telling me I would have to review the resident files when I was done with all the regulations. If I could convince her, somehow, to let me read them tomorrow maybe I could figure out who was assigned as Ciara's mentor. Then I could find her.

I lay back in bed, trying not to think about C and why she was alone in that dark room. My thoughts took me back to the woods, to what had happened with Merick. I could still smell the sweet scent of him all around me. I pulled out his grey t-shirt, which I had hidden in my pillowcase, and breathed in the sweet, clean scent of his soap. "What are we going to do?"

We'll get through this, I promise. I hadn't expected an answer, but his voice filled my mind and I knew that everything was going to be all right. I drifted off to sleep, to thoughts of him—and me.

I was abruptly woken up by the sound of a loud alarm that filled the air outside. It was coming through the sector speaker system that only the Council had access to. When I rolled over and glanced down at my wrist, my monitor reminded me that curfew was still in effect. "Three o'clock in the morning. What could possibly be so important that they're sounding the alarm?" I mumbled to myself.

"Murder!"

"What?" I jumped out of bed. "Who's there?"

Councilman Blake was sitting at the end of my bed, cloaked in the dark shadows. "Anything you want to tell me, Zelina?"

"I—no."

The End for Now

Keep read for an exciting preview of

The next installment of

The SECTOR C Series

By Nina Soden

http://www.ninasoden.wordpress.com
http://www.twitter.com/Nina_Soden

1

"Murder!"

Murder? What murder?

"What?" I jumped out of bed. "Who's there?"

Councilman Blake was sitting at the end of my bed, cloaked in the dark shadows. "Anything you want to tell me, Zelina?" He leaned into the light and his eyes burned with rage.

"I—no."

"Then you leave me no choice." One second Councilman Blake was sitting on the end of my bed, staring across the room at me with those dark black accusing eyes, and the next I was tied up, blindfolded, and gagged, and I was being carried off into the night. I'm not even sure how it happened so fast. I struggled at first, but it got me nowhere. He was too strong or I was too weak. Probably the latter, but it didn't matter—either way, I wasn't getting away.

You need to know when to fight and when to plan. It was something Professor Gunner had said many times over the years. He knew that you can't win every fight by just jumping in swinging. Planning and plotting have a lot to do with whether or not you make it out of a fight alive. I had a feeling this moment would be better served by planning my next move, not by kicking and screaming. Besides, Blake was a Councilman. Fighting him could jeopardize more than just how much sleep I got that night.

I listened as Britt followed behind, chastising him the whole way.

"Didn't I tell you this would happen? Didn't I warn you what she would do—that she was a threat?"

"Did you?" He stopped and turned back to her so abruptly that I almost fell off his shoulder. "What was it you said? Yes, I remember, 'She isn't a threat. It was an accident, I'm sure of it.' Were those not your words, your exact words?"

"No, I never—," she stopped herself. She couldn't defend herself without explaining what had happened. And, she couldn't explain what had happened because she didn't know. She knew she had said those words—but she didn't know why, or what had made her do it. What she also didn't know was that he didn't need an explanation. He already knew. He was just waiting for the right time to expose me, at least that's what I thought at the time. "Father, I—."

"Watch what you say, Britt. You're walking a fine line. I wouldn't want you to get yourself into any more trouble than you are already in."

"But, I—."

"You what? You think Zelina is the only one we've been watching?"

What? They're still watching me? When will this end? I had grown up in Sector C, and cameras were just a part of life. The council watches the sector students until after Selection Week in order to evaluate them. That's how it's always been. But to still be watching me even after I had completed Selection

Week, with flying colors I might add, felt as if they were hoping I would fail—or do something to make them turn on me. As if what I am, what they had made me into, is my fault and not theirs. I shouldn't be punished for their actions—their *choices*.

"No sir, I—I meant no disrespect. I only wanted to explain—." She was backpedaling now, I could hear the pleas in her voice even without her begging words.

"You will have plenty of time to explain when we get to the Council offices."

Well at least now I know where we're going.

"Must I, father? Can't you just let me—?"

"Let you go? Is that what you were going to ask?"

"I—."

"I have been very patient with you over the years, Britt. More patient than I think appropriate. This time, you have gone too far. It is for the Council to determine your fate. I can no longer protect you."

"But—."

He turned and started walking again. At first I didn't think Britt had followed, but then I heard the shuffling of her feet on the road behind us.

I must have fallen asleep or passed out at some point, but I can't say I remember it happening. What I do know is when I woke up I was tied to a chair in the middle of a windowless room that was not a part of any of the Council offices I had seen so far. There was a sharp pain in my arm when I tried to move. When I looked down I noticed a needle, connected to an IV, had been stuck into the inside of my arm.

Instantly, I started to feel nauseous and dizzy. Needles have that effect on me—I can't explain it and I'm not proud of it.

The eight Sector C Council members—Remy, Cruz, Blake, Iris, Serenity, Donovan, Ash, and Phoenix—were all gathered, talking, on the other side of the room. Vampires were standing on one side and lycanthropes on the other. Even in their private meetings they can't seem to play nice.

They must not have noticed that I was awake because they were arguing among themselves. "Why are you even here, any of you? It was a vampire who was killed and a vampire who drained him!" Serenity crossed to Councilman Donovan and spat in his face. "This is a matter for the Vampire Council not the Lycanthrope Council."

"We both know that she is more than just a vampire. The blood of a lycanthrope runs through her veins as well. Therefore, if she had anything to do with his death—."

"Murder," Serenity corrected him.

"Fine, if she had anything to do with his murder, if it was a murder, then we feel that the lycanthrope laws should apply equally. We feel that we should have a say in her punishment."

Punishment?

"There is no proof that the lycanthrope virus has even affected her."

"There is no proof that it hasn't!"

They're both right, I thought, and suddenly I realized Merick had been right. I had been so caught up in what it meant to be a vampire that I really haven't given much thought to the fact that I had also been infected with two of the lycanthropy viruses. He had tried to tell me, tried to show me that the wolf and lion inside of me needed room too, but I hadn't really listened.

"Fine." Serenity turned to Council Leader Remy. "Don't look at this as a Council matter, vampire or lycanthrope. Look at it as a security matter."

"Explain," Remy said.

"It happened within the sector wall, did it not?"

"It did. What is your point?"

"Since it happened within the sector wall, and I am in charge of internal sector security, I believe it falls under my jurisdiction. Had it happened outside of the sector wall I would gladly hand over the responsibilities to Councilman Donovan." Even without seeing her face I could hear the sweet, syrupy smile that she must have been giving Donovan right then. "I think you'll agree, sir, that I should be—."

"Stand down, Councilman Serenity," Remy said.

With those four little words he had wiped the smile and smug attitude right off her face. "But, sir—."

"Now!" He took a deep breath before addressing the group. "We are all well aware of what the child is."

I'm not a child! I decided not to argue, though. I was already in enough trouble—besides, it wouldn't have done me any good.

"What she is capable of is still undetermined. We have all heard Britt's testimony, and although I respect her opinion I do not agree with her recommendations." Serenity became restless, turned away, and leaned against the far wall. She was struggling not to argue her point again. "This is not the first murder we have covered up in Sector C and I am certain it will not be the last."

Then she couldn't stop herself. "Sir, you can't possibly—."

"Stop. Right. There. If you interrupt me one more time, I will have you removed from the meeting and banned from all future Council initiatives."

She turned and took a seat in one of the empty chairs. She had turned her back to the rest of the Council members, so I could see her face as she stared down at the ground. She was flushed with rage, and I couldn't help but tap into her emotions. I closed my eyes, and when I opened them I was there in her seat staring at the floor. I looked up to find my own body, bound and gagged in the chair across the room. I could feel Serenity struggling to understand what was happening to her, inside of her, but she didn't know it was me. She tried to speak, but I stopped her. She turned and I could feel the panic welling up inside of her as she reached for Councilman Ash who stood just to her left.

"Are you all right?" He asked, but something distracted him. He turned to me, to my tied up body and for a second I thought he knew. "If we are finished squabbling among ourselves," he announced, "I believe the child is awake."

Oh no, he does know. He knows.

Also by Nina Soden

The Blood Angel Series

What if everything you thought you knew about yourself and the world turned out to be wrong?

The Blood Angel Series is set in a world very much like our own, yet Atlanta isn't just an ordinary city and Alee Moyer isn't just an ordinary girl. Having barely survived her childhood it will take the death of her father for the truth of her bloodline to come out. Even if it means losing her identity or even her life, she won't be able to escape her true destiny as the first surviving dhampir in history. Surrounded by a new world where the horror films she grew up watching have become reality and the most unlikely characters have become her lifeline, Alee must find herself and her purpose if she hopes to survive.

http://www.ninasoden.wordpress.com
http://www.twitter.com/Nina_Soden
https://www.amazon.com/author/ninasoden

www.ingramcontent.com/pod-product-compliance
Lightning Source LLC
Chambersburg PA
CBHW030019180626
46810CB00001B/118
* 9 7 8 0 9 8 5 8 8 5 3 3 5 *